KU-015-427

DARK RIDERS OF DOOM

DARK RIDERS OF DOOM

Peter Dawson

GUNSMOKE

This hardback edition 2010
by BBC Audiobooks Ltd
by arrangement with
Golden West Literary Agency

Copyright © 1996 by Dorothy S. Ewing.

Vengeance in Shadow Cañon first appeared as *Vengeance in Shadow Valley*. Copyright ©1938 by Street and Smith Publications, Inc. Copyright © renewed 1966 by Dorothy S. Ewing. Copyright © 1996 by Dorothy S. Ewing for restored material.
The Hangtree Rebellion Copyright © 1938 by Popular Publications, Inc. Copyright © renewed 1966 by Dorothy S. Ewing. Copyright © 1996 by Dorothy S. Ewing for restored material.
Long Gone Copyright © 1950 by The Hawley Publications. Copyright © renewed 1978 by Dorothy S. Ewing. Copyright © 1996 by Dorothy S. Ewing for restored material.
Dark Riders of Doom Copyright © 1936 by Popular Publications, Inc. Copyright © renewed 1964 by Dorothy S. Ewing. Copyright © 1996 by Dorothy S. Ewing for restored material.
Lost Homestead Copyright ©1941 by Street and Smith Publications, Inc. Copyright © renewed 1969 by Dorothy S. Ewing. Copyright © 1996 by Dorothy S. Ewing for restored material.

All rights reserved.

ISBN 978 1 408 46285 0

British Library Cataloguing in Publication Data available.

Printed and bound in Great Britain by
CPI Antony Rowe, Chippenham and Eastbourne

Table of Contents

Vengeance in Shadow Cañon   9

The Hang-tree Rebellion   43

Long Gone   101

Dark Riders of Doom   123

Lost Homestead   179

MORAY COUNCIL LIBRARIES & INFO.SERVICES

20 30 65 79	
Askews	
WF WF	

Jonathan Hurff Glidden's first Western story was written and rewritten according to suggestions from his younger brother, Frederick Dilley Glidden, who had established himself in the Western pulp magazines by 1935 under the byline Luke Short. When Fred thought the story publishable, he sent it off to his agent, Marguerite E. Harper, who sold it on March 3, 1936 to Street & Smith's *Complete Stories*. It appeared in that magazine as "Gunsmoke Pledge" in the May, 1936 issue. Harper informed Jon that henceforth his byline would be Peter Dawson (after a brand of Scotch whiskey she drank) and that would be the case for well over one hundred stories of varying lengths, his serials for *The Saturday Evening Post*, and all of his novels.

"Vengeance in Shadow Cañon" was the thirty-third Peter Dawson story to be published and the seventh in Street & Smith's *Western Story Magazine*. It was originally titled "Bullets Bury a Back-Trail" by the author and was sold on April 11, 1938 for $135.00 — a sum computed at the rate of $1^1/2$¢ a word. It was published in the issue dated October 8, 1938. Along with Fiction House's *Lariat Story Magazine*, Street & Smith's *Western Story Magazine* was at the top of the ladder among pulp magazines that published Western fiction exclusively. In the 1920s, *Western Story Magazine* customarily paid its top three authors — Max Brand, Robert J. Horton, and Robert Ormond Case — 5¢ a word and the magazine cost 15¢ a copy. The Depression changed that. The cover price fell to 10¢, and after 1934 the top rate paid for most stories was 2¢ a word, but that was more than most of the competition paid, ever. By the time the Peter Dawson story "Lost Homestead," also included in this quintet, appeared in this magazine, the author was customarily paid 2¢ a word for every story or serial he wrote featured in its pages.

VENGEANCE IN SHADOW CAÑON

I

"DISASTER IN ALKALI CAÑON"

Tim Gilpin counted six riders coming across the pasture. As they started to climb up the slope toward his cabin, he recognized one of the horses. That sent him into the cabin quietly — so his daughter, busy with the breakfast dishes in the kitchen, wouldn't hear — to get his shotgun. He met the six riders down by the corral, well out of hearing of the cabin.

It was Gilpin who spoke first, giving no greeting and receiving none: "Turn around and ride down out of here, Rudd. You aren't wanted."

Mike Rudd, owner of the Whip, was a somber, squat man sitting a silver-mounted saddle atop the finest horse of the lot. His outfit was a black Stetson, broadcloth coat, and fawn-colored trousers stuffed into expensive soft boots. His slate-gray eyes took in the shotgun in the crook of Gilpin's arm, finally came to rest on Tim's blunt Irish face.

"You've got the wrong idea, Gilpin," he said suavely. "It wasn't me that did it nor any of my men. Ask the sheriff here."

Gilpin flashed a look at Bob Scholl, sheriff of Roco Verde County. He had a hearty respect for this lawman, and it was this that made him say, "Bob, you aren't particular who you travel with."

"Now don't go off half-cocked," Bob Scholl warned. His grizzled face was set in a frown, and he was plainly ill at ease. "I came up here to tell you folks that Rudd and ten of his riders was in town all last night. They unloaded two trains of shorthorns yesterday afternoon, spent most of last night at the saloon. Now, Tim. . . ."

"I said to get out of here," Tim Gilpin intoned.

"We'll get," the sheriff said. "Only I want to know . . . have you seen Ed Soule?"

"No. If I do, I'll tell him you're lookin' for him."

"You tell him to see me before he. . . ." Scholl abruptly checked his words as though realizing the futility of talk. He nodded to Mike Rudd and wheeled his horse about. Rudd, after one glance at Gilpin, did the same. His riders followed, and in ten minutes the group had disappeared into the timber two miles below.

That was at eight in the morning. At ten a lone rider crossed the pasture and came on rapidly toward the cabin. This time Tim Gilpin didn't go for his shotgun. He sat on the slab step at the door and called back over his shoulder, "Hope, here comes Ed."

A girl appeared in the doorway, untying her apron and laying it on a chair inside. She took a long look at the approaching rider. "Dad, I'm afraid!" she said abruptly.

"Of Ed Soule?"

"No. Of what'll happen to him . . . to all of us, but mostly to him."

Her father got up without comment and walked out to the hitch rail. He waited there until Ed Soule had come up past the corral and reined in his bay horse twenty feet away.

"Mornin', Ed," Tim greeted. " 'Light, won't you?"

"Haven't time, Tim." Ed Soule was a lanky, tall shape in the saddle, his lean sun-blackened face set bleakly. Eyes that were more gray than green did not lose their hard glitter even when he looked across at Hope Gilpin and touched the brim of his Stetson in greeting. Twin horn-handled guns rested in holsters at his thighs. Tim Gilpin had never before seen him wearing those .45s.

It was this last that worried Gilpin most, for Ed usually

called here to see Hope, and Tim had never thought of him in any other way than as a prospective son-in-law. Here was a different Ed Soule. Tim decided to come straight to the point.

"How many critters did you lose, Ed?"

"All I had, and every horse but this one. It cleans me, Tim. I'm through in this country."

"How about the rest?"

"The same. Baker, Knee, Hollister, and Baggins so far. They cleaned you, too?"

Tim Gilpin nodded. "Mike Rudd was up here an hour or two ago, the sheriff with him," he said.

"Which way did they head out? Above, to see Crippen?"

"No. They headed back toward town. Scholl said you were to see him before you did anything."

"I'll find Rudd when I want him," Ed Soule said flatly. "Why I stopped was to ask you. . . ."

"If I'd side you in a play against Rudd?" Tim Gilpin shook his head soberly. "No, Ed. It'd be suicide. Besides, we haven't proof. We never have had proof against him."

He went on to tell Ed that Rudd and most of his Whip riders had been in town all last night, that the sheriff would back Rudd in that alibi. Ed Soule took this in with little change in expression.

"That about leaves it up to me . . . and to Fred Crippen, if he wants to come along," he said finally.

Hope Gilpin spoke for the first time: "Please, Ed! Don't do it."

There was a tenderness and a pleading in the girl's brown eyes that at any other time would have quickened Ed Soule's pulse. Now he purposely ignored it, for there was no place for softness in him this morning.

"You'll sell to Rudd?" he said to Gilpin.

11

"What else can I do?" Tim Gilpin shrugged. "We're licked. I'll take Rudd's offer, which is fair, and pull out of here."

Ed understood what lay behind Gilpin's words. Tim had responsibilities that made caution and reason come before all else. Tim had Hope to think of. It had been the same with the others whose herds had completely vanished in the roar of the storm's downpour last night. Knee had a wife. Baker was crippled. Hollister and Baggins weren't the kind who would readily take to guns.

"There's two sections in my layout, Tim," Ed declared. "Rudd offers five hundred for them. What good is five hundred dollars to a man?"

"Better than losin' everything, maybe your life too, Ed."

There wasn't any point in arguing that. Ed said abruptly, "Be seein' you," and reined his bay around and started away. Hope called after him, but by that time his pony's shoes were racketing across the gravel out by the barn and her call went unanswered.

Ed Soule heard Hope's voice. But he couldn't let it stop him, for he knew that the things he would say and the look in her eyes would dull the sharp edge of his anger. And more than anything else he wanted to strike back at the man who had ruined him.

It had been nothing but trouble these past three years, trouble with Mike Rudd. The Whip was the biggest outfit in the country, its brand sprawled over fifty sections of good grass range. It was Ed's hard luck, along with the rest, that he'd put all his savings into a land company five years ago — the same land company that had thrown a dam across a steep-walled gorge high in the hills and turned dry and barren Alkali Valley into a rancher's paradise. It was hard luck because Mike Rudd was an ambitious man and resented these small outfits mushrooming out of the waste of what he considered his own private domain. Whip range almost entirely encircled Alkali Valley.

Rudd had made it hard for these small ranchers from the beginning. His hardware store, the only one within two hundred miles, had its own price on any merchandise sold to an Alkali Valley man. Paying twice over for barb wire, nails, tools, and implements meant hardship to the small ranchers. They had patiently put up with it, buying only the necessities and sometimes going without. And they had stoically repaired the damage to their fences and ditches resulting from mysterious night raids made by unknown riders. They had always suspected Mike Rudd, but they had always lacked proof, just as they lacked it now.

Ed Soule was broke, the hope of owning his own brand wiped out in the thunder and wind squalls of a single night's storm. But his pride wasn't broken, and in those early hours before dawn this morning, after he'd discovered his loss, he had come to the only decision his pride could make. He would meet Mike Rudd face to face with a gun, and one of them would go down.

Tim Gilpin and the others had failed him and now Ed was headed above to the last outfit in the valley, old Fred Crippen's. Fred, who worked alone on his place, had a temper as thin as the edge of his razor, and he hated Mike Rudd. Ed knew that Crippen would side him, with his shrewdness, his guns, or his fists. Together, they could wreak enough damage on Whip so that the price Mike Rudd finally paid for Alkali Valley would be high. After that Ed would choose Rudd and have it out with him.

This upper-valley trail climbed the side of an abrupt steep wall at the Narrows, hanging eighty feet above the churning bed of the stream that now ran a torrent of water. It was along this precipitous trail that Ed Soule suddenly reined in on the bay and stared ahead in mild wonder. Forty feet beyond here the ledge of the trail suddenly broke off in a jagged opening. Last night's storm had washed out its foundations, and the rotten rock below had given way to let down a good thirty yards of the ledge.

Ed reined close to the edge, and his glance traveled downward along the scarred path of the landslide. What he saw below brought him swinging quickly out of the saddle and made him run to the drop-off. It took five minutes of careful going before he had climbed below to stand alongside the up-legged carcass of a saddled horse that lay half buried in the loose conical pile of earth and rock on the valley floor. But he paid the dead horse scant attention. Farther out lay a man's broken, twisted body. Ed hated what he was to find, and he had to force himself to walk over there.

It was Fred Crippen, his bearded face twisted in a grimace of pain that made Ed give him one quick look and then take his eyes away. Old Crippen had been a good friend, and Ed didn't like the task he faced of burying him. A rotten rock overhang lay directly above the horse's carcass. He'd bury Crippen and the horse together, probably the way the oldster would have wanted it had he been able to choose.

Lifting Fred's broken body, Ed found the underside of his shirt and vest still damp from last night's rain, and in that sign read his own meaning into this tragedy. Crippen had been riding down this trail during the storm, probably coming for help after hearing or seeing his herd driven off. For Ed had no doubt now that Crippen's herd, like his own, would be missing.

"We'd have made it a good fight, Fred," he murmured regretfully as he lifted the body and started to carry it up under the overhang.

Half way up he thought of something that made him ease the body to the ground once more. He knelt there a long while, thinking, and during the interval he built and smoked a cigarette. As he at last flicked it from his fingers, rising to his feet once more, he looked down at Fred Crippen and drawled: "You'd have done the same for me, Fred."

Half an hour later, after he'd gone up for his bay and led him back along the trail until he could walk the horse into the water of the creek, Ed Soule threw his rope over a cedar that grew high above the spot where the dead horse lay. He snubbed the rope on his saddlehorn and eased the bay into the pull. Then, striking the bay's flanks gently with his spurs, he sat the saddle until suddenly the cedar above tore loose, and tree and overhang thundered down in a slide of earth and rotten sandstone that completely buried the remains of Fred Crippen's horse.

Five minutes later Ed Soule headed up the creek, walking his horse in the stream so he would leave no sign that could be read later. Across his nervous bay's withers hung Fred Crippen's body.

II

"BUSHWHACKER IN THE CAÑON"

It rained again that night and it wasn't until well into the next morning that Tim Gilpin rode into Roco Verde and brought the sheriff the news. Fred Crippen's cabin had been burned. Tim couldn't say when — probably the first night of the rain — but he'd found Fred inside. "He wasn't a pretty sight either, Sheriff," he ended soberly.

Bob Scholl was an honest, if a harassed, lawman. Just now something akin to fear showed in his blue-eyed glance, although Tim Gilpin doubted that Roco Verde's sheriff had ever feared a living thing. "Tim, you don't suppose . . . ?" Scholl broke off.

Gilpin waited a moment for the sheriff to finish. When he didn't, Gilpin supplied the words for him. "That Whip riders killed Fred and started that blaze? You're damned right that's what I think. This makes things different."

"Easy, Tim, easy!"

"Easy, hell!" Gilpin exploded. "This time we've got what we wanted . . . proof. It's there, Bob, and it's up to you to hang this on the right man."

"Does Ed Soule know about this yet?"

"No. I steered clear of his place on the way in here. I wanted to give you your chance first."

"Thanks," the lawman said dryly. "Otherwise we'd have a one-man war against Rudd on our hands. Ed liked old Crippen."

"It won't be a one-man war, not now, Bob. This thing'll bring every man in Alkali against Mike Rudd. The safest place for that sidewinder's in your jail here. Mark my words,

16

you get him in here and lock him up. Otherwise, I'm not answerin' for what'll happen. I'll give you an hour's start on me. There's some things I have to get at the store." Gilpin turned to go out the sheriff's office door.

"Wait, Tim. What's this hour you're givin' me?"

"Before I start back to tell Ed Soule about it."

"That puts me in a tight hole, Tim."

Gilpin laughed harshly, his broad face unsmiling. "Then you'll get a sample of how we've felt for three years now. I thought at first, after what happened to my herd the other night, that I might sell out to Rudd like the others. Now I'm damned if I will! They won't either. We can't sit by and see murder done!"

"This'll take some thinkin', Tim. I wouldn't be too hasty. For instance, like I told you the other mornin', Mike and ten of his men were here in town two nights ago. He left only four of the crew at Whip. Four men couldn't have made that raid on your layouts."

"And what was Rudd doin' in town all night?" Gilpin demanded.

"He had three hundred shorthorns shipped in that afternoon. They unloaded and bedded 'em down out beyond town. Now don't say they could have gone back and driven off your stuff. All but two of those eight were in the saloon until three the next mornin', Rudd with 'em. I know because I had to lock up Fiddle Horn for gettin' drunk and bustin' the front hotel window. I was up all night."

Tim Gilpin was frowning. A moment ago he had been certain of things. Now he wasn't.

"You're askin' yourself who else could have done it," Bob Scholl said. "I don't know yet. But I do know this. Three nights ago Jim Crawford was ridin' home from town when he saw something damned strange. You know his place is

17

out west beyond Whip at the edge of the badlands. Jim says he saw at least half a dozen men ridin' up Shadow Cañon that night."

Tim's look sharpened. "What would take men up there? There's nothin' in that *malpais*."

"I know that. And while you're tellin' Ed Soule about Fred Crippen, tell him about that, too. If your crew is really aimin' to settle this thing, my idea would be to start by havin' a look at Shadow Cañon. I intend to go up there myself."

Ed Soule was that minute having his own look at Shadow Cañon. The night before, a bare half hour after he'd dumped the five-gallon can of coal oil onto the floor of Fred Crippen's cabin and thrown the match that started the blaze, he had been waiting in the timber above the cabin, looking down to make sure he'd done a thorough job. It was while he sat there motionless in his saddle that the bay had lifted his head, ears up in attention. Ed had come down out of the saddle in a hurry and barely managed to clamp his hand over the animal's nostrils in time to stop him from nickering. Then, sounding softly but unmistakably, he had heard the muted plodding hoof pound of a walking horse above him, near the crest of the wooded hill.

No horse could have strayed up there without a rider. And Ed Soule didn't want anyone to witness this thing he was doing. He had planned it carefully as the only way of getting the other small ranchers to come in with him against Whip. He knew that Fred Crippen's place was so isolated and so well hidden that no neighbor would see the blaze. And to make things even better, dark storm clouds now hid the stars. There would be rain before morning, and no man would be able to tell when the fire had started.

Ed's instinct was to go up through the timber and identify that rider. He made a wide circle, walking his horse as soundlessly as he could until he finally came to the spot where he calculated the sound had originated. He was bent over in the saddle studying the ground as best he could in the dark, looking for sign, when suddenly a gun thundered close at hand.

The bullet clipped a one-inch strip of felt neatly off Ed's Stetson. He jerked straight in the saddle in time to see a shadowy figure cut out of the trees ahead. His right hand dipped to holster and came up swinging one of his Colt .45s into line. He thumbed three quick shots at that fading blur of shadow until the flash of his gun blinded him and he couldn't make it out any longer.

Then he recklessly put spurs to his bay and followed the hoofbeats of that other pony. They faded out before he had gone a half mile. Then, knowing that in burning Fred Crippen's body he had neatly framed himself with murder, he waited there on the hill above the layout all that night, his poncho held tightly about him during the brief hard rain. At the first hint of dawn he had picked up the now partly washed-out sign of the other rider and was following it west, down out of the hills.

That sign had held strong all morning. It had swung wide of Whip's north fence, past Jim Crawford's place at the edge of the badlands, and angled down off open range to lead Ed directly into the mouth of Shadow Cañon and across the mile-long punishment of the jagged *malpais* bed that shaped the opening.

Now, he was seeing other sign along with the one he had followed. Interesting sign, too. A mile above the cañon mouth, where the rain hadn't been so heavy two nights ago and where the rock gave way to a thin top soil, the ground

19

was churned by hundreds of hoofs, the sign that a large herd of cattle had passed by.

Ed was beginning to understand the meaning of all this when suddenly from ahead and above him a voice called down, "Jerk 'em up, stranger! Reach!"

Ed's instinct prompted him to roll out of the saddle before that voice had stopped speaking. A shot blasted out, sending its racket up the long corridor of the cañon. Ed hit hard on one shoulder, the sand kicked up by a second bullet which cut his face. He rolled onto his feet an instant later, palming up both of his guns.

Whipping his glance upward, he saw the pale, wicked face of the killer twenty feet above. The man was perched awkwardly on a ledge of rock. There was blood on his shirt, on the hand that held the gun. For a moment Ed Soule hesitated. But, as the wounded man's weapon swung down in line with him again, Ed thumbed three quick shots that cut loose an inferno of sound. Up there the bushwhacker's body jerked spasmodically three distinct times, doubling forward at the waist. It took two long seconds for the man to lose his balance and topple down off his high perch. He hit hard and rolled loosely down the less abrupt slope until he lay spread-eagled and unmoving. When Ed stepped over there, he needed only one glance to see that the man was dead.

A bend of the cañon lay ahead. It was that abrupt angling of the high walls that cut off all sound until it was too late. Hearing the thundering of oncoming horses shuttle down suddenly and loudly, Ed ran for his bay horse thirty feet away. While he was yet ten feet short of the bay, three riders suddenly swung around the bend.

The leader saw him and threw himself out of the saddle, jerking a rifle from its boot. He knelt in the sand and whipped a shot that caught Ed Soule in mid-stride and knocked his feet from under him. Ed tried to get up but a white-hot pain coursed the length of his right leg, leaving it numb and, for the moment at least, helpless.

By that time three guns were on him. He dropped both his weapons and slowly lifted his hands.

"Take a look at Feeney," called the first rider out of his saddle, the one that stepped in and picked up Ed's two guns.

"Four slugs in him," said the man who went over to look at the dead man. "Dead as he'll ever be, and he's come a long ways since he started bleedin'."

"Maybe you ought to tell us about it." This from the last of the trio who now stood in front of Ed, looking down at him.

"I was ridin' up the cañon here when he tried to cut down on me," Ed said. "It had to be one of us."

The obvious leader of this trio was the man who had spoken last, the one who had taken that first shot at Ed and so neatly brought him down. He was a tall man, almost as tall as Ed, lean and with a thin face that was almost handsome. "Suppose you tell us what brought you up here," he now drawled.

Ed nodded toward the body lying a few feet away. "Him."

"And what did Feeney do to you?"

"Stole seventy-odd head of my beef night before last," Ed said, deciding on a bluff.

"Let's get it over with, Stretch!" one of the others growled impatiently.

Stretch waved a hand carelessly to command the speaker to silence. "Be quiet, Tonto. We're paid to steal cattle, not to gun every stranger we meet." He turned and called to the man kneeling beside the dead Feeney: "Joe, come over here and patch this gent's leg so he can ride with us." Then, to Ed: "You won't be able to fork a hull far the shape you're in."

"Because of the leg?" Ed asked.

Stretch grinned significantly. "We'll call it that."

Stretch Dooley rode down to Whip an hour after dark more worried than he admitted even to himself. He was a rustler and not ashamed of it. The stranger's arrival in Shadow Cañon complicated things. As he passed beneath the branches of the tall cottonwood midway the length of the lane, a rider suddenly appeared out of the shadows and called brusquely, "Hold on! Where you goin'?"

"In to buy my girl a hair ribbon," Stretch drawled, pulling his chestnut to a halt. "What's the matter, Pete, you boys spooky tonight?"

"You can get it from the boss," Pete answered. "Go on in. I ain't got any time for talk." His tone was surly.

So Stretch Dooley had a slight forewarning of what was to come. But it was nothing to the explosion that cut loose the instant he stepped into Mike Rudd's office. The rancher was sitting at his desk. When the door opened, he raised his glance and saw who it was. His square, loosely-jowled face took on a quick grimace of anger, and he lunged up out of his chair, planted his fists on the desk top, and glared at Stretch as he said, "You've got guts to come in here! You. . . ." But then the slow hardening of Stretch's face warned him. That, and the lazy gesture of the man's hand that put it within reach of the tied-down holster at his thigh. Stretch wasn't a handsome man now; there was a live anger imprinted on his aquiline face.

Mike sat down heavily, and his voice intoned flatly, "You had your orders! We'd have made this play stick if you hadn't done it. Stretch, I trusted you."

"Suppose you get it off your chest, Boss. After you're through, maybe you can tell me what's makin' you so proddy."

"Proddy!" Rudd blazed. But his anger died out before a mounting shrewdness. "Who did it, Stretch? Name the man that did it, and I'll have him gunned."

"Did what?"

"Burned Fred Crippen's layout, the one at the head of the valley."

"I was up there myself. No one burned it. The old jasper came hellin' down into his pasture after us, but we'd already driven most of the stuff out. We parted his hair with a few slugs and let it go at that. He high-tailed."

"And who went back and cut him down and burned his place? Stretch, this is serious. The law's looking for the man who did that."

Stretch was frowning now, the momentary anger gone from his glance. "Mike, you'll have to take my word for this, but no one of us did it. We made that a clean job. Crippen was the only one that saw us. And he didn't get a close look. If his place was fired, he did it himself."

"And went in there and lay on his floor and let the blaze cook him to a cinder!" Rudd scoffed. But then he understood that Dooley was telling the truth. "All right, Stretch, it didn't happen while you were along. One of your bunch went back later, we'll say. But I've got to know who that man was. I've got to have him dead, to turn over to the sheriff . . . dead, so he can't talk."

"That's another wrong guess. There wasn't a man in the crew left the herd all the way to the cañon hide-out. We hit the breaks about sunup, and it was an all day drive in across that *malpais*. No one of my bunch did it, Mike."

"Then who did?" Rudd queried, plainly baffled.

"I couldn't say, but here's what I came to tell you. A man

23

followed Feeney in today." And Stretch went on to tell of the man who was now a prisoner in the cabin at the hide-out.

During Stretch's brief account of the fight up in Shadow Cañon, Mike Rudd's glance narrowed in deep deliberation. Suddenly he slammed a fist onto his desk. "That's Soule! Tall, a face that doesn't tell much, man crowdin' thirty?"

"That's him. He did say Feeney'd run off with about seventy head of his beef. He made a mess of Feeney."

"Stretch," Rudd breathed, "we've got the man we can turn over to the sheriff for burnin' out Fred Crippen!"

"How'll you make that stick? If this Soule was one of them, he'd be a friend of Crippen's."

"Exactly. I happen to know that yesterday morning Soule called on all his friends and tried to make them come in with him against me. They wouldn't. If we bring this Soule, or his body, in to the sheriff, Bob Scholl can think what he likes. Maybe I can help him decide that Soule and Crippen had it out because Crippen wouldn't help him make his fight against Whip."

Stretch Dooley shook his head dubiously. "It's pretty thin, Mike."

"We'll fix it so something of Soule's will be found up there in the ruins of Crippen's cabin. A spur, maybe, or a. . . ."

"He's got a pocket match case, different from any I've seen around here. It's metal, and he carries it in his shirt pocket. He'd need matches to start a fire!"

"Stretch, you've got a head on your shoulders. I've seen him use that match case." Rudd got up from his desk. "We'll go back and get it from him. This may be the one thing that'll make those ranchers pull out. Soule was the only man of the lot that hated me enough to bring this into the open. Without him, the rest won't fight."

III
"VENGEANCE BOUND"

Rudd and Stretch started west from Whip less than ten minutes later. It took them an hour and a quarter to raise the far-off winking lights of Jim Crawford's place on the edge of the badlands.

"Crawford's up late," Rudd commented as they left the lights behind. "He usually turns in when the sun does."

There was a reason for that light of Crawford's being on. This bachelor oldster wasn't in any way involved in what was happening between Rudd and the Alkali Valley ranchers. Yet a lonely life and an instinctive dislike of Mike Rudd's high-handedness had drawn Jim Crawford's sympathies toward Ed Soule, Tim Gilpin, and the rest. That morning, having gotten a quick look at Soule's bay horse and recognizing it, as Ed struck a straight line for Shadow Cañon on Feeney's sign, Jim Crawford's curiosity had quickened.

Off and on all day, Crawford had watched the north, toward the badlands. Shortly before sundown he had seen a rider come out of the breaks from the direction of Shadow Cañon and head east, toward Whip. Any activity in that direction was odd, for no man ever went into those badlands unless he had to. Two riders, one going in, the other coming out, all in one day, was a little too much for Crawford's peace of mind.

He had eaten his evening meal and had already taken off his boots, ready to turn in, when he suddenly decided that he couldn't sleep unless he had something settled in his mind. That something made him saddle his one pony and ride north toward Shadow Cañon a few minutes later. Two miles from the layout he looked back and saw that he'd left the lamp in his adobe house burning. He cursed mildly at the waste of coal oil that would result but kept on going.

Deep in the cañon a half hour later he had enough warning of Mike Rudd's and Stretch Dooley's approach to cross the cañon floor and put himself and his pony well into the shadow of one wall, his gnarled old fingers clamped about the animal's nostrils. He recognized the Whip owner, and heard the other rider say as he passed, "Mike, you're leavin' me out of this. I'll steal this whole range empty of beef, but I won't be saddled with a killin'." Mike laughed and the echo of that laugh was the last Jim Crawford heard of the pair.

A stroke of intuition told Crawford the meaning of those words. He went up into the saddle, and it took him a full two hours to ride out and make the circle to Alkali Valley. When he pulled in on his pony in Tim Gilpin's yard, the animal was ready to drop from sheer exhaustion.

Crawford was barely out of the saddle before Gilpin's voice sounded from the far corner of the cabin. "Stand where you are! You've got a shotgun lined at your middle, stranger!"

"It's me, Jim Crawford, Tim!"

"It's all right, Hope," Gilpin called. "Light the lamp."

Even before Gilpin walked down into sight a light shone in the cabin's single front window. Crawford didn't wait to get his breath before beginning his story. As a result, it came out in spasmodic, broken sentences that time and time again made Tim Gilpin want to take the oldster by the shoulders and shake the words loose. Hope came out, a quilted robe wrapped about her, to hear the last of Crawford's story. And once she interrupted him to say quietly to her father, "I'll go in and get your guns."

Gilpin threw Crawford's saddle onto a fresh horse, and

the two of them rode at a hard run across the pasture below. Back at the cabin, Hope finished dressing and went to the corral to saddle her own chestnut mare. Her father wouldn't have liked what she was doing, but she was thinking only of Ed Soule now. Thinking of Ed Soule was what made her bring along her father's old Sharps rifle and a handful of shells for it, even though she wasn't certain that the twenty-year-old ammunition would fire.

Gilpin gathered his eight men in a little under an hour. All eight had learned earlier that day of Fred Crippen's death and of Ed Soule's mysterious absence. All of them had undergone a change of heart at these new, ominous developments. Even Baker, who was so crippled that he could keep only one foot in the stirrup, was along tonight. And there was Hollister and his two men, Knee with his fourteen-year-old-son, and Sam Baggins and his brother.

"Crawford, you lead the way," Tim Gilpin said, as Baggins, at the lower end of the valley, rode out to join the rest. "We'll have to take our luck as it comes," he went on. "From what Crawford saw and heard tonight, it's a fair bet that Ed Soule's up in Shadow Cañon somewhere and in trouble. And it's also a fair bet that our missin' herds are in there with him. Gents, tonight'll either see this thing finished, or it'll finish us. If any one of you wants to pull out now, do it, and no one of us will hold it against you."

He paused, and the silence that followed his words was freighted with tension. Yet not a man made a move to swing his pony out of that closely knit group of riders. Finally, Gilpin said, "Then we'll be ridin'," and he followed after Jim Crawford who set the pace at a stiff, mile-eating trot.

Ed Soule doubted that any man in Roco Verde County knew what lay at the head of Shadow Cañon. There was, as Jim Crawford had often put it, nothing to bring a man in here. A mile-long stretch of *malpais* choked the cañon's mouth, the crystalline edges of the lava rock so sharp that they could cut a horse's hoofs to the flesh in five minutes' time unless a man was overly cautious, as cautious as Ed himself had been this morning coming in. Once a man was across the *malpais,* there was nothing beyond, nothing for five tortuous miles of bad up and down going across rock and sand. Even at the end of that five miles there was nothing to arouse a man's interest, unless by chance he took that narrow off-shoot that was no more than a broad crevice in what appeared to be the blank end wall of the cañon.

That narrow off-shoot twisted for another quarter mile between towering walls until suddenly it rounded a sharp bend and opened into a mile-wide basin where fair grass offered temporary feed for six hundred head of cattle now hidden there, Ed Soule's small herd along with the rest. At the basin's far end was a shack built of poles dragged down from one of the low hills three miles away. The shack squatted near the basin's one scant source of water, a weak spring that year after year watered the grass until well into the summer when it finally dried up under the sun's fierce glare.

Ed hadn't been told, but he knew that there was a way out of the back of this basin back, leading into the hills. Once today he'd heard one of Stretch Dooley's men mention Horse Creek, which was the name of both a town and a stream seventy miles across the hills in the next county. If Stretch and the others were from Horse Creek, it was a dead certainty that these cattle would eventually be driven there, their brands changed so that they could be mixed with Horse Creek herds, and forever lose their identity.

"Take it easy on him, boys," Stretch had said on leaving

the cabin before dusk. Stretch was an easy-going man Ed Soule somehow liked despite the fact that he was a rustler. And Stretch's men were typical 'punchers, all but one.

Tonto Keene was the one who had that morning suggested "getting it over with." He was plainly of the killer breed, both in looks and actions. He wore two guns, and they were tied low on his bowed legs. His face was an inscrutable mask of hardly concealed viciousness. He had evidently been the dead Feeney's friend, for after Stretch left the shack at sundown he made several pointed remarks.

"Stretch always was soft," he complained once. "We could gun down this stranger and tell Stretch he made a break for it." He spoke to one of the others loud enough so that Ed could hear.

"Lay off, Tonto. You want to buy some trouble with Stretch?"

Tonto evidently didn't want trouble with Stretch, for he said nothing more about Ed Soule but kept a surly silence and ignored the others. Acting on Stretch's orders, they gave Ed all he could eat for supper that evening and didn't tie him where he lay in his bunk, his leg throbbing with pain from the rifle bullet that had put a hole through the flesh of his thigh. They had taken his guns away from him but not his belts.

"How much is Mike Rudd payin' your crew to drive this herd out of the country?" Ed asked one of Stretch's men.

"Plenty," the man replied, and from there on Ed Soule had at least one slim doubt erased from his mind. Mike Rudd was admittedly behind the rustling.

After they had eaten, four of Stretch's men pulled the slab table out from the wall of the shack's single room and settled down to a game of stud. One man stayed out of the game for two hands to go and gather wood and build a fire in the sheet-iron stove. After that Ed watched the game from where he lay, uncomfortable because of his leg and the stiff bulky shell-belts at his waist. The belts became so bothersome that he finally sat up in the bunk and started unbuckling them. All at once something stopped him, and he fastened the first belt again.

"How's chances on gettin' in the game?" he said to the men at the table. "Or isn't my money any good?"

One of the four, a man called Summers, nodded. "Sure, stranger. Only won't that leg bother you?"

"Did you ever try lyin' down with a toothache?"

Summers grinned. "Once, for about half a minute. It hurt so bad I had to get up."

"This leg's like a whole mouthful of bad teeth," Ed declared, rising from the bunk and stepping across to the table to take the one remaining chair.

He had a little money in his pockets and made it a point to lose consistently. The game reminded him of many others in the bunkhouses of the Colorado outfits he'd worked for years ago. These four were ordinary 'punchers, no different from half a hundred others he had known; they made the same jokes, played the game the same way.

He made it a point to get up out of his chair occasionally and walk the length of the room and back again, "to get the stiffness out of this bum pin," he said the first time. After that they didn't pay him much attention, at least no one but Tonto who sat in a chair in one remote shadowed corner. And Ed realized from their indifference that there was at least one man standing guard outside the shack.

Finally, after more than an hour's play, he saw his chance. He got lazily up out of his chair, hunched his shoulders, and drawled: "That fire could stand some more wood." He limped across and lifted the lid off the stove and dropped some wood in. Then, as he laid the lid back, his free hand shucked two .45 shells from his belt, and he threw them down onto the coals.

His back crawled as he limped slowly back to the table. He noted three things instinctively — that the lamp on the table was within his reach, that the room's single window was set in the wall ten feet in back of his chair, and that Tonto was eyeing him in that cold, inscrutable way that made him the man to watch most carefully.

Ed had barely let himself down in the chair when the blast of the first exploding shell cut loose. Summers, directly across the table, stiffened and stabbed for his gun. A split-second later Ed was lunging up out of his chair and knocking the lamp from the table with a wide sweep of his arm.

The second shell exploded before the lamp hit the floor. Summers yelled stridently, "Watch him! Someone's out there!" and in that brief interval of time Ed Soule had covered the ten feet to the window, dragging a chair along after him.

He threw all his weight into the swing of his two arms that lifted the chair from the floor and hurled it through the window. The glass and frame crashed outward, and with the sound Ed stepped back close against the near wall. Tonto's guns blazed a sudden inferno of sound from the corner, the flashes of the weapons lancing straight for the window. Under cover of the sound, Ed crossed the room and stood to one side of the door. A sudden lull followed.

"Did he make it?" Summers's voice asked harshly.

There was the hurried tread of boots outside, and abruptly the door swung open. The man standing there with a six-gun in his hand had barely time enough to ask, "What's comin' off up . . . ?" before Ed Soule's smashing fist caught him full in the mouth.

Ed lunged through the door, reaching for the six-gun as the man sprawled backward. A gun blasted out behind him, the bullet whipping past his head as he wrenched the gun loose from the guard's grasp. Armed now, he stepped quickly out of line with the door and ran obliquely from the cabin.

From close ahead someone shouted loudly, "That you, Summers?" Ed could just make out the shapes of two riders in the darkness. He brought up his weapon, thumbed two quick shots and saw one horse lunge and fall to his knees. He heard Mike Rudd's voice calling sharp oaths, and then the two were out of sight, wheeling frantically back into the darkness.

The next hour was sheer torture to Ed Soule. His leg bandage loosened and the wound started to bleed so that he had to waste precious minutes binding it up again. He had crossed the floor of the draw and was now on one cedar-dotted upslope, heading in the general direction of the entrance from Shadow Cañon. Time and again riders approached almost close enough for him to see them, only to swing away again and go back down into the draw. Twice he heard Stretch Dooley's voice down there, once Mike Rudd's as the rancher directed the search.

After that first hour, Ed Soule moved carefully, knowing that a single sound might give him away. He was relieved when he found that the weapon he had taken from the guard in the doorway was a .45, and one of the first things he did was to shuck the empties from the gun and reload it with shells from his belts.

IV
"GUNFIRE RECKONING"

It was Stretch Dooley's hunch that took him, his six men, and Mike Rudd to the head of the draw. "He can't get far with that leg," Stretch told Mike. "And the only way out he knows is Shadow. Let's get over there, spread out, and stop him as he tries to get through."

Rudd agreed with this reasoning and went along. Stretch had his men get out of their saddles and leave the horses with one lone guard. Then he placed his men so that either side of the off-shoot entrance was closely watched.

"We may have a long wait. But we want this Ed Soule and we want him alive," he said.

"Dead'll do," Mike Rudd remarked.

"Mike, you'll play along with me on this. Your bargain was for us to get away with anything up to a thousand head of beef. But you didn't hire us as a gun crew. We'll get this Ed Soule and turn him over to you alive. What you do with him's none of our business."

"You can get hung for rustlin' as quick as for killin'," Tonto put in pointedly.

"But if you don't get hung for either, I'd a damn' sight rather think back on alterin' a steer's brand with my runnin' iron than on alterin' the looks of a man's face with a bullet," Stretch drawled. In those few words he summed up his philosophy.

Tonto was a troublemaker. For that reason, Stretch stationed him close in to the opening of the off-shoot and took up his own place nearby. Rudd was across on the other slope with Summers and two others.

They waited there for more than an hour, until Stretch himself began to think that he'd made a wrong guess and that Ed Soule wouldn't try this way out. He was about to rise from where he was hunkered down behind a stunted cedar when he caught the hint of an unmistakable sound slurring out of the opening between the high walls of the off-shoot that led up from Shadow Cañon. Two seconds later he had identified the sound as the muffled hoofbeat of several ponies. Then, before he could shout a warning to the others, that sound suddenly increased in volume as Tim Gilpin led his small posse of ranchers out of the opening and into the draw.

Tonto's gun spoke sharply, its explosion slapping back off the high walls with a flat detonation. Jim Crawford, close behind Gilpin, lurched in his saddle and fell stiffly to the ground. Someone behind Gilpin answered Tonto's gun with a quick shot from a Winchester and, opposite Stretch, Mike Rudd's six-gun suddenly blasted three times in a staccato burst of sound.

Gilpin spurred his horse down out of the way, giving those behind him room to fan out on either side of the narrow opening. He wheeled and headed for the spot where the gun had a moment before sounded. Suddenly a shape rose from behind a low-growing *chamiza* bush close in front of him, to be outlined a moment later by a burst of gun flame. A bullet caught Gilpin high on his left shoulder, yet he lifted his Winchester, took cool aim, and brought the man down as his horse plunged by.

A hundred yards short of Stretch's position Ed Soule was startled by this sudden burst of sound across a silence that had a moment ago been complete and ominous, a silence that had taken him to his knees to crawl warily toward the off-shoot opening in the full knowledge that a trap might lie ahead. Now he rose to his feet, stood there a moment undecided, catching an occasional glimpse of an unmounted rider, twice seeing men on foot running down from the shelter of the clump of cedars footing the opening.

Far across to the other side came Tim Gilpin's shout, "Ride 'em down!" and with the sudden knowledge that these mounted riders were his friends, Ed Soule swung up his six-gun and fired once at the shadowy figure of a man running back from the shelter of the trees.

His bullet grazed Tonto's left arm. The rustler stopped, arced both his guns upward to line at that wink of powder flame that had for a split-second spotted Ed's gun. The weapons bucked in Tonto's hands, his bullets whipping with deadly accuracy at that now blacked-out target. But Ed Soule had instinctively stepped aside as he shot, so that Tonto's bullets whipped the air close to one side of him.

By the flashes of those twin guns, Ed recognized Tonto and, as those bullets cut closer toward him, he threw one more blasting shot with the .45. The explosion of his weapon sounded at the exact instant a bullet caught Ed in his wounded leg and knocked him off his feet. Abruptly the rustler's guns ended their staccato rhythm. Tonto dropped both six-guns, his hands clawed his shirt open at the chest, suddenly his knees buckled, and he fell hard on his face, his hands still clenching his shirt with the stiff grip of death.

Below, Gilpin and the others had fanned out and now came sweeping back toward the off-shoot's entrance. Ed, unable to move his leg, saw three empty-saddled broncs go plunging wildly off into the darkness before Gilpin's riders opened their fire again at two men on foot who made a wild break from the cover of the cedars and tried to run down to the spot where they'd left their ponies. Seeing that they couldn't make it, these two abruptly stopped, and their guns blasted at Gilpin and the others. One rider melted out of the saddle, another dropped his rifle and clutched his side before the pair on foot were finally cut down.

The sound of the guns faded for a moment and was then taken up again two hundred yards below. Two rifles down there were throwing shots at a rider who suddenly cut out from the knot of horses that had an hour ago brought Stretch Dooley's men up here. In another ten seconds those rifles were quiet, and Gilpin's two riders came up from below. A voice Ed recognized as Charlie Knee's called, "That's the last of 'em, Gilpin. He got away. Now we'll try and find Ed Soule."

"Up here!" Ed Soule called faintly.

Gilpin, identifying the voice, reined his pony up the slope. Ed called once again, and in half a minute Gilpin was alongside him and coming out of his saddle.

"You hurt?" Tim said as he knelt beside Ed.

"Don't know, Tim. I can't feel much down there."

Ed tried to lift himself up onto his knees, but Gilpin reached out and pushed him down again. "Easy, Ed. You're bleedin' like a stuck pig." Gilpin took out his knife, slit the leg of Ed's Levi's and took a quick look at the wound. Then he came onto his feet and called down to the others. "A couple of you get up here and build a fire so we can see what we're doin'. The rest take a look for Jim and Hollister."

"You go along and help, Tim," Ed said. "I saw Jim Crawford leave his hull close in near the off-shoot. He may need doctorin' a damn' sight worse than I do."

It took twenty minutes after the fire of dead cedar branches started blazing to account for the last of Tim Gilpin's posse. A bullet had broken Baker's forearm. One of Hollister's men had a flesh-wound in the calf of his right leg. John Baggins was missing the lobe of one ear, and

Gilpin himself had a bullet-grazed shoulder. And after a long search they found Jim Crawford's lifeless body wedged between two jagged rocks near the mouth of the off-shoot.

Tim Gilpin helped carry Crawford's limp form down to the fire. "Never knew what hit him," he said quietly, his voice edged with bitterness. "I counted four others up there that make it up a little for losin' him. The rest are gone."

"Anyone see the gent that took off on that pony?" Ed Soule asked from where he sat alongside the fire, his right hand holding the tourniquet Hollister had wrapped about his leg. He was thinking of Mike Rudd and of Stretch Dooley.

"I did," Knee spoke up. "Had a good look at him. He was about your size, big and leggy. Funny thing about that. He had a clean chance at me and didn't take it."

Ed Soule smiled, knowing at once that it was Stretch Dooley who had ridden down the draw. He was somehow relieved to think that Stretch wasn't one of the four dead men. Then he had another thought that made him ask quickly, "And how about Mike Rudd?"

"How about Mike Rudd?" a deep-noted voice spoke out from beyond the fire. There was a quality of harshness in that voice that brought the eyes of all these men swinging there to identify it. An instant later a wide, low-built shape came into the range of the firelight.

It was Mike Rudd. He had a six-gun in each hand, weapons that swung slowly in tight arcs that menaced them all, made them lift their hands above their heads. Rudd's square ugly face was gray-looking and twisted with pain. His black broadcloth coat was unbuttoned to reveal a smear of red on his white shirt front, high up and to one side. That was the damage done by the first shot Tim Gilpin had thrown in the fight.

Rudd came on a step or two until he stood directly opposite

Ed Soule. And it was on Ed Soule that his bleak, gray-eyed glance finally rested. Now that he was closer they could all hear his breathing, a rattle that was the unmistakable sign of a lung wound.

"You nearly got away with it, Soule," he said bleakly. "Before I shoot your guts out, tell 'em about Crippen! Tell 'em who burned his place."

Ed Soule told them soberly, explaining the reasons for what he'd done as briefly as he could. He hadn't raised his hands as the others did at the threat of Rudd's guns. And as he talked, he edged his right hand in toward the holster at his thigh. When he finished speaking, the thumb of his hand was touching the walnut handle of the weapon.

Mike Rudd saw that, smiled twistedly. "Go ahead, Soule. Make your play!" And, to emphasize his words, he thumbed back both hammers of his guns.

Ed felt his forehead bead with perspiration. He was staring across at Rudd, not at the man's eyes but into the black holes of those twin gun muzzles. He knew he didn't have a chance, but he knew, too, that in another second those guns would blast flame at him and that he'd have to make this one futile try.

His right hand lifted, his forefinger snapped out the gun. Suddenly from far behind Rudd the darkness was spotted with a purple burst of flame and a low-throated explosion blasted the silence. Ed, staring at the two six-guns, saw them jerk to one side as Mike Rudd's body jumped. Then the guns exploded, Ed's own .45 swung up, and he emptied it with a prolonged burst of sound that slapped out across the draw in a series of repeated echoes. It was over then, Mike Rudd down off his feet, his shirt front torn ragged by Ed's bullets, and now more red than white.

Ed struggled to his feet. "See who's out there, Tim," he

said, peering into the darkness behind the spot where Mike Rudd had a moment ago stood.

"Dad! Dad, are you all right?"

It was Hope Gilpin's voice. The sound of it brought Tim wheeling around, running away from the fire.

Ed Soule, remembering the jerk of Mike Rudd's guns a split-second before they had fired, hobbled to the other side of the fire, and threw a blanket across Rudd's still body.

Tim and Hope came into the firelight, the father's arm about the girl's shoulders. Tim held the old Sharps rifle in his other hand.

Abruptly Hope Gilpin stopped, her horrified gaze riveted to the blanket and the shape that lay beneath it. "I . . . I killed him!" Her voice was barely above a whisper, a hint of hysteria touching it. She buried her face in her hands and turned to put her head on her father's shoulder. "He was . . . he would have shot Ed, Dad. I had to do it."

"But you didn't," Ed Soule said. "You missed. Your bullet kicked up the dust off there beyond the fire."

Hope raised her head, wonder and relief in her eyes. "You're sure?"

"Sure as I'll ever be of anything," Ed told her soberly. "Rudd must have felt how close that bullet came. He waited just long enough to let me get my gun onto him. He was dead right when he pulled his triggers."

He flashed a glance at the rest, a glance that was at once understood, for John Baggins spoke up: "That's right, Miss Hope. Either the sights on that old smokepole are twisted, or you're a poorer shot than your old man."

Ed Soule had only a hazy recollection of what happened from then on. He knew that they put him on a horse and that Hope rode close beside him on the way back to the shack, once or twice putting an arm about him to keep him in the saddle. And he had a dim, fevered memory of climbing out of his saddle and walking a few steps and falling onto something that was softer than the ground and that immediately invited sleep.

It was nearly noon of the next day before he opened his eyes. Hope had just stepped in through the shack's doorway and was looking toward the bunk where he lay. She met his glance and smiled.

"Better?" she asked softly, coming over to him.

Instead of answering, he reached out and took one of her hands. Her face took on that tinge of color and the smile that made her beautiful. "Dad's gone to town for a doctor," she said.

"I don't need a doctor. Hope, that mornin' I rode up to your place so riled I couldn't see. . . ."

"Yes, Ed?"

"Well, I remember the way you looked. It was . . . it was a little like the way you look now." His grip tightened on her hand.

"How do I look now, Ed?" She bent down under the pull of his arm.

"Good enough to. . . ." But probably Ed realized the futility of words at that moment, for suddenly he was finishing what he had to say without speaking.

"The Hang-tree Rebellion" was the thirty-fourth Western story that Jon Glidden published. He completed it on March 30, 1938 and his agent sold it to *.44 Western*, one of the Popular Publications group, for $108.00 on July 5, 1938. Jon's original title for this story was "Hangman's Helper," but Ralph Perry, who edited *.44 Western*, changed it to the title that has been retained for its first appearance here since it was showcased in first position on the cover and in the table of contents of the issue dated 11-12/38. Fred Glidden had continued to exert some influence on the kinds of stories Jon wrote when he was starting out, but by 1937 Jon had already found the direction his own unique talent would take him.

THE HANG-TREE REBELLION

I

"ONE LESS FOR BOOTHILL"

The cottonwood towered better than sixty feet skyward, its out-flung branches casting a shadow broad enough so that not a man of the twenty-seven riders had to stand his horse in the full glare of the beating sun that slanted into the cañon. There was even enough room in the tree's shade so that on horseback Bill Peace, the prisoner, felt pretty much alone as he twisted his neck against the prickly rub of the hemp rope and looked fully at Judge White.

"You're the last man I'd expect to catch at a lynchin', Judge," he remarked bitterly.

White's grizzled face lost its hard set for an instant. "I hate it as bad as anything I ever did, Bill," he said softly. Then, seeming to feel the uncompromising glances of the others, a subtle change rode through him. He stiffened and added, louder this time: "Damned if I do! I hope you take a long time chokin' your life away at the end of that rope!"

Peace smiled thinly, his gray eyes unafraid, his lean, weather-burned face set stonily against the searching glances of these men who hoped to see some hint of fear there. "Get on with it," he said at last.

Sheriff Ralph Fowler, a wide, heavy shape alongside his prisoner, reached across to draw the knot tighter so that it cut a hard line past Bill Peace's right ear. The others shifted restlessly, stirred by an impatience to get this done with.

Peace's smile broadened as his neck-muscles took up the savage pull of the tightened rope. "Sheriff, I've got one regret," he said. "It's that I didn't take the trouble to beat your brains out with a gun butt long ago! I'd try it now . . .

only you've got my hands tied."

Fowler clenched a fist and raised it. But before he could strike, Judge White said sharply: "None of that, Ralph!" The lawman relaxed once more and glared in cold, silent anger.

"There's one thing missin'," Peace went on tauntingly. "Where's the rest of your friends, Sheriff? Miles Root, for instance? He'd glory in seein' this."

Judge White intoned: "Neither Miles Root nor anyone else had anything to do with this, Peace. You built your own noose around your neck. We're responsible citizens savin' the county and state the expense of a trial. Maybe we're stoppin' a war that would cost a dozen lives. We'll know that later." He squared his shoulders, thrust out his white-bearded chin in a stubborn gesture. "Is there anything you have to say before . . . before we . . . ?"

"Before you walk my horse out from under me?" Peace put in. "No, not even good bye to Joyce. She wouldn't care."

The judge's face lost color. "It's a shame I'll never live down, but she will care. It makes me wonder if she's really my own flesh and blood."

For a fleeing instant Bill Peace's features softened to betray an inner emotion. Then, as though something deeply within him was taking too strong a hold, he breathed shortly: "I said to get on with it!"

Sheriff Fowler grinned wickedly. He reined closer and raised his hand, about to slap Peace's horse over the hind-quarters. There was a mixture of brutality and cunning in his glance. It was plain he was enjoying this. So were the rest, for a lesser measure of the sheriff's feeling held them all.

As the lawman's hand ended its upward arc, paused, and started downward in a stiff-armed blow, a voice from directly above sounded down sharply: "Hold it, Fowler!

44

I've go my sights lined on you."

The sheriff's square-built body went abruptly rigid. He rocked back his head so that he looked up into the leafy mass overhead, toward the sound of that voice. It took him, and most of the others, a good five seconds to see the speaker. There, thirty feet overhead, sitting easily in a branch-crotch near the solid trunk of the huge tree, was a man who hugged the stock of a Winchester .30-.30 to his cheek. The blunt snout of the barrel was lined directly down at the lawman.

Fowler choked, "Al Sisson!" Involuntarily, he ducked his head to one side.

The rifle-barrel swung a fraction of an inch to cover this move, and the stranger above said: "You'll all shuck out your hardware, gents. Fowler, reach over and loosen that hemp necktie. Peace, see that they shed their irons."

As Bill Peace's glance swung upward to take in this outlaw whom he had never before seen but had heard much about, Judge White said sharply: "Don't move, Fowler! One of you others make a try at Sisson."

From above Sisson's voice sounded in a low chuckle. "Sure, make a try at me! Make a try and one of my hands will cut you down. They're up above on the rim, lookin' down at you over their rifle sights!"

Twenty-seven pairs of eyes jerked their glances from the leafy mass overhead and swung far out and up to the cañon rim. Bill Peace saw no sign of life up there nor did the rest. But when Sisson called down again, "How about that rope, Sheriff?" Fowler moved with a frightened quickness that made him look a little ridiculous.

In ten seconds the lawman's shaking hands had flipped the noose from Peace's neck and untied the rawhide thong that bound his wrists. Once his hands were free, Bill Peace reached across to lift one of Fowler's heavy Colt .45s from its holster. He swung the weapon into line with the nearest man.

"Unbuckle your belts, friend," he drawled, and the threat of his gun seemed to bring the others out of their inaction. One by one, a little hurriedly, they loosened their belts and dropped their weapons to the ground.

It was then that Bill Peace had his first good look at Al Sisson. The outlaw came down off his high perch and swung lithely to earth. He moved quickly among the riders, gathering their weapons and threading them by the trigger guards on the belt he took from his own waist. Al Sisson had already become a legend in this country. Bill Peace was satisfied as he studied the man's unhasty but efficient moves.

At length, approaching Fowler, Sisson said: "Climb down, Tin Star! I'll fork your horse out of here."

The lawman obeyed with surprising swiftness, and in five seconds Sisson was astride the bay. Judge White suddenly reined in closer alongside Bill Peace and struck him an open-handed blow in the face. Peace drew away, the color draining from his lean visage. He let the hand that held the six-gun fall to his side.

"You're the only man who could do that and live, Judge," he said tonelessly.

"We'll hunt you down like a killer wolf," White breathed.

Sisson laughed softly and put in, "A couple years ago you made the same talk about me, Judge. For a man with brains, it's takin' you a long time to see the straight of things. Peace didn't kill Wes Stanley."

White ignored the outlaw, his glance fixed on Bill Peace. "You may live a month, maybe two, Peace. Sooner or later we'll finish what we started today."

Peace abruptly wheeled his black and rode beyond the margin of the encircling riders. One man made a stealthy move, and Peace swung up his weapon and thumbed a shot that sent blasting echoes along the corridors of the cañon. On the heels of that sound the rider jerked spasmodically in the saddle, and his right arm fell to his side. His gun spun out of his grasp to fall into the dust. A splotch of red showed at his shoulder. He brought up his other hand to clutch at it, rasping: "Damn you for a sidewinder, Peace!"

Sisson swung wide of the group, rode in, and picked up the fallen weapon. "You're lucky to be alive, stranger," he remarked dryly. He came back and handed the weapon to Peace. It was then that Peace spoke once more to Judge White.

"If you'll ride herd on your temper long enough, you might like to take a closer look and find out who really killed Wes Stanley. Sooner or later you'll know I was framed."

"We'll have a reward of two thousand on your head before sundown!"

Bill Peace considered that, certain now that nothing would ever change the hot hatred these men felt for him. Fate had fed the flames of that hatred so that not even this group, honest, respectable, the pick of this wide range, could temper its hostility with reason. He was all at once impatient to ride out of here, to put behind him once and for all the misery of these past eight months.

Al Sisson must have sensed his feeling, for he said crisply: "We'll ride upcañon and pick up my bronc."

He looped his belt of weapons over his saddlehorn, drove his spurs into the flanks of Fowler's bay, and sent the animal into a leaping run. Peace whirled his black about and followed. As the outlaw rode diagonally out across the cañon floor, putting distance between him and the cottonwood, he reined his bay from side to side, cutting a zigzag course. Peace, close behind, read the reason for this and dogged the outlaw's tracks. He was none too soon, for shortly a hollow, muted blast cut loose behind and a plume of dust spurted up ten feet to one side of them. Someone in the posse had hidden a gun and was now using it.

Once Peace turned in his saddle and emptied his six-gun in a staccato burst that turned back four pursuing riders who suddenly streaked out from the cottonwood's shadow. Seconds later he and Sisson swung around a turn in this high-walled cañon and for five minutes held their horses to a steady hard run. Abruptly, Sisson reined to one side, slowed the bay to a walk, and swung into a narrow off-shoot, calling, "Wait here for me."

In a quarter-minute he was back again, mounted on a rangy dun gelding. The belt-load of guns was no longer slung from his saddle.

"Dropped 'em in the spring up there," he explained as he reined up in front of Peace. He cocked his head and held it that way for a long moment, finally smiling as no sound of pursuit broke the afternoon's utter silence. "They'll come along slow, expectin' us to fort up and hold 'em back. It'll take half an hour to find their guns, and by that time we'll have covered plenty of ground."

Peace said: "What about the others . . . your men up on the rim?"

Sisson laughed softly, shrugged: "I've never traveled in any company but my own. It's safest that way."

Bill Peace's gray eyes widened. "Then what's this talk about your wild bunch?"

"Just that, talk!"

Sisson's smile broadened at the expression of surprise that came to Peace's face. The outlaw wheeled away and lifted

48

the dun into a fast walk that soon became an easy mile-eating trot as Peace fell in alongside. They rode steadily, saying little for two full hours. Alternately trotting and walking their horses, they put distance behind them without tiring their animals. They neither saw nor heard sign of the posse behind.

II
"A DANGEROUS DECISION"

It was Sisson who chose their direction once they gained
the upper reaches of the cañon. They cut west into the broken
hilly country that was the north boundary of Steeple range.
It flanked the high spire of snow-capped Steeple Peak that
rose three thousand feet above the lesser mountains.

During those two hours Bill Peace reached a decision he
fought against making. He was through with this country.
He didn't want to be, but a man with a price on his head
had little choice. His regret wasn't for the ten-section ranch
that had been his home for the past eight months since he
had come onto this range. The bank still owned all but a
small part of that land, and there would be more and better
land in a new country. Rather, he was losing a thing he
would never find in his life again when he rode away from
Twin Rivers — Joyce White.

He told himself that he had been a fool ever to think of
her seriously. From the first he had seen that fate would
line him against her father. He had had the misfortune to
stake out his ten sections along the banks of a dry wash,
known for years as Snake River. That was two months
before a government dam, high in the hills, had broken
through its foundations, washed out the side of a cañon,
and sent the waters off those snowy peaks spilling down
the mountainside to make a green, fertile land of the Snake
River bottoms.

His ten sections suddenly increased in value to a hundred
times their former worth. So had the value of other small
outfits along Snake River, that of the dead Wes Stanley

among them. Overnight, this land was priceless for the raising of alfalfa, for the pasturage of yearlings, and for the remudas of the bigger outfits. Some of the big brands bought out a half dozen of the smaller spreads, paying a fair price. But Miles Root, owner of the Quarter-Circle R, didn't do things that way. He made a low offer for Peace's ten sections, then for others, and had been refused. It caused hard feelings between Root's high-riding crew and Peace and the others. Two men were killed from ambush — both Quarter-Circle R riders — and several hundred head of Root's steers vanished into thin air. It looked as if a small war was shaping up between the big and the small ranchers, with the Snake River outfits forcing Root's hand. Root had the law on his side. He was Judge White's friend and apparently in the right. Yes, Peace had made a mistake in ever thinking of Joyce White.

"We'll circle back to Wes Stanley's layout," Sisson said at sundown.

By then they were high in a rocky country, long ago having lost their sign below where the thin soil gave out in an uptilted, barren stretch that ran for a hundred miles at the foot of the high peaks.

Bill Peace was fast developing a respect for this outlaw. It had taken guts to make that play at the cottonwood, foresight even to be on hand for the attempted hanging. Peace was intrigued with the mystery of the outlaw's presence there but decided to wait until later to put his questions. Just now he thought he saw a method in Sisson's wide circle back onto home range. The last place the law would look for them would be at Wes Stanley's — within five miles of Twin Rivers.

They rode by the light of the stars for a full three hours. Finally, Sisson led the way to a rocky, high-walled gulch a

51

mile behind Stanley's place. There they made camp, even had a fire, for this country was wild, and the towering steep walls of the gulch hid the light of their blaze. Sisson's saddlebags yielded jerky, beans, flour, salt, and coffee — enough for two.

After they had hungrily wolfed their meal in silence, Peace lit his pipe and hunkered down with his back to the stump of a lightning-blasted cedar, well out of the circle of light. He studied Sisson for many long minutes. Then, abruptly, he mentioned what was on his mind.

"I want to know all about it," he said. "How it comes you're in this country, how you know I didn't kill Wes and burn his place, how you came to be there at the cottonwood this afternoon?"

Sisson was busy with the making of a cigarette. He didn't reply immediately but studied his hands as they shaped his quirly. When he had lit it, flicking the match into the hot coals of the fire, he looked across at Peace. He smiled thinly.

"By rights I should have let you hang. Wes Stanley brought me in to bushwhack you."

For an instant Peace was confused. At length he queried: "Did Wes hate me that bad?"

"He did," Sisson nodded solemnly. "And he had good reason, from what I can learn. You were against Wes and the others along the river, thought you ought to make your choice between them and the big outfits. They thought you were double-crossin' 'em. Wes spoke of one of your neighbors bein' burned out two weeks ago. They figured you were the only one who could have told Miles Root that neighbor would be gone from his layout that particular night. It was Root's crew they blamed for that fire . . . Root and you."

Peace shook his head, meeting the outlaw's level glance

52

squarely: "And what do you think?"

"I don't think you did it . . . or killed Wes, either."

"Thanks for that. But how come you don't agree with Wes about me?"

Sisson chuckled softly, looking at his cigarette once more. "Wes was a good man in many ways, a bad one in a few. The way I figure it, he was in the wrong. Most of the men he chose as his friends were these small ranchers. Maybe it wasn't his fault, for a man has to have friends, and the way things are he couldn't be too particular. But his friends are a mangy crew, mostly squatters who've never had a dollar and don't know what to do with their money now that they have it."

"That's puttin' it a bit strong," Peace said cautiously.

"But it's the truth, nevertheless . . . and just about the way you've sized 'em up." Sisson eyed Peace shrewdly. "The pack of 'em wants to fight Root openly. You're smart enough to know they'd be licked. Wes Stanley wasn't. That's why you wouldn't throw in with 'em."

"But I didn't side with Miles Root."

"I know," Sisson nodded. "And I'll tell you how I know. Two years ago Root 'gulched his foreman and framed me with the killin'. I can't prove it, but I'm sure that's the way it was. Root's always swung a sticky loop, although not many people know it. He made the mistake of hirin' an honest man to rod his outfit. The ramrod discovered his crookedness, and so Root had to get rid of him. He framed me for killing that man. Only I broke jail, and they've never found me. Wes was my friend. A week ago, when he saw things shaping up this way, he sent for me, knowin' I'd side with him. I don't think you're the kind that'd trust a man like Root."

"You still haven't said why Wes hired you to get me."

"Because he and the rest didn't think they could make a play against Root without your comin' in with 'em. And so long as you wouldn't . . . so long as Wes was sure you'd double-crossed them . . . he wanted you out of the way."

Sisson paused, and Peace waited. He wanted him to tell his story in his own way. At length, the outlaw went on: "Wes primed me into thinkin' you were ten kinds of a coyote. Late yesterday afternoon I was forted up in that grove of cottonwoods behind your place, with a rifle, waitin' a chance at you, but I couldn't get a sure shot. When you went into your cabin about dark, I went back to Wes's place, decidin' to wait for another try. That's how I know you didn't kill Wes. You were at home when Wes was murdered, and his house fired. I even saw the tobacco tin."

Peace couldn't hide his amazement. "You mean you understood what it meant, why it was put there?"

"Not at first. You see, I rode down to Stanley's place shortly after the fire started. Whoever did it must have ridden away only a few minutes before I got there. I had a look at Wes, lyin' on the floor, but I couldn't get to him because of the blaze. But I did see the empty tobacco tin in front of the door."

"You might have seen it, but you couldn't have guessed what it meant . . . that it was put there to frame me."

"I partly guessed it. I know Wes, and I know he's a neat man, one who wouldn't let trash lie around square in front of his door. Wes didn't smoke. And another thing that gave it away was that the brand of tobacco is one you almost never see in this country. So last night I rode to town and talked to a stranger or two. It didn't take much talk to learn that you're the only one man around here that smokes that brand . . . you have it mailed in from Kentucky."

Peace was frowning. He had pieced together all but the

last fragments of this puzzle: "But how come you were up the cottonwood?"

Sisson smiled tolerantly. "Since it looked to be a frame-up, I went back to Wes's place to make sure it was you they were framin'. The sheriff rode out with a posse late this mornin' and picked up that tobacco tin and headed for your place. I hung along the posse's back trail. They got you and started back to town, and I saw Fowler arguin' with Judge White."

Peace nodded: "I heard most of that argument. White wanted to jail me . . . Fowler won the argument."

"When they swung to the south of the trail, I figured it that way. It's a treeless country and, when Fowler took his rope off his saddle, it looked like they were headed for the big cottonwood. So I rode on ahead, hid my horse, and climbed the tree."

For a long moment Bill Peace was silent, too full of emotion to put his thoughts into words. Finally he drawled: "Sayin' thanks is a poor way of payin' off this kind of a debt."

"You can do it another way," was Sisson's answer. "Stay here and help me fight Miles Root . . . instead of headin' out of the country." Sisson paused, watching Peace carefully. Then he added: "It won't be easy. Wes's bein' gone knocks the props out from under this fight his friends were buildin'. We'll be alone. Those squatters will stick close to home and keep out of this. Root has 'em buffaloed."

It was five seconds before Peace made his answer. What he said was: "Those squatters wouldn't have been much help. I think we can win anyway. They'll think we headed out of the country." He looked squarely at the outlaw. . . . "I'll stay here as long as you do."

55

III
"MONEY BUYS DEATH"

Judge White stabled his horse at about the same hour Peace and Sisson were making camp near the Stanley place. The judge had ridden into town alone.

Late that afternoon the posse had lost the sign of the men they followed. After that Sheriff Fowler had split his twenty-five riders into three groups, sending them in different directions to search for sign. These groups, in turn, had divided into pairs to cover more ground. They hadn't met after dark but headed directly for town. White's companion had left him two miles from town, heading south to his small ranch.

The judge was a man who prided himself on his honesty and fairness, not openly of course but merely as a way of answering to his conscience. Just now, as he crossed his back yard and walked up the steps of the rear porch, his conscience was troubling him. Although Peace was a comparative stranger in this country, the judge had grown to like him. This afternoon a subtle mob feeling had gripped the whole posse, fed by Fowler's arguments after they had taken Bill Peace. It was that mob feeling that had finally made White give in to the lawman and agree to the verdict of a cottonwood jury. This was a rugged country; a man was either right or wrong; and Bill Peace had been obviously guilty. Once convinced of that, a hanging seemed no stranger to White than it did to those others. But now that fatigue had sobered him, he wasn't so sure. Bill Peace hadn't fought, hadn't had a chance. Yet his nerve hadn't broken, and time and again he had proclaimed himself innocent.

Then, too, White was remembering Al Sisson's words, *Peace didn't kill Wes Stanley.*

Since Sisson had broken jail and made himself an outlaw, White's original respect for the man hadn't diminished. He told himself that there was no need for Sisson to have said that this afternoon — no need, unless what he said was the truth.

The judge hoped he wouldn't have to face Joyce tonight. His daughter loved Bill Peace, although they'd never openly discussed her feeling for him. So, when he went in the back door of his house, he sprung the latch softly and swung the door open gingerly. He was glad he had made it a habit to keep the hinges oiled.

As he stepped into the kitchen, he heard voices from the front of the house. One was Joyce's voice, and his disappointment was keen. He had ridden up the back alley and hadn't been able to see the lights in front. Now he'd have to talk with her, explain what had happened, why he'd made himself a member of a lynch mob.

But two seconds after he had softly closed the door, his regrets vanished before a sudden curiosity. From the living room up front he made out a voice he recognized as Miles Root's. The rancher was saying: ". . . may be too soon to mention a thing like this, but I mean it, Joyce. I want you to marry me."

Joyce's answer came to her father, low-throated and filled with an emotion he couldn't identify. "Miles, I'll never marry you. But I do thank you. I feel honored."

"Is it Bill Peace?" Root asked.

There was the scrape of a chair. Then Joyce's voice sounded more vibrant this time as she said: "That's a question I needn't answer!"

"Remember, Joyce, I wasn't a part of what happened

today. For all I know, Peace may have been innocent."

"He was innocent!" she flared. "He's too good a man, too much of a man, to commit murder."

For a long moment a strained silence hung on. At length the sound of Root's steps crossing the room shuttled back through the house.

The judge heard the rancher pause at the front door, saying clearly: "I'm a clumsy fool, Joyce. I won't mention this again, not for a long time. But someday, when you've forgotten what's happened today, I'll ask you this same question. I think I could make you happy."

"Perhaps you could, Miles." Joyce's tone held a measure of tenderness. "But I can't think of it now . . . I can't think of anything. Please understand."

Shortly there was the soft closing of the front door, Joyce's light step as she crossed the room. Before the judge could rid himself of the amazement that held him at what he had heard, Joyce came into the kitchen, holding a lighted lamp in her hand. She stopped abruptly, just inside the door, her eyes wide in surprise.

"Dad!" she breathed. "Dad, you heard!"

He nodded guiltily. "I didn't mean to. I just came in, thought I'd get a bite, and go to bed without wakening you. I thought you'd turned in for the night."

The girl shrugged lifelessly. "Of course you didn't mean to overhear." She stepped across to the table to place the lamp on it then went on lifelessly: "There's some cold chicken you can eat. You must have had a hard day."

White, for the moment, was wordless, held by an emotion of tenderness toward his daughter. She stood there — tall, erect, with none of her pent-up emotion showing in the set of her strong aquiline face. But it did show in her deep brown eyes. There was a hurt look in them that somehow carried to him the fact that she was suffering deeply. With a sudden impulsive gesture he stepped over to her and took her in his arms. She let her head sink against his chest, her chestnut hair softly caressing his face, turned coppery at the edges as it caught the glow from the lamp.

"I'll get over it, Dad," she whispered, her voice steady and low.

Somehow he knew that she wouldn't give way to her grief, that it was too deep to be relieved by tears. He admired her for that stubborn check to her emotion, strangely enough convinced in his own mind that she couldn't be entirely wrong about Bill Peace.

He pushed her gently from him: "I'm hungry, Joyce. How about that chicken?"

There was a fire in the range, and she warmed his meal and set it before him. Her silence was a relief, for his thoughts were still too confused to try and frame into words. But when she had taken the chair opposite, and after his first few mouthfuls of food had dulled the sharp pangs of his hunger, he said, looking at his plate: "You're sure you don't want Miles, honey? He's a good man."

"No, Dad, I don't want Miles." Then, after a long awkward silence: "Bill Peace will be back."

The conviction in her voice startled him. He looked at her squarely. Her head was held proudly, a tenderness mirrored in her eyes that made him proud she was his.

"You heard about it?" he queried. "About Bill . . . escaping?"

She nodded.

"Maybe we all lost our heads today," he said, feeling the need of explaining his actions to her. "Fowler talked me into it. The evidence against Peace was so convincing . . . and then we all thought a lot of Wes."

"You thought a lot of Bill, too, Dad," Joyce reminded him,

her tone lacking the bitterness of a moment ago.

"I know, but there was a lot against him. Tonight I've been thinkin' . . . thinkin' over a few things Bill and Al Sisson said. I think I'll go down and have a talk with Ralph Fowler. There might be a thing or two we'd find out at Wes's place if we looked a bit closer."

The happiness that shone in Joyce's eyes somehow tempered the feeling of self-loathing that had been like a cancerous growth deep within Judge White during these past few hours — since his knowing that he had been in the wrong on the long ride today. He wasn't a man who often made mistakes, and he was too old to admit an error readily. This helped, for in trying to satisfy his own doubts of Bill Peace's guilt, he was bringing happiness to the one person in the world he loved.

He finished his meal quickly, even forgot to take out his pipe and light it as he put on his Stetson and went out the front door. He headed down the street for the jail and Ralph Fowler's office. He wasn't sure what he'd say to the sheriff, how he'd convince him there was a reasonable doubt — but he would try. Joyce's parting — "Good luck, Dad!" — made him realize even more strongly that this was a serious thing.

Miles Root was lighthearted as he left Judge White's house and walked up the street. Soon he was striding beneath the awnings in front of the stores along the plank walk. After the heat of the day the cool night air was bracing, and the fragrant richness of the expensive cigar he smoked tasted good. Tonight was only the beginning with Joyce White. She cared a little for him — it was easy to see that. And sooner or later she would forget Peace.

He was startled out of his thoughts as a figure loomed out of a narrow passageway between two stores a few feet ahead of him. Instinctively his right hand streaked up and slid under the lapel of his broadcloth coat. It settled on the butt of the .38 at his arm-pit.

A familiar voice drawled softly, "It's me, Trank!"

Miles Root's tense muscles relaxed, and he brought his hand down empty. But an instant later hidden relief gave way before a rising of cold anger. He stepped closer to that lone figure.

"I thought I told you to leave the county!" he said, barely audible.

He was close enough now so that he could make out the expression on Ed Trank's gaunt face. It bothered him a little to have to look up at this high-built man. Trank was well over six feet, a full head the taller, and his height subtly robbed Root of a certain dignity.

Trank said: "Wait'll I tell you why I didn't go. Can we talk here?"

Root's glance swiveled up the walk. Then he turned and scanned the shadows behind, seeing that the street was deserted. "We can if you make it quick. What do you want?"

"Money," Trank said and smiled wickedly, his thin lips parting over yellowed teeth.

Miles Root's square-built frame went taut once more. He knew how to deal with this breed of man, and his glance settled on Trank's hands. He watched for a hint of a move there as he intoned: "No understrapper ever blackmailed me and got away with it, Ed!"

"This isn't blackmail, Boss! It's somethin' I seen last night."

Root's curiosity came alive. "Something you saw? What?"

"I'd want my pay first."

The rancher waved a hand in a quick gesture of irritation. "You've always been well paid, haven't you? What was it you saw?"

"Someone was there last night right after I got the blaze goin'."

"Who?" Root snapped the word, his black eyes beady. His jaw muscles corded, giving his rugged face an ugly expression.

Trank lifted his thin shoulders in a shrug. "How would I know? I'm a stranger here. But he was there and tried to get in and pull Stanley out. The flames was too strong. And he saw that tobacco tin, picked it up, and looked at it."

"And you let him get away?"

"I was on that slope above the place and only happened to look back. It was too far to make sure of a shot with a plow handle. By the time I'd got out of my hull and worked closer, he was gone. So I stayed on today, thinkin' you'd want to know."

On the way to town, late that afternoon, Root had talked with a member of the posse, heard the details of what had happened. Now he was fairly certain that the man Trank had seen was Al Sisson. His confidence of a few minutes ago gave way to a troubled feeling of irritation and uncertainty.

"The money, Boss," Trank all at once reminded him.

Grudgingly, Root reached to his hip pocket and took out a wallet. He handed Trank two crisp new twenty dollar bills. "Here's forty dollars," he said. "You'd better put plenty of distance behind you tonight. Tomorrow mornin' there'll be a hundred men on the hunt for Peace and. . . ." Abruptly he broke off, toying with an idea. Then he added hastily: "No, you're not to leave. Maybe I can use you. Ride up to Stanley's place and hole up there and wait. I'll send for you when I want you."

"For how much?" Trank queried, grinning mirthlessly.

Root took two more banknotes from his wallet. "We'll talk

about that when the time comes. This ought to make it interesting enough for you to stay. Wait at Stanley's a week. If I haven't sent for you by that time, slope out of the country. Now get goin'."

Trank took the money, touched the brim of his Stetson in a gesture that might have been one of courtesy but wasn't, and stepped back into the shadows of the alleyway. Then he was gone.

IV
"RUNAWAY LAWMAN"

When Root went on down the street, his lighthearted confidence of minutes ago had vanished. He was sure it was Al Sisson that Trank had seen, and he was very disturbed over how much the outlaw knew. He had planned the events of this day for weeks, and it was his habit to make sure that anything like this went off smoothly. Today it hadn't. First there was Peace's escape. Now the unknown quantity of Al Sisson's being in the country and against him. Root was remembering Sisson and knew that it wasn't in the man's nature to be forgiving. And he knew too that he had given Sisson enough reason to hate him.

He was walking leisurely toward the livery stable when he saw the light in Fowler's office — a low-built adobe behind the jail across the way. Being in the frame of mind he was, he decided to have a talk with Fowler. His entrance into the sheriff's office was abrupt. It brought Ralph Fowler out of his chair in a lunge, hands swiveling up to the twin holsters at his thighs. When the lawman saw who it was, he eased back down into his chair with a sigh of relief.

"Guess I'm jumpy tonight, Miles," he muttered. "I've had a hard. . . ." He caught the expression on the rancher's bleakly set face and stopped his talk.

After a brief interval that seemed interminable to the lawman, Root said: "You made a mess of things today, Ralph."

"A mess?" The sheriff bridled. "What I did was the same as you'd have done . . . or anyone else!"

"You could have rammed a cutter into Peace's middle and

had both of them cold! They outbluffed you."

"The hell they did!" Fowler exploded. "Sisson had half a dozen guns on the cañon rim. You think I'd be damned fool enough . . . ?"

"Jerry Bates rode up there and claimed he couldn't find any sign. Sisson outbluffed you. He was alone."

Root's tone was so positive, the expression in his black eyes so like granite, that all at once the lawman sighed gustily. All the fight was gone out of him. "All right, they bluffed me. But you're rid of Peace, and in two weeks' time you can buy both outfits from the bank. That's what you wanted in the first place . . . what you're payin' me for."

"I'd forgotten that," Root drawled pointedly, taking the wallet from his pocket for the second time that night. This time he counted out ten of the twenty-dollar notes. He stepped across to lay them on Fowler's desk. "There it is, two hundred. It was to be for hangin' Peace, but I'll never have a man sayin' I'm close with money."

Fowler was undecided. He looked greedily at the money, not the first he'd taken from Root. But a deep inner conviction made him hesitate to take it. "Pay me what you think it's worth," he said. "Hell, I don't take money for somethin' I don't do!"

Root shook his head slowly, his smile full of meaning. "It's yours, Ralph. All I ask is that you make a big play tomorrow of huntin' down those two. And you'd better give out orders for the posse to kill them on sight. Peace could talk, and I've a hunch that Sisson knows enough to blow this whole thing sky high. Have 'em brought in dead, if they're brought in at all."

Root stood there only a second, letting his glance add weight to his meaning. Then, before the sheriff could reply, he abruptly turned and went out the door. His leaving was so sudden that Judge White had barely time enough to step back out of the light before the window outside. He hugged the wall's shadow, not daring to breathe until Root had rounded the corner of the jail and gone on down the street.

For the second time that night Judge White had stumbled upon a scene he wasn't supposed to be witnessing. Only this time he had seen, not heard, Miles Root. Five minutes ago, coming down the alleyway beside the jail and intending to go directly to Fowler's office, he had chanced to glance into the single window of the sheriff's office on his way to the door. He had seen Root in there. It was the look on Root's face that had stopped him. He hadn't heard anything but the muted undertone of their voices, but he had seen that Root had paid the sheriff money, for what he couldn't even make a guess. A growing curiosity held White rooted to the spot, watching the lawman.

Inside, Ralph Fowler was mopping his perspiring forehead with a trembling hand. These past few minutes had left him more shaken than the rifle Al Sisson had trained on him this afternoon. It was not because of what Root had said, but because of what he hadn't. Ralph Fowler had the average measure of brains, but it had been his misfortune to use them in the wrong way. He still squirmed at remembrance of the first time he had taken money from Miles Root, years ago. On that occasion Root had paid him handsomely to be at the other end of town at a certain hour one night when a killer was broken out of jail. Since then, Root's money had been wisely spent on taking the sting out of the law. Fowler could remember a dozen times when he'd been paid a flat hundred dollars to overlook freshly altered brands in making a shipping count for Root at the railroad's loading corrals.

Tonight Fowler stripped aside his pretense and took a

good look at himself. Beneath the floorboards of his back room at the hotel, nicely wrapped in a strip of oil cloth, was close onto three thousand dollars he hadn't dared deposit in the bank for fear of arousing suspicion. That three thousand had come to him over a period of eight years, too small a sum to make up for the risk involved in collecting it. Now he was Root's man, cleverly bought and at little expense. Letting his thoughts run on, unhaltered by his usual weak self-assurances, the sheriff had a clear look into the future — down the trail his greed was leading him. What he saw made him afraid. Miles Root would use him just as long as he had need for him. And then?

No man ever lets an understrapper live too long or know too much, Root had once said over a bottle on the evening of a particularly large and successful shipment of stolen beef. Fowler remembered the rancher's words now, attached a grim significance to them. The thought made his palms moist with a clammy sweat, made the small of his back tingle. It would take only one bullet, a hired bullet perhaps, to rid Root of a man who knew too much about the secret of his sudden rise to wealth and power on Steeple range.

The full realization of how deeply he had involved himself sent a flood of momentary panic through Fowler. That emotion gave way to speculation and, after a half-minute's deliberate consideration of the fate that was in store for him, he knew what he must do. The border lay seventy miles south. His three thousand wasn't much but would be enough to take him far beyond Root's reach. By sunup he could be fifty miles on his way. He was through here, and a wise man would leave while his skin was whole. No sooner had the idea come to him than he got up out of his chair and began clearing out his desk, sorting through his few personal belongings and dropping them in an empty saddlebag that he found in a pile of gear in one corner of the room.

Outside, his gaze held fascinated and his conscience eased by the knowledge that he was witnessing something unique here, Judge White watched Fowler through the window. As yet he was not quite able to grasp all that he was seeing. But when the lawman had finished rummaging through his desk and was filling the saddlebag, when he went to the gun rack on the rear wall of the room and took down an extra pair of Colt .45s and a saddle gun, the judge knew: *He's headin' out of here . . . for a long stay!*

By the time Fowler had blown out the lamp, the judge was hidden better than he had been five minutes ago when Root had left. He let Fowler get clear of the alley and far down the street before he moved from his hiding place in the deep shadows underneath a barred window of the jail. From the mouth of the passageway onto the street, he watched Fowler drop his saddlebag in the darkened door-way of a store and cross to the hotel. Waiting there, sensing that the lawman would be back, ten minutes later White saw the sheriff come out of the hotel, cross to pick up the saddlebag, and then walk quickly down the street to the livery barn. But he was only half way guessing the truth when Fowler left town, turning south at the intersection of Twin Rivers' two streets.

V
"IN THE LOFT"

After breakfast the next morning, Bill Peace said: "We'll need grub. You'd better ride over to my place and pick up what we need. There's enough there to last us a week. And while you're there, turn the stock out of the corral."

Sisson nodded. "And what'll you do?"

"Take a *pasear* down to Stanley's place. I want to look around. Did they bury him?"

Sisson nodded. "The posse took care of that. But if you expect to find anything to steer you onto who did the job, you won't get far. I had a look myself, yesterday."

"It'll be spendin' time," Peace said. "Another thing. While you're at my place, go to the barn and dig down into the bottom of the feed bin and bring back that box I cached there. It's money. Tonight I'll take it into Twin Rivers. Someone I know there'll go to the bank tomorrow and pay up the interest on my note."

"Then you're stayin' for good?" Sisson queried. Peace's answering nod brought a broad smile to the outlaw's face. "I've heard about the girl and, from what they tell me, she's worth stayin' around for."

Peace's lean face took on a shade more color. He hadn't consciously been thinking of Joyce this morning, but he knew now that she had been at the back of his mind ever since he'd crawled out of his blankets.

Later, riding down the gulch toward Stanley's place — after Sisson had left — he told himself once again that it was foolishness to be thinking of Joyce. But something deeply within him kept that hope alive. Tonight he would see her, and he would know then whether or not she thought him guilty like the rest. Remembering the sober hatred of those twenty-seven men in the posse, he was filled with a momentary dread of seeing her. But he put it down, hating to recognize the possibility that he might be losing the one real thing in his life.

As the walls of the gulch fell away into the gradual down slope behind Stanley's place, he came within sight of the layout and drew rein, warily studying what lay below before he went on. To all appearances, the place was deserted. The spot where Stanley's cabin had stood was a black scar against the clay-colored yard — a few timbers thrusting up their gaunt, scorched outlines to mark the shape of the foundations.

His glance traveled onto the corral. It was empty, doubtless thrown open by a member of the posse. Two horses, both Stanley's, grazed below the corral in the small two-acre pasture. The weathered frame barn stood open, its loft doors swinging slowly in the breeze.

Certain that he was alone, he rode on. And, as he swung around a far corner of the barn, scanning the ground for sign, he sat relaxed in the saddle. Suddenly a gruff voice spoke to one side of him, from the barn door. It brought him all at once rigid.

"Lookin' for something, stranger?"

When he slowly turned his head to look at the speaker, it was to see Ed Trank leaning idly against the frame of the door, a whittled stick in one hand, an open clasp knife in the other.

Peace was too surprised for a moment to speak. His silence was what saved him, for the next moment Trank said: "Don't tell me the boss sent you after me already."

"No. He sent me to take a look around," was Peace's quick, noncommittal answer.

Trank's glance narrowed as he regarded Peace, a faint suspicion edging it. "Maybe I spoke out of turn," he drawled. His gray eyes shuttled to take in the black's jaw brand. On sight of it he suddenly stiffened. His right hand opened, let go the knife, and dropped toward his holster.

Bill Peace drove his spurs into the black's flanks, tugging at the reins with his left hand as his right swept upward, palming out his gun. The black took a quick, nervous step that moved Peace out of line, so that Trank's whipping shot went wide. Peace's weapon swung down and into line and echoed the explosion of Trank's gun.

The gunman all at once dropped the gun and made a hurried stab at his chest. He tottered weakly back against the boards of the barn siding. His knees gave way, and he slid down to a sitting position. By that time Peace had thrown himself out of the saddle and was standing ten feet away, his Colt lined at the gunman's chest. His shot had been a lucky one, for it was thrown quickly with his arm unsteadied by the lunge of the black.

Sitting there, Ed Trank coughed pulpily, and blood flecked his lips. His hand came away from his chest to show a red smear centering his shirt, one that spread outward slowly. He cursed viciously time and again, pausing only to gasp for breath. At length, he eyed Bill Peace coldly. Then, faintly smiling at some inner thought, he drawled: "Damned if this isn't luck! You're Peace, ain't you? That brand gave you away. The first time I ever had a chance to collect a reward that wasn't on my own head, and I fumble it!"

Peace said: "Your mistake was in goin' for your iron."

Trank laughed softly, and even that effort brought on a spasm of coughing. He shook his head. "No, my mistake was in ever staying in this country. It was the money that did it."

"Whose money?"

After a moment in which lines of pain robbed Trank's twisted smile of its mirth, the gunman said: "I never yet double-crossed a man. You go to hell!"

"You're Miles Root's man?" Peace queried, voicing his only logical guess.

"Who's Root?" Trank asked blandly. Then, again: "You go to hell!" As he spoke, his right hand edged slowly outward to take a hold on the handle of his fallen gun.

Peace saw that gesture and warned: "Don't make me throw down on you again."

But Trank said: "Why not? I'm cashin' in anyway." He raised the weapon.

It was sheer suicide, Trank's last gesture in defiance of having been beaten by a better man. Awed, hating what he must do, yet knowing that it was either his life or the gunman's, Bill Peace thumbed back the hammer of his .45, his gaze riveted to that upswinging gun of Trank's. Suddenly its feeble upswing ended, and the hand that held the weapon went limp and loosed its grasp. Ed Trank's chin rested on his chest. He was dead.

It took Peace two hours to dig the grave in the brick-hard clay down by the corral. When he had finished lugging rocks from the cabin foundation, rocks he put over the grave, the sun had topped its slow arc to the south and was lowering toward the uneven horizon to the west. He was hungry, sobered by this quirk of fate that had forced him to kill to defend his own life, so that he rode away from the layout without giving a thought to his purpose in going there.

Twenty minutes later he had unsaddled and hobbled the black and was gathering dry wood for a fire. He opened Sisson's one remaining can of beans, heated them in a pan, and hungrily devoured them. Then he settled down to wait, vaguely troubled by the outlaw's prolonged absence. It was only six miles north to Peace's layout. Sisson should have returned long ago.

The reason the outlaw didn't return was that two members of the posse that spread out in all directions from Twin Rivers that morning had been sent to keep a watch at Peace's place. Sisson had left his horse in the grove of cottonwoods nearly a half mile away, walking the remaining distance, keeping to cover as best he could and wanting to make sure that no one was around. He found the place deserted and set about his first task, turning loose the three broncs in the corral. Once done with that, he went to the barn and thrust his hand deeply into the oats in the feed bin and found the box containing Bill Peace's money. Next, he went to the slab-sided cabin and had half filled a flour sack with provisions when he heard riders approaching. A quick look outside showed him two men had ridden directly into the yard. When they dismounted, they were close enough so that he heard one of them say: "This'll be better than ridin' all day."

One rider stayed in the yard, blocking the outlaw's chance of escape. The other took their horses to the corral. By the time he was back once more, Sisson had climbed into the low-roofed loft above the beamed ceiling of the cabin's single room.

The loft was dark, the air close and hot from the beating sun on the roof. Al Sisson endured his discomforts with a time-trained patience as the two riders below made themselves comfortable.

At first there was little talk. One of the pair found a pack of cards and for two hours they played pinochle, sitting at a table directly below the spot where the outlaw lay. Through a space between the crude sheathing of the ceiling he could look down onto the table and watch their game. In a way it relieved the slow torture of the heat and his consequent thirst.

It wasn't until the two below gave up their game and started cooking their noon meal on Bill Peace's sheet-iron stove that either of them said anything interesting. Sisson, his senses dulled by the heat, had closed his eyes and was nearly asleep when he heard one of them say: "You got any more ideas on what happened to Ralph Fowler?"

The second man grunted his disgust. "Your guess is as good as mine." He didn't appear particularly interested.

But the first was in the mood for talk. "It ain't like Ralph to skip out and leave a job like this to a deputy."

"It ain't!" the other snorted. "You ought to have been along yesterday. Fowler had his chance to take them two and missed it. Slim, I'm beginnin' to think this county needs a new sheriff!"

That was all — until the middle of the afternoon. Al Sisson had been dozing, his mind utterly weary yet not relaxing completely due to a long-trained wariness. Because of this half alertness he heard the hoof pound of the running horse while it was still a good distance below the cabin. The sound jerked him into complete wakefulness, his first thought being that this might be Bill Peace riding into a trap. He reached down and took his pair of Colt .45s from their holsters and crawled to the loft opening. He'd jump down into the room and help Peace if the two down there made any move to threaten the approaching rider.

VI
"OVERTAKEN"

An instant later the gruff voice of one of the pair below brought an immediate relief. The man was standing at the door, looking out, and he called to his companion: "Looks like Jerry Bates. He's in an all-fired hurry, too!"

After a brief pause his voice sounded from outside the cabin, muted by the distance as he greeted the newcomer who had ridden into the yard in front.

Sisson holstered his guns once more, irritably deciding that he would be cooped up for several more hours. But five seconds later he heard the quick pound of boots in the hard-packed yard outside, and the man who had spoken a moment ago called: "Slim! Goddlemighty, Slim, listen to this!"

Slim's chair scraped across the floor. He went to the door. The three of them stood there talking, their voices plainly heard by the outlaw.

"Slim, it's about Ralph Fowler! He's been kidnapped!"

"The hell you say!"

"Tell him about it, Jerry."

"It didn't happen until after Brady'd sent the posse out this mornin'," came a new voice. "Brady was in the office when Miles Root came in, about noon. Miles listened to what Brady had to say then went over to the hotel. Later it come out he'd got suspicious and thought he ought to take a look at Fowler's room. The sheriff's bed hadn't been slept in, and Root found a sheet of paper lyin' on it. It was printed so as to disguise the handwriting of the man that left it there. But what it said was plain enough. We're takin' your sheriff along just in case someone tries to collect the reward."

In the brief interval of awed silence that followed Jerry Bates's words, Al Sisson lay there, taking in the full significance of this news. For the first time here was clear proof of Miles Root's cunning.

"It means Sisson and Bill Peace. . . ."

"It means they've got Ralph Fowler and that his hide ain't worth a plug nickel!" Bates put in. "You gents climb into your hulls and get on back to town. I'm roundin' up as many of the boys as I can find. Root's takin' charge."

"What does he aim to do?"

"He hasn't said. But there's a meetin' in town at five. If you ride hard, you can make it."

In five more minutes Slim and his partner were pounding away from the corrals below. Jerry Bates had three minutes ago ridden in the opposite direction, north, obviously in a hurry to locate as many members of the far-flung posse as he could.

Al Sisson was in the saddle in twenty minutes. He had left the provisions and Bill Peace's money in the cabin. He was in too much of a hurry to bring them with him now. They could wait until later — until after he'd found Peace and told him the news.

He rode hard, cutting back through the hills directly for the gulch instead of using the winding, roundabout trail that flanked the course of Snake River. Had he taken the easier way, the trail that followed the river for four miles before cutting in toward Stanley's place, he would have met Bill Peace. For Peace, anxious because of the outlaw's absence, had decided to ride to his layout and find him.

When Al Sisson arrived at the gulch camp, he saw that Peace had already been there and left. He tried to follow his friend's sign, but the rocky floor of the gulch made that impossible. So he came back to camp, knowing that Peace would eventually return.

Peace approached his cabin cautiously. The signs in the trampled yard meant only one thing. At least three riders had been here today. Al Sisson had undoubtedly been taken prisoner. Although at first unwilling to believe that, he was convinced when he found lying inside the doorway on the plank flooring the sack of provisions the outlaw had gathered. The money-box was in the bottom of the sack, the evidence plain. Al Sisson had been surprised and caught helpless as he went about his errand. That was the only explanation Peace could give for what he found.

"If he's alive, he's in Twin Rivers' jail," was his logical reasoning.

Persuaded of this, he took the three sheaves of paper money from the box he had cached in the feed-bin, stuffed them in his pockets, and headed down the trail. Six miles put him on the Twin Rivers road. He kept the black to a steady, mile-eating run, forgetting all caution, intent only on his single purpose of helping Al Sisson if it wasn't too late.

Had he tempered his haste with wariness, he wouldn't have been surprised. As it was, he sighted the group of riders better than a mile ahead before they had seen him. He swung immediately off the trail, intending to take to the broken tree-protected country two miles to the north before he made his swing in toward town. But far to the north, Jerry Bates had found five more members of the posse and had sent them riding hard for town. Now they rode out of those trees two miles to the north — just as Peace headed toward them.

One of the five saw Peace as he right-angled from the trail and came toward them. At first this rider's curiosity was mild, held vaguely by the sight of the distant horseman whose black horse streaked across the sweep of range below at a hard run.

"Someone's in a hurry," he stated to the man in the saddle alongside him. "This meetin' of Root's will have every jasper on Steeple range rarin' up on his hind legs, headin' in toward Twin Rivers. I wouldn't give a peso Mex for Al Sisson's scalp right now. Peace's either!"

His neighbor smiled mirthlessly, eyeing the rider on the black far ahead. But suddenly his gaze hardened. He looked at the black horse intently, then breathed: "That black has four white stockings. Bill Peace owns a horse like that!"

The first rider's glance narrowed suspiciously. He muttered softly, "It couldn't be!" Then, louder: "Damned if it isn't!"

He rammed blunt spurs to his pony's flanks and sent the animal into a fast lope. He swung diagonally off to intercept Peace, who was now nearer. The rest, urged on by the shouts of the second rider, strung out behind.

Bill Peace had been too interested in the group of horsemen on the trail far ahead. He saw these others too late as they streaked down out of the dark shadows of the tree-margins to the north. He wheeled the black around and drove his spurs cruelly in an effort to outrun this remnant of the posse.

At first the black responded, keeping his distance, making the run of his life. But these last six miles at such a killing pace had robbed the animal of his wind. Gradually, the distance between Peace and the others lessened. From behind came the brittle, distance-muffled crack of a gun. Then another.

The second bullet was thrown from a rider who had stopped and taken careful aim. Luck was against Peace. He felt the black's high frame shudder as the bullet took him. He had barely time to kick his feet clear of the stirrups before the black's forelegs buckled.

Peace was thrown clear. He lighted on one shoulder in a practiced roll. But as the force of his fall carried him over onto his back, his head struck hard against the ground. He fought to keep that curtain of blackness from blotting out his senses; but it hung on, dimming his sight, making his thoughts a hazy jumble. Then his body relaxed into unconsciousness.

VII
"THE KILLER'S TRAIL"

Judge White was in the most enviable position of his life. Mystified by Root's call on the sheriff and by Fowler's consequent disappearance, he had gotten out of bed that morning and carefully watched the shaping of events. He saw Stud Brady, Fowler's deputy, reassemble the posse and give the riders their directions and send them out on the hunt for Bill Peace. He speculated idly with the loungers along the awninged walk as to the reason for the sheriff's disappearance.

Later, when Miles Root rode into town, the judge inconspicuously dogged the rancher's every move. When Root turned up at the sheriff's office with the note he claimed he'd found on Fowler's bed in the hotel, White was an eager listener in the crowd that quickly gathered at the jail to hear Root publicly read the kidnapper's message and then send Jerry Bates and two others out to call in the posse. White had his reasons for suspecting Root now but, being a man of long experience in the subtleties of intrigue, he chose to watch developments rather than denounce Root immediately.

At five o'clock, when the heat of the dust of the streets was being swept away by a gusty wind out of the black-clouded horizon to the east, most of the riders of the posse were back in town. They mingled impatiently with the crowd, awaiting Root's promised speech. The street in front of the jail was impassable, crowded from walk to walk with a mass of grim, silent men — even those small ranchers who had until now taken side against Miles Root. Root, always showing a flair for drama, wasn't going to miss his opportunity this evening. During the afternoon he had ordered a platform built of foot-wide planks on barrel ends before the jail's entrance. Now, having secluded himself at the hotel all afternoon, he suddenly put in an appearance when the crowd was thickest.

A hoarse cheer from across the street welcomed his approach. A lane opened in the crowd, and he walked through it with his wide shoulders squared, a sober set to his rugged face that was plain indication of the seriousness of this affair. When he had climbed to the platform, he held up a hand, commanding instant silence. Judge White stood directly below, in the front line of the men who crowded out into the street and filled the walks on either side of Root's crude rostrum.

"You all know why we're here," Root began, his voice deep throated and carrying clearly to the most distant of his listeners perched on the wooden awnings across the street. "Some time last night our good friend and sheriff, Ralph Fowler, was forcibly taken prisoner by two men who yesterday made themselves outlaws, Bill Peace and Al Sisson!" Root waited until the crowd's angry murmur had died, then he went on: "A message was found in Fowler's room at the hotel today . . . a message of warning, threatening the sheriff's life if we should make any attempt at capturing the outlaw who committed the crime. I'm here to ask you what you think we ought to do about it!"

This time the roar of protest that met his words took longer to wear itself out. Root made no attempt to stop the angry outburst. Knowing what was coming, he wanted to fan the smoldering tempers of the men to a white-hot flame. At length, across the utter stillness of the street, he spoke deliberately and solemnly: "Regardless of that warning, I am for. . . ." His words ended as suddenly as they had begun, for his glance was attracted by the approach of a knot of fifteen or twenty riders coming into the far end of the street off the west trail. As he hesitated, a shout came from one of the riders down there, and the cavalcade lifted their horses out of their trot to a fast run.

In another five seconds, the shouts of those oncoming horsemen could be heard and understood. What they were shouting was: "We've got Peace!"

Instant pandemonium cut loose as the crowd surged along the thoroughfare to meet the riders. Those at the outer fringes of the mob ran. Those behind pushed their neighbors in a frantic attempt to see what was going on now.

Judge White let the mob break from around him before he stepped up onto the walk and ran as hard as he could to come up with the leaders of the crowd. A numbing premonition of what might happen set up a panic within him that mounted higher each instant. Soon he was close enough to see the leaders of the mob run in between the horses and up to the pony across whose saddle Bill Peace's limp frame was roped.

Someone grasped at the pony's reins, holding the frightened animal, while others lifted Peace's inert bulk down. Judge White saw all that with a feeling of acute dread. Suddenly he was striding down off the walk, pushing his way through the gathering crowd to its center. As he came nearer, he reached into his coat pocket and pulled out the stubby Derringer he had thought to bring with him that afternoon. When he could force his way no further into the mob that now crowded in around the frightened horses of the posse, he lifted the Derringer high over his head, cocked it, and squeezed the trigger.

The blast ripped along the corridor of the street, attracting instant attention. Someone saw who had fired the shot and shouted: "Let the judge through!"

When White stood in front of the two men who were holding erect Bill Peace's loose figure, he held up a hand to command silence. It was a tribute to the regard these people held for him that those nearest backed away a step or two, recognizing his authority, and turned to silence those behind. The word went back through the packed crowd that Judge White was up front, taking things in charge. Everyone there knew that White had been at the cottonwood the day before. Now they remembered his outspoken hatred of Bill Peace and decided that here was a good man to act as their leader at this time.

A few shouts of "Hooray for the judge!" and "Let White handle this!" went back through the crowd. And, in their eagerness, the leaders were calling: "Quiet down! Let's hear what he says!"

Someone helped White up into the saddle of the horse that had carried the unconscious Peace into town. From there, where he could look out across this sea of faces, White said in a loud, steady voice: "Here's what we wanted, men! Here's Bill Peace, alive, the best bait for a hang noose the law of this country ever had!"

A roar of grim satisfaction broke in on his words, falling away to a quick, restless silence as his upraised hand again commanded attention. When he spoke now, it was hurriedly, for he saw Miles Root making his way to the front of the crowd. "But I'm askin' you why we stop with the job half finished? Take Peace to jail and keep him there until he can talk! Then we'll make him lead us to where Al Sisson's hidin' our sheriff!"

The low, restless undertone of heated argument that broke loose was unreadable for long moments. Judge White tried to speak, couldn't make himself heard. Then Miles Root stepped into the cleared space around the posse's horses, and White thought he had lost. As though to bear out his fears, Root threw up his hands and through the sheer force of his personality silenced those standing nearest.

What he said was: "Why wait? We'll take care of Peace now and Sisson later!"

A cold, relentless anger mounted up in Judge White. He looked down at the rancher. "What's the hurry, Miles? A play like that might spoil our chances of taking Al Sisson."

The crowd agreed, and shouted its approval. For once in his life Miles Root was faced by a greater will than his own. His face was white in anger as he realized it. Grudgingly, he gave in and made no protest as Peace was carried out through the crowd and taken to the jail. Root even made a pretense of helping clear the way. They threw Bill Peace onto the cot in one of the two iron-barred cells.

"Get Doc Baker," Judge White said to one of the men nearest. "The sooner Peace comes around, the quicker we'll finish the business." Then he looked out into the crowded jail corridors. "The rest of you clear out. We'll take care of him."

After the corridor was cleared of all but a half dozen men, Miles Root among them, White said to the rancher: "Miles, I'll leave it up to you to throw a guard around the jail."

When Root was gone, the judge felt a great relief. But when Doc Baker came in, his concern returned. Baker was one of Twin Rivers' oldest citizens, an honest man, a friend of the judge's. Yet White wondered what the medico would say to the thing he had in mind.

Baker was efficient as he examined Peace. "Nothin' but a bump on the head," he finally said. "He'll be out of it soon."

White, standing alongside the medico, said softly, so that those in the corridor close by couldn't hear: "Send the rest out, Doc. There's something I have to say."

Baker looked surprised, puzzled, but he got up off his chair and looked out at the others. "White and I will see to Peace," he called gruffly. "The rest of you clear out. And open that window before you leave. This man has to have fresh air."

In another minute, White and the medico were alone with the prisoner.

"What's eatin' you, Judge?" Baker asked.

White gave him a level stare, deciding all at once to let this man in on his confidence. "Peace is innocent," he said. Then, before Baker could recover from his amazement and interrupt him, the judge told the medico all he knew — of Miles Root, of Fowler's strange disappearance, of his doubts about the message Root claimed to have found. He finished by saying: "So it's up to you and me to see that Peace isn't in shape to be seen tonight. Or if he is, to keep these others, especially Root, out of here."

Bill Peace stirred faintly where he lay on the cot. Judge White leaned down over him just as he opened his eyes and stared around in bewilderment. The judge put his hand over Peace's mouth, said in a low voice: "You're goin' to be all right, Bill. Just don't try and talk." As he took his hand away, his voice droned on and on, Doc Baker nodding his approval at rare intervals. The bewilderment gradually went out of Bill Peace's intent stare.

Five minutes later, Doc Baker came out onto the walk in front of the jail. Miles Root was there, along with many others.

"You're all out of luck tonight, gents!" the medico announced to them. "Peace has a bad concussion. It's a cinch he won't recover consciousness tonight, maybe not for days. You'd all better go home and rest easy." He glanced down the street and out across the open sweep of range to the far eastern horizon. Out there, black thunderheads were banking high into the sky. What he saw made him chuckle. He added: "It's a poor evenin' for a hangin', anyway. Goin' to rain."

Miles Root was disappointed. Yet he accepted this un-looked-for development stoically. Immediately he asked himself how he could upset Judge White's plan of talking to Bill Peace when he recovered consciousness. Finally he knew what he would do. He started along the walk toward the livery barn at the far end of town. Half way down he met Joyce White face to face.

She had been at home all afternoon, her hopes shattered by Ralph Fowler's disappearance and Miles Root's discovery that so ominously explained it. Her father had been too uncertain of what he knew to tell her anything that would have revived her hopes earlier in the day. During the past hour he had been too busy. Only a minute ago one of their neighbors, returning home after the breaking up of the mob, had told her of Bill Peace's predicament. And that neighbor had mentioned hanging. Her oval face was pale, and her brown eyes flashed in anger as she found herself suddenly confronting the man she instinctively blamed for all Bill Peace's trouble.

Miles Root had barely time enough to greet her, "Evenin', Joyce," before she said bitingly: "You should be proud of yourself tonight, Miles! First you gather this mob, then you talk of hanging an innocent man!"

"But Peace is guilty, Joyce. Ralph Fowler was my friend. I'm doing a public duty."

"Bill Peace isn't guilty!" came her heated protest. "None of you knows what you're doing! The whole country has gone mad!"

All at once she caught the hint of amusement in Miles Root's glance that betrayed his sober set of countenance. At sight of it, she knew he was inwardly laughing at her, that she could look for no help from him. It sharpened her anger.

"I think you're really liking this, Miles. I'll remember it." With that she strode on past him, her glance holding nothing but an obvious scorn and loathing.

Root stood there a moment, watching her tall, proudly-erect figure as it disappeared into the crowd. He hadn't wanted this to happen and now cursed himself for a fool in speaking against Bill Peace. It would have been better to pretend sympathy for Peace, even after it was all over.

While he stood there, he felt a touch on his arm and turned to confront Peter Kennedy, owner of the bank. Kennedy said: "So there's nothin' more doin' tonight?"

Root shook his head irritably. "They want to talk to Peace before they hang him."

"Which reminds me, Miles. When this is over, I'll have twenty sections of that land you've been wantin'. You figure to put in a bid on it?"

"At what price?"

"At your own price," Kennedy said. "We want to get our money out of it."

Here was something that made up a little to Root for his meeting with Joyce. He thanked the banker, told him he'd see him in a week or so, and then went on to the livery stable. Yet the more he thought about it, the more unsatisfactory it seemed to be. He was getting one thing without the other. He'd had high hopes, up until now, of making Joyce White mistress of one of the largest landholdings in this country. And, like a fool, he'd narrowed his chances a minute ago by one badly chosen run of words.

His temper running high and thin after getting his horse, he punished the bay unmercifully on the eight-mile ride that took him out to Wes Stanley's place. The makings of the storm behind suited his dark mood. He would pay Ed

87

Trank well for what he would do tonight. He'd have Trank wait until late, until the town had quieted down. Then the gunman could climb onto the roof of the saddle shop across the street from the jail. From there a man could look directly into the single window of the jail.

If Root remembered correctly, the cot in the cell Peace occupied would almost exactly center that window. A bullet couldn't miss a man who lay upon it. After Trank had finished that, he could head for the border on another errand. Miles Root had shrewdly guessed that Ralph Fowler was gone for good, and why he'd gone. *He'll head for old Mexico* was his judgment.

Al Sisson waited two hours for Peace to return. Then, more troubled than he cared to admit, the outlaw rode down to Wes Stanley's layout. It took some time for him to locate Peace's sign. From there on what he saw utterly mystified him. There was a splotch of dried, darkened blood smeared low down on the weathered boards of the barn, alongside the door. Higher up, a bullet hole showed. The full significance of what had happened didn't come to him until he noticed the newly dug grave near the corral. Then, frantically dreading what he was sure he'd find, Al Sisson performed the distasteful task of opening that grave.

Sobered by sight of the dead stranger's face in the fading light of dusk yet relieved to find that it wasn't Bill Peace, he rode out from Stanley's burned cabin toward the gulch camp since to wait there would be the surest way of finding Peace. Something Peace had said that morning brought him added relief. *Like as not, he's gone in to see that girl,* he decided.

From a few hundred yards out along the faint line of the

trail, Miles Root sighted Al Sisson riding away and recognized him barely in time to escape discovery. He let the outlaw get out of sight before he made a wide circle and followed. Well into the gulch, he warily climbed from the saddle, leading his bay far up one slope. There he rein-tied the animal to the gnarled trunk of a piñon and last of all drew his rifle from the boot under the saddle. He knew this gulch and his shrewd observation was: *Their hide-out is somewhere close.*

Less than an hour later, walking soundlessly through the darkness, careful of where he placed each foot as he went slowly forward, he sighted the winking light of Sisson's fire through the cobalt shadows up ahead. He circled to the left and, from above the camp, looked down over his rifle sights at Al Sisson's darkly outlined shape.

He squeezed the trigger. The brittle report of the gunshot slapped sharply up the gulch, and he saw Al Sisson double at the waist and fall forward in a loose sprawl. For a brief interval he watched Sisson's inert form lying there. Then, satisfied at what he had done, he made his way back to his bay horse and climbed into the saddle. He rode down the gulch, directly to Stanley's place. As he came within sight of the barn's dark shadow, a few pelting drops of rain fell out of the leaden sky.

He called loudly, "Ed!" and heard the echo of his voice slapped hollowly at him. Once more, "Ed!" and his only answer was that echo.

At length, as a gusty wind whipped the rain into a downpour, he reached around and untied his poncho from behind the cantle and put it on. He buckled it tightly against the stinging bite of the storm.

"So he high-tailed?" he muttered, half aloud. He had never been too sure of this Ed Trank, and the gunman's absence left him somehow unsurprised. At the worst all it could mean was that he himself would have to do the work he had intended for Trank. *And maybe it's better this way, too,* he mused, reaching down to caress the stock of the rifle.

As his hand touched the smoothly rounded heel-plate of the Winchester, a sudden thought slowed his pulse. He remembered the day, better than a week ago, when he had last used the Winchester. He had been on his north range and sighted a coyote at better than two hundred yards away. He had drawn the Winchester, raised the back sight, and killed that coyote at the first shot. But had he lowered the sight again?

Frantically he drew the .30-.30 from its scabbard and laid it across his lap. He looked at it, squinting his eyes against the wind-whipped rain. No, the sight was still raised, to the third notch. Did that mean that he had thrown his bullet high back there in the gulch — that it hadn't hit Sisson squarely in the chest?

"You're spooky!" he said aloud. Then he remembered another thing. He had been shooting downhill and hadn't aimed below his target to compensate for the natural tendency to shoot low while aiming downward. He had been in too much of a hurry to think of such things. *But he caved in like a pole-axed bull* was his final thought. Reassured then by the memory of Sisson's loose fall, he turned his attention back to Bill Peace.

From there on, on the long uncomfortable ride to Twin Rivers, his desire to remove this last obstacle, Bill Peace, became a thing that twisted his mind to near madness. With Peace out of the way and those two small outfits along Snake River thrown in with his already far-ranging spread, nothing could keep him from becoming the biggest man in this country.

VIII
"WITNESS WANTED"

The storm struck Twin Rivers with a ferocity greater than most men could remember for a late-summer rain. With it came lightning that seemed to pick the town as its target. Time and again the bolts struck with deafening, prolonged blasts that shook the ground and left the few remaining saddle horses at the hitch rails terror-stricken and shaking with fright. At the height of the storm, when the water was streaming down in foggy sheets that made it impossible to see across the street, a jagged streamer of lightning hit the barn in the livery stable corral at the edge of town. And even for all the rain that poured upon its roof, its baled alfalfa and loft full of hay were soon a roaring mass of flame.

The word whipped through town: "Beck's barn is on fire! Get the horses out!"

The remnants of the crowd that had assembled that afternoon now crowded the saloons, safely out of the storm. But many of these men had horses in the big corral along-side the barn. With the spreading of the news, the saloons emptied and every able-bodied man in town ran out into the rain and toward the corral to save the half a hundred head of terror-stricken broncs that might, even now, be trying to break down the corral-poles and be inadvertently plunging into the roaring inferno of the barn's blaze.

The guards at the jail were the last to leave. But, as the rain suddenly slacked off to a misty drizzle and with the livery barn's rosy flames mounting higher into the sky, one of the guards said: "To hell with this job. My blaze-face

91

and my saddle are down there!" He set off at a run, and his leaving was a signal for the others.

Inside the jail, Bill Peace and Judge White had pulled a cot to the single window and were watching the blaze. As White saw the guards run off down the walk, his face took on a bitter smile.

"Their bad luck is our good luck, Bill!" he whispered. "The way's clear outside. I'll go get your guns."

He was gone from the cell room for a few seconds, and Peace heard him moving about in the small cubicle up front by the door. Soon he was back with Peace's twin gun belts slung over his arm — the same guns Peace had taken from Ralph Fowler yesterday afternoon at the cottonwood.

"Strap 'em on, Bill. This is your chance for a getaway."

Reluctantly, Bill Peace took the belts. "What about you, Judge? They'll blame you for this."

As Peace uttered these words, Miles Root was turning his bay in to the hitching rail two doors above. He had just entered the street in time to see the guards lean their rifles against the jail's adobe wall and run down the walk toward the fire. He understood immediately what this meant. With the jail left unguarded, the rancher gave up his idea of climbing to the roof of the saddle shop opposite and waiting for his opportunity to send a bullet through the jail's window at Peace. Here was a sure way, a quicker one. He would walk straight into the place, finish with Peace, and be out of town before the gunshot had attracted the attention of those at the burning barn. He smiled.

He left the Winchester in its saddle scabbard. Instead, after he got down out of the saddle, he paused to take his .38 from its shoulder holster and examine it to make doubly sure that five of its six chambers were loaded. Then, the

92

weapon still in his hand, he came on down the walk and turned in at the jail door. He was just in time to hear Judge White's deep-toned voice say: "But you've got to, Bill! They can't do anything to me. I know enough about Miles Root to send a posse out after him. When we have him here, we'll get the truth out of him if we have to bend a gun barrel over his head! Now you get out of here!"

Root waited no longer. The light of a lantern shone through the door to the cell room, and now he stepped into that orange rectangle of light. The sound of his boot tread brought White and Peace wheeling around to face him. They stood in the corridor between the cells, the judge with the keys still in his hand, Peace with his twin .45s strapped to his thighs.

Peace's right hand made a short, quick stab toward his holster; but Root's upswinging .38 cut short that desperate motion. Slowly, Bill Peace's hands came up to the level of his wide shoulders.

"So you'll gun whip me, will you, Judge?" Root drawled, his stocky frame outlined by the door opening in which he stood.

White didn't answer for a moment. His hawkish, grizzled face drained of color. At length, he breathed, "Damn you, Root!"

The rancher's low chuckle was full of a strident menace. The weapon in his hand was held rock steady, his thumb on the hammer. Yet he was glorying in this moment, in seeing these two strong men so powerless in his grasp. Outside, the street was quiet except for the muffled crackle of the flames and the mutter of the crowd far out along it. There was plenty of time.

"How much do you know, Judge?" Root queried silkily. Then, when White made no answer, the rancher added:

93

"Out of curiosity, I'd like to know."

It was Peace who supplied the answer, his drawl soft against the stillness of the room: "Plenty, Root! First, I didn't kill Stanley. You, or one of your men, did. Today I had to cut down a man at Stanley's place. I think he was one of your hired guns. Last night you were seen handing money to Ralph Fowler. Fowler was seen leaving town in a hurry, headed south."

"Much obliged," Root muttered. "I wasn't sure which way Ralph left. Now I'll know where to find him." His thumb drew back the .38's hammer, the click of its catch sounding loudly in the stillness. "So you killed Ed Trank, eh? He's the one I hired to 'gulch Stanley."

That hammer-click worked a visible change in Judge White. He seemed to become a smaller man. The slack expression of his visage was plain evidence that he had lost all hope. "You can't do this, Miles," he intoned. "You won't live another day when they hear what I have to say."

"But you won't have anything to say. Dead men don't talk!" Root laughed harshly as he saw the sudden frenzy that took possession of the judge's glance. "You'll be found here, alongside Peace, one of his guns in your hand. It'll look like the two of you fought it out. They'll make a hero of you, Judge."

During the interval that followed, Bill Peace's hands edged slowly downward. "I'm goin' to make a try for you, Root!" he drawled.

"Sure, make one, Peace! I'll wait until your iron's free of leather. Then you'll get lead through your. . . ."

All at once his words broke off as the hard pound of boots sounded on the walk directly outside. A sudden indecision dilated Miles Root's black eyes. He stood transfixed by a sudden paralysis of fear for one instant. Then his glance swung around, and he turned his head and looked back over his shoulder.

In that split-second Bill Peace's hands streaked downward and up. When Root's head jerked back again, Peace's guns were clearing leather.

"Root!"

The voice came from the outer doorway of the jail. It was Al Sisson's.

Root lunged sideways, clear of the doorway. His .38 blasted away the silence in an exploding burst of sound.

The thunder of his gun seemed to push Bill Peace backward, break the upward swing of his two hands. But before the concussion had died, his twin Colts were lancing flame in a pounding riot of sound that beat outward at the walls.

Judge White threw himself to one side, out of the way of those guns. He felt the air whip of Peace's bullets as they fanned past him.

Once more, Root's .38 exploded, its feeble roar deadened by the staccato blast of Bill Peace's .45s. That shot of Root's was his last, for already his Colt was slanted toward the floor. Twice his body quivered spasmodically at the hard impact of lead. His eyes stared wide and horrified at Peace, the hatred in them wiped suddenly away to be replaced by one of utter bewilderment. Blood flecked his lips, until all at once a bullet made his mouth a misshapen, pulpy mass.

He tottered weakly out from the wall just as Al Sisson, six-gun in hand, appeared in the doorway. Then, slowly, the rancher's right knee gave way and his body swung to the right in a half turn. Some inner strength guided his hands, for even as he saw Sisson, his .38 raised a full two inches and his thumb had the power to draw back the weapon's hammer and let it fall.

But he was already dead, falling loosely, as the gun

blasted the momentary silence. Its bullet ripped a channel down one of the floor planks. His fall tore loose the Colt from his grasp so that, when he finally lay spread-eagled on his back, his outstretched hand had the appearance of making a futile reach for the gun.

Judge White's fascinated, horrified gaze finally tore itself from Root. He looked at Bill Peace, saw the jagged circle of red smearing his shirt low on one side. "Bill, you're hit!"

"It can wait." Peace looked across at Al Sisson. "You drew it pretty fine, gettin' here when you did, Al. You saved our lives."

Sisson seemed not to have heard. His hard stare regarded the prostrate form at his feet. "After all these years it had to be someone besides me that handed you your last poison!" he breathed. There was a thinly disguised regret in his tone. But all at once he looked up at Bill Peace and smiled. "Next to me, I don't know anyone I'd rather have seen do the job."

For the first time Peace saw that Sisson's shirt was torn at the shoulder, that the edges of the torn cloth were edged with red. "Who cut down on you, Al?" he queried.

The outlaw nodded toward the floor. "Our friend Root . . . out in the gulch. He tried a bushwhack but threw his shot too high. I played dead and, when he left, I followed him here."

From out on the street shouts echoed suddenly, the sound of boots pounding on the plank walk.

Hearing that, Judge White stepped around Peace and through the inner door, saying: "I'll have some fast talkin' to do."

The judge was partly right. But he had a helper out there in the person of Doc Baker. Between them they silenced the crowd that had heard the shots and run for the jail. They took turns telling the story, what they knew of it. Doc Baker made it his job to answer any objections from the crowd as to what the judge had to say.

Later, when Baker had taken Peace and Sisson home to the office in his back room to bandage their flesh wounds and while the crowd was moving slowly down the street following the four men that carried what was left of Miles Root, Judge White came to the door of Baker's office. He looked in at Peace and said: "Bill, you've got a visitor out here."

Peace got up from the chair where he had been sitting, his move jerking the roll of bandage from the medico's hand. Peace didn't notice that, didn't hear the medico's half-amused oath. Beyond the door was Joyce White.

She stood tall and straight, her brown eyes shining with a light that meant a new world to Bill Peace. He took her in his arms. Judge White softly opened the front door and went out.

Afterward — it couldn't have been longer than two minutes — the front door opened once more and Judge White stepped in, a little breathless. He had a black book in his hand.

Joyce raised her head from Peace's shoulder and looked at her father and understood. A soft tide of color deepened the flush in her cheeks.

White glanced beyond them, into the medico's office, calling: "Doc, you and Sisson get out here! You're needed as witnesses."

"Long Gone" was one of the last Peter Dawson short stories to be published. It appeared under this title in the March, 1953 issue of *Zane Grey's Western Magazine*. Don Ward was editor of that digest-sized pulp magazine, and he subsequently selected this story to appear in the Western Writers of America story collection he edited titled BRANDED WEST (Houghton Mifflin, 1956). It was adapted for the screen by David Chantler and Daniel Ullman and filmed as FACE OF A FUGITIVE (Columbia, 1959) directed by Paul Wendkos and starring Fred MacMurray, Dorothy Green, and James Coburn. As so many scenes in Peter Dawson's Western fiction, much of the action in this story takes place at night, amid the yellow gleam of lamplight.

LONG GONE

The blast of the locomotive's whistle shrilled back over the rhythmic clanking of the gondola's trucks, and at once Ray Kindred stirred from a wary lethargy, shifting his long length to ease the prod of a .44 Colt against hipbone. When the whistle sounded again, he came to his knees and then slowly, with an infinite care, he raised up out of the creosote-stenched pocket among the butt ends of the ties until his pale gray eyes were staring outward. This was but the second time in over eleven hours he had risked a look anywhere but straight upward from his hiding place. And now he was weighing against a cool apprehension the friendly beckoning of a dusk-blurred pattern of nearby pine slopes.

He had caught this freight laboring slowly along a cañon grade in a bleaker, drier country early this morning, and he had sensed no beckoning on taking that first outward look. Then, at midday, the train had been stopped at a way station and tank along the flats. There had been a prolonged interval of frozen uncertainty for him while a crewman slowly paced the length of the train toward his car. Kindred had waited, squatting on his heels, the .44 held idly in hand, until finally the man tapped the gondola's journal boxes and went on.

Two sobering possibilities had been in his thoughts constantly throughout the long day: one, that a man catwalking the cars could easily stumble on his hiding place, the other that the train might be stopped and searched at any time. Kindred had accepted these likelihoods stoically and with a customary fatality, though also with a measure of self-disdain, for he had made the concession of lying most of the time with the Colt drawn and his arm propped idly so that the weapon slanted in line with the upward edges of the ties.

Ignoring drowsiness and thirst had been hardest of all. The thirst he could endure. But each time he briefly dozed he was seeing the eyes again, a pair of blue, kindly eyes with a stare of death creeping into them. And the nightmare would invariably jerk him awake, cursing and with a raw temper.

He was trying to put that haunting vision of the eyes from his mind as a rearward glance showed him the caboose almost obscured by the settling darkness, the glow of its lanterns plainly visible. Some of the tautness was leaving his nerves then as he looked ahead. His back straightened in surprise at seeing the scattered lights of a town winking through the lodge poles, the locomotive already running past a gray-lined clutter of cattle pens at the settlement's outskirts.

An eager, gloating look at once shaped itself on his narrow face. He was thinking of the prospect of buying grub and a horse and saddle — or of stealing them — and then of losing himself in the high country to the north. Now was the moment for deciding whether to stay with the train or leave it. The choice wasn't difficult, and there was no hesitation in his reaching down for his wide gray hat, beating the dust and cinders from it, and then pulling it hard onto his blond head against the rush of smoke-tainted air. He pushed the .44 more snugly into the trough ahead of hipbone, a hard-fleshed pocket grown callused over the years of constant use. Then, hunching low, he lifted a leg over the gondola's swaying side.

The freight was slowing jerkily now, and as the first loading pen came abreast Ray Kindred vaulted out and down. His boots hit the graveled embankment with a force that drove him to his knees, sent him skidding on in a smother of dust, and down into a weed patch. He came stiffly erect and took three deliberate steps in on the nearest corral. With his back against the poles he reached down and brushed the sand from his trousers, watching the caboose trundling in on him.

He saw the brakeman's silhouette in the cupola window, saw the man staring straight ahead. A down-lipped and disdainful smile patterned his narrow face. He brought up his right hand, its fingers outspread, and touched nose with thumb in a parting salute as the caboose lanterns went away.

For two full minutes after the rumble of the train had died against the stillness, he stood there hungrily breathing in the cool and pine-scented air, listening, his senses keening the evening, trying to judge it. He caught the yapping of a dog from the direction of town, and from somewhere above in the timber a cow's bell toned in a slow, unrhythmic note. A faint breeze whispered from the pine crests. The sounds were peaceful, as friendly as any could be to Ray Kindred. And finally, as he walked on along the corrals in the direction of town, his wary instincts had passed a momentary affirmative judgment.

He found a windmill and log trough at the townward end of the pens, and there he drank his fill from the trickling feed pipe. Afterward, he sloshed water on his face and scrubbed away the grime. The feel of beard stubble along his hollow cheeks made him frown, for he was a vain man. And, thus reminded that he'd left all his possibles in the pouches of the saddle he'd hidden there in the cañon thicket this morning, he was feeling a strong disgust.

It had been a close thing, his jumping the freight, and in his hurry he'd thought only of the bundle of bank notes bulging the inside pocket of his coat. Looking back upon that crowded half minute, he knew he could easily have taken a few more seconds to get the razor and some other things. The disgust in him now was targeting an uneasy awareness that he'd been close to panic; and panic was a thing he couldn't abide, something he considered as deadly as a bullet to any man who lived so constantly with danger as he had these past years.

When he presently started on along the lane paralleling the tracks, he was thinking chiefly of a shave, of whether he should risk one in a barber shop or wait until later and shave himself with the razor he intended buying along with the other things. He was pondering this minor detail as he followed a turning of the lane and came abruptly to its joining with a road that became the head of the street.

He passed some houses, built of log mostly and, by the time he reached a plank wall fronting the first few stores, he had decided that the town held no danger for him, provided he remained inconspicuous, made his purchases, and left. Just then he spotted the red and white pattern of a barber pole gleaming in front of a lighted window several buildings ahead. Its invitation instantly made him qualify the resolve to avoid giving anyone a close look at him. His pace quickened. Then the next moment a tall man turned toward him out of a lighted doorway to this side of the barber shop and came on at a slow walk, coat hanging open. And, just as the man was striding beyond the widow's glow, a dull gleam of light was reflected from metal along his shirt front.

Ray Kindred caught that gleam and his stride almost broke. But then that same prideful arrogance that invariably froze out any trace of fear in him at moments of real danger carried him on at a casual, easy saunter.

As they passed, the man said pleasantly, "Evenin'."

Kindred drawled, "It's a good one," and walked straight on.

A chill rippled along his spine. He listened to the other's steady boot tread going away against the planks, listened for any break in it. There was none. Then shortly he came abreast the barber shop window. He looked in to see the barber alone, sitting in a chair by the wall reading a newspaper in the light of a coal-oil lamp hanging from the ornamental tin ceiling. He turned toward the door.

A deliberate glance back along the walk showed him the tall shape far up the street, still going away. He went on into the shop and let his breath go in a slow sigh of relief as he was closing the door.

The barber said, "How goes it?" and Kindred only nodded as he shrugged out of his coat.

He eased into the single barber chair and only then spoke: "Shave and a trim."

Most of Ray Kindred's remembered life had involved a crowding of his luck either by ignoring danger or fleeing from it. Tonight he was ignoring it, no longer fleeing. He was ignoring it even this moment, knowing the chance he took in having hung his coat there so openly on the rack by the door with all that money in the pocket, knowing the .44 to be in plain sight at his belt.

The barber had been waiting by the chair, apron over arm. Now he reached over toward Kindred's waist, asking, "Lay it aside for you?"

"No."

That clipped, uncompromising word made the man draw his hand quickly away.

Kindred lay back in the chair and crossed his boots on the padded rest, scarcely noticing. He was lying there under the apron with a hot towel steaming the lather into his face before the barber spoke again.

"Rest of the boys come down with you to see the fun?"

"What boys?"

"From up the Buckhorn. From Miller's."

The man waited for a reply. When it didn't come, he went on, "You got the stink of that tie-camp in your clothes, stranger. Not that it ain't a right good smell. Clean like. Always did take to a good whiff of creosote now and then."

"Never hurt a man." Guardedly then, Kindred asked: "What's the fun you mention?"

"The dance. Down at the school, next to the Baptist meetin' house. Nesters and homestead folk from Alder Valley mostly. Reed Williams aims to bust it up single-handed. Bill Shepley allows as how Reed had better keep clear."

"Haven't been around long enough for names to mean much." Kindred's scratchy voice was muffled by the towel. "This Reed now. Who's he?"

"Reed Williams. Runs the Brush brand. Alder Valley has been his private bailiwick up to now. Government land or no, he says, no one moves in there. The homesteaders have, right enough, and Reed's been layin' for 'em. Tonight he aims to pay off."

Kindred's interest was lagging, though he asked, "And who's Shepley?"

"Hell, you must have heard of young Bill Shepley even up on the Buckhorn. Sheriff. Was deputy before old Cromer passed on. Good man. But with Reed on the warpath he's

106

liable not to be much of anything for long."

"Think he'll stand up to this Reed . . . ?"

"Williams, it is. That, Bill will! And a damn' shame, too.
Might be the last of him. He runs cattle, and he's got a fine
girl all set to marry if he'll only give up the law. She hates
his wearin' the badge. But he's mule-stubborn. Says he's
obliged to serve out the term as sheriff. And he won't quit
so long as Reed Williams crowds these grangers. Looks like
real trouble."

"The usual."

Kindred spoke without any real interest, the warmth of
the towel and not the strop-slap of the razor at the chair's
side lulling him to a deep relaxation. He supposed it must
be this Bill Shepley he'd met up the street. The man must
be a fool, in the first place for not noticing strangers
appearing in town around train time, secondly for backing
a bunch of stray farmers against his own kind. *He was sure
a fool not to give me the once-over* came Kindred's thought
as the towel was taken away and his face wiped clean and
then relathered. He felt almost safe now at this double
assurance of the sheriff's poor abilities, so secure that he
didn't even open his eyes at the touch of the razor along
the side of his face.

The first strokes of the blade were long, unhesitating, and
clean. Its touch felt good. Abruptly then the barber was
saying, "Wasn't the usual that caught up with old Ben
Sadler down to Burnt Springs this mornin'."

Kindred's eyes came wide open, that name sawing at his
nerves. He warily searched the barber's face for any hint
of a hidden emotion or double meaning. There wasn't any
he could see. The man was painstakingly watching his
razor's upstroke along the underlip.

Kindred waited until the blade was being wiped before

107

asking carefully, "Should I know this Ben Sadler?"

"Reckon not, since Burnt Springs is two hundred mile south." The razor was back again, working under the chin. As Kindred's awareness of it sharpened, he was once more being stared at by those gentle blue eyes, not the barber's but the ones that had haunted his fitful snatches of sleep throughout the day, the ones with the look of death creeping into them.

"Ben's an old-timer from these parts. Rode shotgun for Wells Fargo till he lost a leg in a smash-up when the Windrock road caved from under his coach. They gave him the Burnt Springs office soon as he could hobble 'round again. He's run it ever since. Or did. Got him a busted skull this morning when he come to open up the place."

Kindred waited for more, almost flinching now against the razor's keen touch. When the barber remained silent, he finally asked: "Why would he get a busted skull?"

"For the company money. Why else? They found him layin' along of his open safe, cash box cleaned. What men won't do to lay hands on a dishonest dollar! Beat the bejesus out of a crippled old man! God A'mighty!"

There was something to be decided here, and Kindred considered it with the fingers of his right hand inching from the chair arm until they touched the handle of the Colt under the apron. There was a sudden dryness in his throat. He started to swallow. The razor left his neck with a jerk.

"Brother, you damn' near lost your Adam's apple that time! Get 'er swallowed."

Now Kindred did swallow, telling himself that if the man knew who he was the razor would already have struck deep. Nevertheless, as the silence dragged on and he felt the blade keening along his throat again, he was wishing he hadn't

108

come here. He couldn't keep his hands from knotting, his long frame from holding rigid. It took a real effort to crowd back the urge to sweep aside the apron and run on out into the shielding darkness.

He realized suddenly that he was nearly panicked and for the second time this day. The thought brought with it a brittle anger. Gradually, it steadied him until his nerves were under control again.

Finally he was calm enough to drawl, "Maybe this Sadler asked for it. You don't place a bet or even call if the deck's stacked against you."

The barber lifted the razor, frowned down at him. "Meanin' what?"

"The old boy could've got cashed in because he was scared. Because he ran or something when he should've just stood there and let it happen."

"Ben scared? When he's met up with . . . ?"

"Or there might have been a iron in the cash box he went for," Kindred cut in, telling himself — *He won't know he's hearing the truth!* — as he went on hurriedly: "These hardcases don't want to hurt no one nine times out of ten. If they do, it's because they're crowded into it. Like with old Sadler. He likely lost his head and made some fool try, and this bird had to clip him. Yeah, that's it. He lost his head, got in a panic."

"Who's to know?" The barber shrugged, wiped his blade clean, and then closed it. He tilted the chair up and re-arranged the apron. "Anyway, a good man's gone, and the one that did it'll be dodgin' brimstone on into eternity. You say you want a trim?"

"Even it up all around." Kindred sat straighter, right hand resting idly on the chair arm again. "Have they caught this hardcase yet?"

109

"Nope. Shepley got the word along about noon. To watch the railroad, that is. But they ain't at all sure the sidewinder come this way. Seems he'd rightly head off into the desert. There's a world of animals down there he could've stole."

Kindred considered this over quite an interval. Finally, in a tone utterly casual, he said, "Ought to be easy to close up the country. Mountains and all to this end, desert on the south."

"Oh, she's closed tight as a barrel bung a'ready. Ain't hardly a man between here and Alkali but what would gladly spend a week ridin' to square it for Ben if he's called on."

"What's Shepley done at this end?"

The scissors were clicking over Kindred's left ear, and he was breathing shallowly as the answer came: "Closed all the pass trails. Got a big crew stoppin' the trains up there. He'll be there hisself, come mornin'. If he's able, if he comes through this trouble with Reed Williams."

Kindred accepted the information stoically, with scarcely a ripple of inner excitement. He was weighing his chances coolly now, knowing them to be far slimmer than he'd realized. But slim as they were, he would think of something to improve them. Meantime, he was wondering if there was anything more the barber could tell him.

All at once a startling notion made him chuckle softly. Then he was drawling, "Might be interestin' to take a couple days off and tag along with Shepley. Think he could use another man?"

"Sure thing. Want me to speak to him about it?"

"No, I'll look him up myself." As he spoke, Kindred was telling himself, *The joker might fall for it at that.*

His thinking was pretty much on dead center by the time he left the chair, paid, and pulled his coat on. The bulge at the right side of his coat put a friendly pressure against his stringy chest muscles as he closed the door. Once out on the walk again, his instinct sent him into the nearest shadows under the wooden awning fronting the adjoining, darkened store. He was hungry with a real gnawing at his middle. But the risk of showing himself a second time as openly as he had at the barber shop would mean he was putting himself alongside the sheriff in being a fool.

Tobacco was the thing to dull his appetite, and now he took a sack of dust from his pocket, rolled a smoke, and lit it with his face toward the store wall, killing the match quickly. His back was still turned to the street when a voice sounded from across the way: "Everything all set, Bill?"

"All set."

"You still don't want any help?"

"Not any, thanks."

Kindred faced slowly around, seeing a pair of figures idling at the opposite walk's edge, another coming on past them. He recognized the shape of Bill Shepley in the lone man and, thinking back on his conversation with the barber, a strong and sudden impulse carried him on out across the walk.

He was half way over the street and trying in his eagerness not to hurry when he called, "Sheriff?"

Shepley stopped, turned slightly to face him as he came on. "Yes?"

Kindred instantly recognized the wary stance the man had taken for exactly what it was, noncommittal at the moment but one that had nicely dispensed with any necessary preliminary move but the upsweep of hand for unlimbering the weapon along his thigh. Kindred enjoyed seeing that equally as much as he did the absolute certainty that his .44 could be lined at Shepley before the man's hand had lifted past holster. He came on, his stride more deliberate now that he had Shepley's attention. Shortly he ducked under the tie-rail and stood within three strides of the man.

"You don't know me, Sheriff," he said. "But the barber across there tells me you're headed for the hills tonight and could use more help. If you can fix me up with a horse, you got yourself another man."

He felt Shepley's glance probing in at him and was thankful for the shadows. Abruptly the sheriff asked: "You wouldn't be a friend of Reed Williams, would you?"

"Who's Reed Williams?"

"If you are, now's the time to show your stuff," Shepley insisted.

"Man, you got me wrong. Whatever's botherin' you?"

Shepley took that in without any break in his impassive expression. "Where you hail from?"

"Miller's camp up on the Buckhorn." Moving his left arm slowly — so that his intention would be plainly understood — Kindred raised it and sniffed at the sleeve of his coat. He chuckled. "Can't you smell it on me?"

Shepley's square face lost its hard set. He smiled all at once, reminding Kindred of nothing so much as some carefree young ranch hand. "All right," he drawled, "you're on. Hang around down by the school, and you can head out with me after I've finished one more chore. There's a chuck wagon up the pass, so never mind about grub."

He nodded and started on past Kindred. Then, as he came abreast, he halted abruptly and, almost within arm's reach now, leaned over and drew in a breath quite audibly. "That's creosote, right enough," he said. "See you later." And he turned and walked away.

Kindred laughed softly, delightedly at realizing how smoothly his bluff was working. But then he sobered.

112

Shepley might be a fool, an overgrown kid beyond his depth in trying to deal with a situation beyond him, but he was nevertheless a likable fool. Kindred gave the man a grudging admiration for the positive word that they would be heading out together after he had finished his "one more chore" which must be his meeting with this Reed Williams. He hadn't betrayed by word or look any concern over the outcome of the meeting.

Yet the spot Shepley was in mattered little to Kindred now as he sauntered on after the younger man. Instead, he was thinking of the strangeness of the circumstances, of this being the first time in his life he had ever depended on a lawman for anything but suspicion or hostility. The incongruity of Shepley's having become the means of his salvation filled him with smugness. Shepley would post him at some point along the pass he would be supposed to watch. His appearance with the sheriff would be his passport to the far side of the mountains. *By sunup they'll find me long gone,* he told himself.

"Long gone." He spoke aloud, smiling broadly, liking the sound of the words.

He had gone on a hundred yards past the spot where he had encountered Shepley before he caught the first faint strains of music sounding from far down the street. Shortly the lilt of the tune strengthened until he was walking in time with it. He passed a lighted saloon, aware of several loungers on the walk who scarcely noticed him; only when he was past a feed mill several doors farther on could he forget them. And now up ahead he made out the shadowed outline of a church with its spire thrust sharply against the stars. Beyond, lighted windows came into sight, silhouetting the headstones of a graveyard in front of the church.

The street rails by the lighted building were crowded with

saddle horses and the teams of light rigs and wagons. The music was coming from there. This must be the school, the dance.

A picket fence fronted the school lot, joining a head-high locust hedge separating it from the churchyard. Kindred walked in on that fence corner. From there he could see couples moving in the lighted room beyond the windows. He noticed one couple in particular, the man with head thrown back in silent laughter as he gyrated from sight whirling a girl whose dark curls swung outward with the turn.

Kindred was suddenly and powerfully longing for the feel of his arm about a woman's slender waist, any woman's and, in his rancor over the hopelessness of that longing, he tried to shut from his hearing the cordant strains of fiddle, concertina, guitar, and mouth-harp. He realized then that he was standing in plain sight, and he eased on down the line of locusts into the grassy graveyard. But he went only far enough to put himself in the deep shadows and out of sight of any passers-by. There he squatted on a mounded grave, his back to the high headstone, thus placing himself so that he could look through the thick lower branches of the bushes and keep an eye on the street.

Long gone. The phrase came back to him suddenly, out of nowhere and, as the minutes passed, he was idly trying to imagine what it would be like to be free again, free to come and go as he pleased, with money in his pocket, and for a time not to have to keep his eye and mind so everlastingly on his back trail. The voices from the other side of the hedge, a man's and a woman's, reached him only as a muted undertone at first. He wasn't quite sure of the first moment he became aware of them, and then he wasn't even curious enough to look toward the back of the lot and try to see who was speaking. He supposed it was a couple courting in the shadows. Then all at once the woman — her voice sounded like a young girl's — spoke in a choked outburst:

". . . thought it through! You aren't in your right mind!"

"But I am, Laura."

With the man's first plainly audible word, Kindred recognized him. It was Bill Shepley. The sheriff's tone was calm, unruffled, not even remotely the voice of a man afraid. His next words put emphasis to this quality in him as he added, "My head would hang the rest of my life if I stood aside and let Reed make this stick."

There was a moment's silence before the girl spoke again, lower than before, her words miserable, impassioned. "None of this concerns you, Bill. None of it! You have the ranch. You have me. You'll have neither if Reed Williams kills you." Her words jarred Kindred, corded the muscles of his face as his jaw set hard. "Or even if you make an enemy of him."

"There's never been the day when I was afraid of Reed."

"Make him your enemy, and we have a burden to bear the rest of our lives," she went on, ignoring his positiveness. "And our children will have it to bear. Can't you look ahead and see what it all means, Bill?"

"That's what I am doing . . . looking ahead. If I back down to Reed now, it'll be to other things later. Alder's big enough for these people and Reed, and more. Let him boot 'em. . . ."

"Then get help, Bill! Call on some of your friends."

"They've offered, and I've turned 'em down. Reed Williams is just one man, isn't he?"

"Suppose he doesn't come alone?"

"He will."

Kindred waited out a longer silence now, one that kept him on edge, leaning forward, listening intently. And shortly the girl's voice came once more: "You were never intended to be sheriff, Bill. Let the next sheriff do this after election."

"After Reed's sent all those people on their way, kicked 'em off land that's rightfully theirs? No, honey. No." Shepley's tone was gently ungiving. "It happens I'm the one to stop him. They'd laugh me out of the country if I backed down now."

"Then you're . . . you're lost, Bill. He'll kill you! As surely as. . . ."

The girl's words laid a shock through Kindred, one that for long seconds numbed him against understanding just why her voice had broken off so suddenly. Then, over his apprehension, he was hearing the echoes of hoof-falls along the street, imagined echoes of real sounds he had ignored some seconds ago in his concentration on catching what was being said.

His glance swung sharply streetward. He saw a pair of riders idly sitting their horses to this near side of the animals at the rails. They were in the light from the windows, looking this way, in the direction out of which Shepley's and the girl's voices had sounded.

At that moment came a cry that echoed Kindred's thought: "You see? He's not alone, Bill!"

"Never mind."

Those quiet words of Shepley's were overlaid with the sound of boots crunching against gravel beyond the hedge. Kindred saw a shadow moving past him on the far side, past him toward the street. And with a sudden foreboding he lunged erect and started on after Shepley.

He reached the fence corner, the cinder walk at the street's edge, and came around the end of the hedge. He saw Shepley standing there inside the fence not ten feet

116

from him. The glances of the riders swung sharply from the sheriff to him. The light from the windows thinned the shadows here. He could plainly catch the hesitation of the pair at the street's edge now.

His sudden appearance had thrown them off balance. He wanted it that way. He asked: "Which one's Williams, Sheriff?"

"Keep clear of this, stranger." Surprise edged Shepley's tone.

"Which one is he?"

"I'm Williams." It was the stockier of the two, the nearest, who had spoken. He was heavy bodied, his full face wearing a stubborn, bulldog look as he asked abruptly: "You sidin' Shepley in this?"

"I am."

Kindred could plainly see the effect of his words. The far man, a hawk-faced oldster, now glanced uneasily at Williams who came straighter in the saddle. Kindred told himself, *They're already licked,* pushing aside an uneasy awareness that neither man appeared particularly ready to drop this and ride away.

That unsettling awareness crowded into him saying, "So now we're even, gents. Who'd care to call the turn?"

Shepley said quickly, "Stranger, this is my. . . ."

"You're wastin' your wind, Sheriff."

Kindred spoke sharply, derisively, for Shepley's words were spoiling the play, weakening it to Reed Williams's advantage. There was still the chance that this pair would back down now that the odds were no longer in their favor. If it came to a shoot-out, Kindred was ready, confident. Whichever way it went, the all-important thing was to see that Shepley came through this with a whole skin. Never before had the life of another man even remotely mattered

117

to Kindred. Shepley's did now.

He could see that Williams was about to speak. He didn't give the man the chance, saying in a taunting way, "Isn't what you planned on, is it? So now what? Do you play out the hand or fold?"

For several seconds Kindred thought that his bluff had carried, thought Shepley safe. And over those seconds it was as though he stood apart, witnessing all this. Then suddenly from that onlooker's viewpoint he was struck by the absurdity of his being here at all, of his risking his neck for a man he didn't even know, didn't care about beyond the using of him.

He understood then that he, not Shepley, was the fool. He was making the same mistake old Ben Sadler had made this morning. He'd let himself be panicked into making a foolish move. He caught the sudden tightening of Reed Williams's face and instantly knew his bluff hadn't carried. A coolness flowed along his nerves as he sensed the violence about to erupt.

It came unexpectedly. Williams's partner simply lifted his off arm into sight, swinging up a two-barreled shotgun. Kindred's right hand slashed his coat aside. The moistness of his palm surprised him, for a split second slowed his draw. A voice inside him cried — *Hell, you're not scared!* — and afterward his draw came smoothly, fast.

He saw his bullet smash through the hawk-faced one's jumper. The man buckled at the waist, and his shotgun slanted downward. Both barrels thundered at the dirt ahead of Williams's horse.

Williams was moving now as his animal reared. His gun dropped into line uncertainly. At the same instant an explosion alongside made Kindred hesitate. Shepley had thrown his first shot. Too late he saw Williams untouched,

118

saw the man's weapon settle its swing straight at him. He hurried the squeeze of trigger. He was staring into the rosy-blasting mouth of that other Colt as his own bucked sharply against his wrist.

A slamming weight hit his abdomen. He was thrown back off-balance into the hedge. He cried out hoarsely in triumph, seeing Williams sagging loosely in the saddle. Yet that fierce exultation at seeing his second kill was instantly dulled by stark terror. He was falling. He could see the stars wheel from overhead until he was looking straight at them. Their brightness faded. And then his staring eyes saw nothing.

As Williams's frightened animal bolted off into the darkness, Bill Shepley's glance left the two inert shapes sprawled at the street's edge, and he stared through the fence at the dead stranger. He heard Laura's quick step coming in behind him. Still, he stood looking down at Kindred.

"Bill! Bill!" He felt Laura's grip on his arm yet didn't look around at her. Then, in a low, awed voice, she was asking, 'Who was he?"

Shepley's head moved from side to side in a slow, baffled way. He sighed wearily, and only then thought to lift the gun hanging in his hand and drop it in its sheath.

"I'd decided he was the one that killed old Sadler," he said. 'Now I'm just not sure who he was, Laura."

"Dark Riders of Doom" was Jon Glidden's second Western story, somewhat longer and more ambitious than the first. It was sent by his agent to Popular Publications where it was bought for *Big-Book Western* on May 12, 1936. The author was paid $126.00 (a penny a word). However, upon review and, notwithstanding one rather contrived and melodramatic episode, the story was considered too fine for that magazine, and instead it was published in the more prestigious *Star Western* in the August, 1936 issue. Already here Glidden was making capable use of the shifting points of view and the interactive characterizations which were to mark his Western fiction with a dimension of dramatic suspense absent from so many one-dimensional stories in which the protagonist's viewpoint is the only perspective provided a reader. This early story also makes an interesting contrast with "Long Gone," one of his last stories, indicating how much he had grown as a master of narrative and yet how many elements that characterize his best work were apparent from the beginning.

DARK RIDERS OF DOOM

I

"A SUMMONS IN THE NIGHT"

The smoke-fogged room wavered uncertainly before old Matt Weir's eyes as he looked momentarily beyond the tent of light in which he sat at the green-felted table. The quiet disinterest of his face was no betrayal of the inner uneasiness that told him he had been drinking too much. He blinked once, then focused his eyes back to the cards clutched narrowly fan-wise in his bony hand. Three queens and a pair of sevens.

"I'll call," he said thickly and spilled his last stack of chips into the pile at the table's center.

"Hell, I'm out of this!" the man who sat at his left growled and threw his cards across into the discard.

Matt took no notice but glanced up and met Crump Mundy's gaze of smug vacancy. Crump squinted one gray eye to ease the smart of the smoke that curled up from a cigar clenched in yellow teeth. He eased his bulk forward and pointedly regarded the empty table-arc in front of Matt.

"That cleans you, Matt?" he asked, his voice flat and expressionless.

"Uh-huh. 'Til I've won this hand."

"Don't like it!" Crump growled. "You come into my place and throw away a year's work in dust. You ain't playin' your cards, Matt."

"The way I play poker's my own damn' business!" Matt flared.

"I know. But you've lost a two-thousand-dollar poke. You ain't goin' to like it when you sober up. You'll talk. Won't help my business any." Crump folded his cards and laid them face down before him.

The man on Matt's left smiled thinly and shot Crump the hint of a wink.

"I'm not beefin'," Matt said belligerently. "There's three hundred on the table there. I'm callin'. Show your tickets."

Crump shrugged and slowly turned his cards face up with his plump left hand. Four eights and a five of hearts.

Matt's eyes widened a trifle. "Four of a kind? Danged if I ever seen such ornery luck!" He tossed his cards onto the table face down, shrugged resignedly, and pushed himself up out of the chair. He stood unsteadily, only the lower half of his spare frame caught by the circle of light. "Stake me to a drink?"

Crump jerked his pear-shaped head in the direction of the bar. "Tell George your drinks are on the house tonight. Sorry, Matt." Nothing but concern showed in his eyes.

He and the two others at the table watched Matt stagger to the bar and lean heavily against it.

"Nice dealin', Squire," Crump said, his glance still on Matt. "What did he have last hand?"

"Full house," answered the sallow-faced little man, sitting with his back to the wall. Matt's cards lay untouched where he had thrown them face down.

Crump's glance shuttled over the early-evening crowd. He nodded approval when he saw the four miners at the faro table. George, the bartender, leaned lazily across the bar, talking with two 'punchers, and the ring of their mellow laughter fit perfectly the half-empty bottle before them. Crump's eyes settled on the batwing doors, on the shadowy outline of the high-heeled, low-cut boots of a man who stood outside. Idly he watched the boots as the man stepped into the room. A sudden quiet made him raise his glance to examine the newcomer. He stared squarely into the muzzle of a leveled Colt.

Crump stiffened and stayed that way. The tall, flat-hipped stranger stood carelessly alert, his face masked by a black bandanna that covered all but his shadowed eyes. He took one step aside to allow a second masked figure to take his place at the door. Then, disregarding the others, he walked toward Crump, nodding briefly in the direction of the back offices. Crump's pink face flushed with anger but, understanding what was meant, he got up and walked across the still room. As he opened the office door, the stranger said, "Hold on!"

Crump stepped to one side, and the man edged into the dark interior.

"You're against the light, Crump," the outlaw's soft drawl cautioned.

Crump entered warily and lighted the lamp.

"Shut the door," came the curt bidding. "Open your safe."

Crump, his nervousness leaving him, bent over the safe, saying, "Why the mask, Larry?"

"Who's Larry?" the outlaw countered, shifting his broad shoulders nervously. The tumblerclick sounded as Crump spun the dial. "That's enough," he snapped. "I'll finish. Might be embarrassin' if you went for the iron in there."

Crump, always seeing ahead, sighed resignedly, and the expression on his face brought a mirthless chuckle from the other who bent down and deftly turned the dial until the door swung open. He raked out onto the floor a .45 Smith and Wesson, several bundles of paper, and a cash box that disgorged a great many silver dollars, a few gold coins, a bundle of greenbacks.

"Where's the gold?" asked the outlaw whose eyes had never strayed far from Crump.

"Gold?" Crump asked blandly. "There may be a couple of ounces in the cash drawers out front."

"I mean Matt's poke . . . what you stole from him this evening."

Crump flushed and straightened from his slouch. "Now see here, Larry . . . !"

"Get it!" rasped the other, cutting off the saloon owner's rising voice.

"Go to hell!" Crump shouted but checked himself as he caught the glint of the shadowed eyes beneath the gray Stetson.

The look made him move quickly to the wall. He swung outward on its hinges the only picture in the room — a brightly painted thing showing a sternwheeler crawling away down a blue stream between clashing green banks. Crump reached into the cubicle behind the picture and brought out two heavy deerskin bags. Lamplight glinted brightly from the blued steel of a six-gun he had wisely chosen to leave undisturbed.

The man took the bags from him, threw them on the desk, and opened one. A quick glance satisfied him of the contents and, with a flick of his .38, he motioned Crump from the room. As the other passed out through the door, the outlaw holstered his gun, stuffed the bags into the pockets of his Levi's, and followed.

Old Matt was the only one at ease in the barroom. As the outlaw strode past him, he turned unsteadily from the bar, gazed fixedly at the man's retreating back. He jerked aloft a glass of whiskey in a secret toast and gulped it down. Abruptly his knee joints gave way and he slumped to the floor, sitting there with the bar for a backrest, his bearded chin on chest, snoring loudly.

Unexpectedly, on the heel of Matt's fall, the outlaw half

turned, his hand dipped to his gun, and it came up in a thundering roar. The man alongside the Squire at the poker table jumped, shrieked once, and clamped his hand to a shattered wrist as the gun he had drawn clattered to the floor.

Without a word the two masked men backed out through the doors. The quiet hush of the room held for long moments, to be broken at length by the soft cursing of the wounded man. Voices started a spasmodic hum of conversation that soon settled to a nervous undertone. Crump looked once at the wounded man, sneered with disgust, and walked over to stare belligerently at the sleeping prospector. With one nervous foot he pushed Matt sideways to the floor and glowered down at him.

"Another evening wasted! Squire, take him out and tie him to his burro. She'll head for his shack." Then he faced about and swept the room with a glance. If anyone had been smiling, Crump did not see it now.

Outside, in front of the Aces Wild, the two outlaws were joined by a third who emerged from the shadow of the awninged walk. Bandannas were pulled down, and the three hurried to the half light of the street where their horses stood haltered at a rail. But their exit down the street was unhurried and unnoticed. In two minutes they had passed the town limits of Whitewater and were trotting their horses up the night-shadowed cañon road.

"We sure picked the right time with the sheriff outta town. Did he kick up a ruckus, Larry?" one of the riders asked.

"No. Crump's waitin' for a sure thing," the leader answered. "You wait here, Quill, and see that Matt makes it home all right. They'll tie him onto Jinny's back and start her up the road. Leave the dust in his saddlebags."

Larry Scott reined in as he spoke and let Quill come

abreast of him. The deerskin sacks changed hands. Larry and the third horseman rode on until Quill dropped out of sight in the blackness.

An hour later the two were threading their way over the boulder fields of Miller's Pass. The biting chill of the wind that swept down off Ermine Peak discouraged any conversation. Down the far slope the first belt of stunted cedar thrust up out of the gloom. They pushed the horses steadily, fast, anxious to get down into the warmer low country. The bluish disk of the rising moon pushed up above the far line of the foothills and brought out the jet folds of the cedar-covered slopes. Their way turned south, at right angles from the line of the mountains, dipped into a cañon to cut off the hint of light the moon had afforded.

A half mile farther on the walls fell away around a sharp bend, and once again the moon showed in front. As they were crossing from the rocky cañon mouth to the tall cedars beyond, the screech of a night hawk brought them to a halt. Larry answered the call, wildly, accurately, and listened as the slap of the echo came back at him. He squinted to bring the dim shapes ahead into sharper outline, until he saw the moving bulk of a shadow come out of the trees. The oncoming form took on the shape of a rider. He came up quickly and reined in alongside.

"Soapy Wilson just rode in. Dave Martin wants to see you at the Box M tonight."

Larry jerked his slouched body erect. "Anything wrong?"

"Soapy couldn't say."

"Can't make it before midnight," Larry thought aloud. "Twenty miles. Can't Dave wait?"

"Soapy said he'd be expectin' you to ride over tonight . . . alone," the man repeated.

Larry looked ahead for a long moment upon that broad

sweep of gently rolling land that lay south of the foothills. A silent night bird swooped across the silver pattern below and was gone. As he looked, it was as though he could pick out the buildings of the Box M from the misty distance.

From far away drifted up the wailing bark of a coyote, and it seemed to him as he sat there in the stillness that the cry made more ominous the word his rider had just given him. So Dave Martin had finally sent for him. His pulse quickened and, now as he turned in the saddle to face his two riders, he had a foreboding that they were all heading into trouble. Yet when he spoke, his voice was calm and quiet.

"Soapy was wrong. We'll all go."

II
"OUTLAW'S BARGAIN"

"See anything yet?" Jake Rivers called out. He stood in the darkness of the wide porch of the Box M ranch house.

"Nothin', Boss," a voice drifted back from out front where cottonwoods arched a lane over the road leading from the building.

Jake, foreman of the Box M, sucked nervously at the pipe clenched between his teeth. "Reckon he ain't comin' tonight," he said, speaking to a man who stood near him, leaning against the adobe wall. His voice had scarcely broken off when he heard the scrape of a boot behind him. He turned quickly around and saw the outline of a man showing against the lighter adobe of the moonlit yard.

"That you, Frank?" he asked tersely.

"No," came the soft spoken answer. "It's Larry, Jake."

Jake's quick intake of breath betrayed his astonishment. "Larry!" he said with a welcome ring in his deep voice. But when he spoke again, his tones were gruff and more controlled. "Dave's waitin' for you inside."

Larry did not move. Instead his brown eyes surveyed Jake's solid figure, finally settled on the mustached, wrinkled face he knew so well. It was too dark for him to catch any hint of an expression.

"No hurry, Jake," he said. "Seems you're proddy tonight. Comin' in I thought I saw a few of the boys planted. Their cutters loaded for me?"

"You'll have to get it from Dave, Larry," Jake answered tonelessly.

The man who had been standing near Jake stepped off

130

the porch and walked across the yard in the direction of the bunkhouse. Only when he was fifty yards away did Larry motion Jake to lead the way. The two of them walked the half length of the porch to an open door that flooded a rectangle of yellow light onto the clay floor. Jake stood to one side.

Larry edged sideways into the little room that served as Dave Martin's office and stepped out of line with the door. A hasty glance showed him that Dave was dozing at his desk. Although Larry's entrance had been noiseless, Dave stirred now and jerked wide awake.

"Larry!" came his hearty greeting.

"Howdy, Dave," Larry smiled warily. He stood leaning against the wall.

Dave noted his position and quickly understood, his sun-wrinkled face flushing in embarrassment. He moved over to close the door, waving toward a chair that stood in one corner. "Have a seat."

The two of them sat down. For a long moment Dave Martin studied the face of his former 'puncher, now turned outlaw. Something he saw in that sun-blackened, square-jawed face of the younger man brought a sigh from him.

"It's good to see you," he said finally.

"First time in two long years, Dave."

Dave coughed nervously and ran long fingers through his gray hair. He lifted his gaze to meet that of the younger man. "Larry, I've brought you here to bargain."

Larry frowned and raised his brows in silent question.

"It's about the stock I've been losin' . . . ," the rancher went on, then paused as though he expected an answer. Larry waited, saying nothing. The fingers of Dave's left hand drummed an uneven tattoo on the desk top, and for a space of moments the two sat eyeing each other. "How much will you take to call your men off?" came Dave's blunt question.

A widening of the eyes was all that gave a hint of Larry's surprise. Then came a sudden understanding of the question, and a hot retort rose to his lips. He throttled it.

"So that's why you have the place guarded. Afraid I'd bring my wild bunch with me?" Larry queried accusingly. "Dave, not one of my men has ever run off a Box M steer."

"I'm losin' a hundred head a week lately!" Dave insisted.

"My boys are out of this," Larry said evenly. "You should know better, Dave."

"Larry Scott, you . . . are you runnin' a sandy on me?" Dave asked slowly, suspiciously.

"Have I ever lied to you, Dave?"

The rancher stared at him for a long moment then leaned back in his chair. "Never," he said gently. He raised a hand in bewildered protest. "But . . . look. It's. . . ." His voice faded to silence, and he waved a hand as if to dismiss what he said. His head sagged to his chest, and he stared moodily at the floor. Then he sighed. "Son, I'm licked."

"Licked?" Larry echoed.

"I thought it was your bunch. Thought I could make you pull your boys off 'til I was on my feet again. If it isn't you, who is it that's runnin' my herds into the hills?"

"I've known about it, Dave. You aren't the only one who figures it's me." Larry evaded a direct answer.

"They've started in on the Slash B herds now. Baxter lost two hundred head a week ago."

For the second time surprise showed on Larry's face. A dark look crossed his brow but was gone before Dave could define it "So Baxter's havin' his troubles, too? Queer!"

"Queer?" Dave raised his eyebrows.

"You'd think he could protect his stock with that bunch of hardcases he has ridin' for him."

"Oh, that," shrugged Dave. "I've tried guardin' my stuff, too, but it don't make any difference. The boys can't be in every pasture at the same time. It's always the one we leave unguarded that they raid." Dave sat pensively for a moment. "I didn't see how it could be you."

"You spoke of trouble?" Larry asked, frowning.

"Plenty. I was managin' fairly well until lately. Looked like we'd have a good roundup this year . . . like I'd be able to pay off my note to Baxter and have a little to run the place on besides. But now. . . ." Dave threw up his hands.

"I didn't know," Larry murmured. "Why didn't you send for me before?"

"You're an outlaw, Larry." Dave's blunt statement was not accusing.

"I see," nodded Larry. "Folks might not understand."

"Oh, hell!" Dave blurted out. "It wouldn't matter ordinarily. But I have to watch myself these days. Baxter would be on me in a minute if he knew I had any dealin's with you. You were my friend . . . always. I know that you didn't kill Ozzie Weir, and I'm stickin' by you. But the law says you did, and you chose to take to the owlhoot 'stead of standin' trial."

"I had my reasons. They'd have lynched me that night." Larry ruminated. He reached for his tobacco and papers and did not speak until he had made and lit a cigarette. "Dave, it means a lot to you to have this rustlin' stopped. It means somethin' to me, too, for everyone, includin' Sheriff Parsons, thinks I'm the one swingin' the sticky loop. They haven't a charge against me 'cept that killin' of Ozzie Weir. I reckon I better see to it they don't pile anything on top of that."

"How about your raidin' Whitewater last winter? They have that against you."

"No. The Aces Wild is the only place we ever touched in town. Crump Mundy would never swear out a warrant against me. He's forked and knows that a word from me in the right place would put a noose around his neck. He'll let me alone . . . until he has a chance to drygulch me. I don't regret robbin' him. It kept my bunch from starvin' last winter."

"Not only your bunch but a lot of those nesters and prospectors up in the hills," added Dave. "People up that way say some mighty fine things about you, Larry."

Larry stared in thoughtful vacancy at Dave for two long seconds then abruptly sat forward in his chair. "I'm takin' a chance sayin' this, but I'll see to it you don't lose any more stock."

Dave was incredulous. "You mean, you know who's runnin' it off? Who is it?"

"I've got my reasons for not tellin' you, Dave," Larry countered. "One more thing," he went on, brushing off the crown of his hat with a nervous excitement. "About the money you owe Baxter. I . . . that is . . . will he be too hard on you? He and Mona . . . ?"

Dave Martin got up slowly and looked fixedly at Larry. When he spoke, it was with an almost menacing tone. "Get this. Mona's marryin' Sid Baxter don't mean a damn' thing except that she loves him. If I thought she was doin' it for me, I'd lock her in the house to keep her from it. They've been in love since the first day he hit this country three years ago. Don't forget it!"

"No offense meant," Larry apologized. "I remember the day she met him. Since then there's been no one but Sid with her. But I heard they busted up after a while . . . right after I took to the timber."

"Didn't mean a thing," Dave informed him, softening in

134

his manner. "Just a quarrel."

Larry turned to the door. "Well, Dave, I'll be high-tailin'. You know where to find me."

They walked out onto the porch and, after Dave had mumbled an awkward thanks to the man who had promised him so much, Larry disappeared in the direction of the barns.

III
"CROSSED TRAILS"

For weeks Mona Martin had each morning ridden the circle that brought her to the top of the bald ridge overlooking Fenton's Basin. Today, pausing there to blow the chestnut gelding she had named Dawn, she realized that for days she had been missing the freshness and mystery of the country below. Lush grass pastures climbed gently up to the darkly green, mist-shrouded carpet of the foothills while above them towered the jagged, snow capped peaks of the San Martinas.

An early morning breeze from the hills pressed to her slight figure the blue blouse that so well matched her eyes. The sun caught the burnished gold of her hair and shadowed her smoothly tanned face. She breathed deeply, relishing the crispness and fragrance of the chill air. Once again, she was glad to be alive. And this was partly because of Larry's visit, his first to the Box M since he had taken to the owlhoot two years before to become an almost legendary figure in the country. It seemed strange to her that this boy who, under her father's guidance, had once roped and ridden and shot himself into the top cowhand of the whole range should now be riding the dark trails. But it was stranger still that he should come to them with an offer that meant her father's salvation . . . and hers.

Her impending marriage with Sid Baxter, owner of the Slash B, had lately become a symbol of her defeat and helplessness, but she was chained by necessity. Baxter had told her that the ten-thousand-dollar note he held against the Box M would be destroyed the day they were married and, notwithstanding the fact that Dave Martin would have lost his ranch rather than sacrifice her, she had consented. But if Larry went through with his promise, she would never go through with her marriage to the Slash B owner.

Once, long ago, she had believed that to marry dark, handsome, and gentlemanly Sid Baxter would bring happiness to any woman, but lately she had glimpsed his petty cruelties, his iron will, his arrogance, and she knew she could never grow to love these things in him. More than that, she had come to fear him and his ways.

Her thoughts were interrupted as she caught sight of a moving speck below on the trail. As it approached, it took the form of a rider and, a few moments later, she saw it was Sid Baxter. He waved now, and she saw it was too late to run. As she waited for him, she could not repress a feeling of admiration for his horsemanship. Baxter was big and rangy. He sat his Steeldust as though he were part of the animal, his broad shoulders back, his solid body in perfect balance as his horse slogged up the rocky slope. As he reined up before her, he swept his Stetson off in mock courtesy, a half smile on his bland, dark face. His black eyes were mocking, arrogant.

"You're very beautiful, my dear," he greeted her.

Mona flushed at the intimacy of the words, but she checked herself. " 'Morning, Sid," she said quietly.

"You look mighty happy this morning," he continued.

"It's all this," she said, indicating with a wave of her arm the green and purple haze of the mountains. "Do you wonder?"

"It's just as it always is, far as I can see," Baxter replied, watching her curiously. Then he added: "Maybe everything looks different to you this morning."

"Maybe," she said noncommittally, wondering at his quiet, shy smile.

"Couldn't be something that happened last night, could it?" he asked easily, avoiding her gaze as he rolled and lighted a cigarette. When he got no answer, he went on, "Understand Larry Scott paid the Box M a visit."

She could not hide her surprise. "How did you know?" she asked suddenly.

Baxter laughed shortly. "One of the boys."

"Spies, you mean?"

"Spies?" he echoed, his voice bland. "That's not a pretty thing to accuse your future husband of."

"Not yet, Sid," Mona said hotly. "You're not my husband yet! You forget the conditions of our bargain."

"Which were?"

"That it was purely a business deal. I was to marry you if you tore up that note. I could choose my own time."

"You still can," Sid said easily. "Only people are beginning to wonder. It's inevitable. Why not face it?"

"Sid," Mona said, suddenly serious. "How can you want a wife that wouldn't love you? You know I don't love you . . . like a wife should love her husband."

"You will," Baxter replied confidently. "Just give me a chance. We might as well be married tomorrow. Waiting won't change things."

"Are you sure of that?" Mona asked quietly. "Larry Scott said last night he could stop the rustling and, if he does, Dad can pay you that note. There'd be no reason for our marrying, then, would there?"

"I reckon not. But Scott's making too much money with that running iron of his to throw it away because your dad asks him."

Mona flared up. "Larry's no rustler!"

"And a killer," Baxter added.

"That's not true!"

It was their old quarrel again, and Baxter rehearsed his points with cruel delight. "No? Why is he on the owlhoot? Everyone knows Ozzie Weir and Scott argued over something Larry wanted a secret. Ozzie was hunting these rustlers that are cleaning out your dad. Everyone but you knew Larry was swingin' a long rope while he was working for the Box M. And when Ozzie was found dead on the edge of the *malpais* with a thirty-eight slug in his back, everybody but you knew Larry did it. He's the only man in this country that carries that caliber six-gun, and he's the only man in the country that had any reason for wanting Ozzie to keep out of the *malpais*. Do I have to tell you why?"

"No, you don't, but you probably will."

"I will," he corrected her. "It was because he was driving all his rustled stuff through there . . . stuff that he stole from your dad, from me, from four or five other spreads!"

"That's never been proven, Sid!"

Baxter sneered. "It has to everyone but you. Why do you think that mob tried to lynch him after Sheriff Parsons had locked him in jail?"

"I don't know, but a mob is always wrong!"

"To folks too blind to see the truth," Baxter added, with smiling insolence. "No, Mona. That tinhorn, gun-slick badman will never get you out of this for the simple reason that he's the one that got you in it."

"If he won't, nobody will!" Mona flared up. "Not even you, Sid. At least Dave Martin and his daughter will go down without having to bargain with you! I'm through . . . through for good!"

With that she wheeled the chestnut and left Baxter, riding down towards Fenton's Basin. Baxter leaned forward, his right forearm resting on the saddlehorn, and arranged the gaudy neckerchief he was wearing. The expression on his face was smug and knowing.

"You'll be back," he murmured. "You can't live on pride, my lady."

IV
"GUNS FLASH IN THE MOONLIGHT"

Matt Weir's cabin topped a spruce-covered knoll that lay four miles up Jackrabbit Cañon from Whitewater. At the foot of the knoll a sun-splashed stream passed under the handrail bridge that brought the trail to Matt's side of the cañon. Matt was a solitary man and had chosen a solitary spot for his home. Back of the cabin the sheer rock wall climbed a hundred feet to the stellar blue of the sky. Half way up its precipitous side was the opening to Matt's mine. He was sitting at the mine entrance, smoking and resting his aching head, when he saw the rider coming up the trail.

He picked up his Winchester, let it hang in the crook of his right arm, and started down the path to the cabin, surveying the rider the while. He was in the cedars and hidden from view before the rider crossed the bridge. Matt quickened his pace, worked around to a vantage point along the trail, and waited.

When the rider came up even with him, he said: "Howdy, you tinhorn badman!"

The rider was Larry Scott who turned abruptly in the saddle to face Matt.

"For a ranny that put away a quart of Crump's liquor last night, you're feelin' right smart," he retorted, swinging easily from the saddle to saunter over to where Matt was standing, leaning on his rifle. "Did Jinny get you home all right?"

"Sure thing. Had a little more than I could pack last night. First thing I knowed this mornin' was when that loco jackass tried to scrape me off alongside a cedar stump."

Matt reached down to rub his bruised thigh. "Found my dust, too . . . in the saddlebags."

"I promised you that you'd get it back," Larry said. "What did you find out?"

"Plenty!" Matt answered, his face suddenly gone pensive. "They raid the Box M tonight. Late. After midnight."

Larry looked up from the cigarette he was shaping in his long fingers. "Let's have it, Matt . . . from the beginnin'."

"Juan Mercado, that rib-stickin' Manuelo's kid brother, come foggin' up here yesterday mornin' and told me he thought his big brother was gettin' ready to be away a few days with Crump's bunch of gunnies. I'd told Juan I'd pay him plenty to let me know when Manuelo started whettin' his knife and packin' his roll. So I showed up at the Aces Wild 'bout sunset, met Quill there, and sent him out to get the news to you, as you know. After that I starts flashin' my dust sacks and slackin' a godawful thirst. Wasn't long before they asked me into a game. From then on it was easy."

"How do you know it's tonight?" Larry asked impatiently.

"Crump," Matt answered and shrugged. "He's got the idea I can't take more'n a pint without losin' my senses. Soon as he thought I was too sozzled to keep my eyes open, he started talkin' to several of his quick-fingered *hombres* that came in. Told 'em to meet tonight at The Notch, up in the Box M east pasture about midnight. That was enough for me. I got so damn' drunk I can't remember much else, but I didn't care. I knew they was playin' marked cards ag'in' me, but then I remembered you said you'd get the dust back for me, so I just set back and watched the fireworks. Everything in the United States happened in that game! Four of a kind was only tol'able. They skinned me sudden."

"Will Crump ride with 'em tonight?" Larry asked.

"No. The Squire," Matt answered. "Crump's keepin' his back trail clear."

Larry flicked alight a match and touched it to his cigarette. He walked over to hunker down with his back against a cedar, frowning a long moment before he spoke. "Matt, I'm afraid the end's in sight."

"Afraid?" Matt queried.

"Yeah! Afraid." Larry's gaze was locked with Matt's now. "It's goin' to hurt someone I think a lot of."

"Mona?"

Larry nodded soberly.

"I know," said Matt, "but it's better to hurt her now than to let her marry the polecat and find it out later."

"If we can prove it's Baxter, I'll be a free man once more, Matt. I'll have to leave the country. Can't go back and face Mona."

"Hell, she'll get over losin' Baxter!" Matt insisted. "Maybe she knows already what a sidewinder he is. No one could be around him long without findin' it out." Matt hesitated, watching the hurt look in Larry's eyes. "You've taken enough for that girl, son! Tryin' to save her feelin's. The very day you took to the hills you knew Sid had killed Ozzie .. killed him because he'd found their hide-out. Don't forget .. Ozzie'd told me about it, and I could have gone in and cleared up the whole works with lawman Parsons. I've waited two long years to see Baxter get what's due him. You forget Mona and her feelin's."

Larry sighed and rose to stamp out his cigarette. He walked over to where his big, shad-bellied roan stood ground-haltered.

"Maybe you're right, old-timer. Leastways, I'm with you to the finish."

" 'Pears to me like the finish'll be when Baxter's got a rope

143

'round his neck, his feet swingin' clear of the ground."

After he left Matt's, Larry spent the rest of the day rounding up his men and making sure they knew their jobs in the coming showdown. For showdown it was, Larry knew, and all his distaste for facing it could not be put off.

The Notch was a place perfectly named. It was a V-shaped pass, the only way within miles of gaining the top of the rocky rim that right-angled south from the mountains to form the eastern boundary of the Box M. Further out onto the plain the rim fell away, its place taken by a fence that enclosed Box M lands all the way to the river, five miles south. The east pasture, bordered by the rim, was a choice one, although at a great distance from the ranch buildings. Here Dave Martin kept a herd of yearlings and, because it was so remote, he had even now failed to put a heavy guard on the herd.

It was bright moonlight, shortly after midnight, when Larry, Quill, and Fay saw the little knot of horsemen that threaded their way through The Notch and into the Box M pasture.

"They'll drive back this way," Larry told them. "It's their shortest way through to the cañons. Quill, you and Fay cross over to the other side. Remember what I told you about the Squire. I want him."

Larry watched the two go afoot across the smooth, narrow opening to the other side and lose themselves in the rocks. In five minutes the moon-shadowed boulders looked deserted. It was a full hour before Larry heard the low rumble of the herd on the move. The sound increased in volume, and he knew that the Squire and his men were driving the herd fast for The Notch so that dawn would see them well into the cañon country.

Soon the moving shadow crept into view. Almost before Larry realized it, the point was close enough so that he could make him out. He waited minutes more until the rider and two score of cattle had passed beneath him and into The Notch. Then he thumbed back the hammer of his Winchester. He had counted eight riders going into the pasture — more men than necessary to work the small herd — and knew that there would be keen eyes among them searching out signs of any moving thing. He saw now that only two men were riding the swing positions, so he lowered his rifle until the five drag riders came into full outline behind the bawling, tangled mass of animals.

The swing riders were passing below as he fired. The sharp crack of his .30-.30 seemed to knock sideways one of the five in the dust cloud of the drag. The rider had not yet fallen clear before the two guns across from him took up the echo on their own. Larry saw that Quinn, the best rifle shot of their trio, had shot the horse from under the smallest rider in the drag. That would be the Squire, for he was a small man, and it had been Quinn's job to take him alive.

In less than two minutes the shooting was abruptly over. Directly below, one of the swing riders lay where he had fallen among the rocks, his horse fast disappearing with the half-crazed animals of the herd that had stampeded back into the pasture. One gunny had wisely wheeled his horse, when the shots spoke out, to streak back into the pasture again and disappear in the half darkness. Three drag riders lay a hundred yards out from The Notch, two instantly cut down by the rifles, a third trampled badly by the terror-stricken animals. The Squire had taken to cover, limping, and now the hollow snort of his Colt lanced flame from behind a huge outcropping of rock.

Larry, half nauseated by what he had just seen yet knowing the justice of his action, started working down the slope toward the Squire. He took advantage of all cover crawling, running. Once he had to drop ten feet onto a narrow ledge directly in the Squire's vision, but he moved quickly and was well hidden before the gambler heard the falling gravel and sent a haphazard shot at the sound. In five minutes he was within twenty feet of the Squire, behind him.

"Reach, Squire!" his voice lashed out. The Squire straightened up tensely from where he had been crouching. Cautious always, he hesitated then slowly his fingers unclasped from the butt of his Colt, and he dropped it.

"Walk straight ahead, Squire," Larry ordered. "Remember I don't like gamblers."

They had walked perhaps twenty steps toward The Notch when Larry heard the faraway sound of pounding hoofs. This new sound was puzzling and unexpected, since the herd had wandered off out of earshot. Several riders were approaching, coming up fast.

"Behind the rocks!" Larry breathed and, when the two of them were crouched down, he thrust his .38 into the gambler's back, giving an unspoken warning that the Squire would not ignore if these were more of Crump's riders.

It was only seconds before they came into sight and swept on past. Larry recognized them as Box M riders, Dave Martin among them, yet he made no attempt to hail, hoping they would go on through The Notch without seeing the signs of the fight. But they spotted the bodies of the dead rustlers and slid their horses to a stop in a swirl of dust Larry sighed and said, "Come on," and they walked up to the Box M crew. He told his story briefly while Martin listened, saying nothing.

"Take him to the house, boys," Dave ordered, as though it had become his affair.

"Dave, let me take him. I want to work this thing out my own way," Larry cut in, for the moment worried at what the gambler might tell if threatened by the Box M hands. A thought of Mona was in the back of his mind, yet he at once sensed the futility of trying to keep his secret any longer. It was only delaying the eventual outcome, and he knew that could lead to only one thing — Baxter's exposure. So, with a shrug, he answered Dave's remonstrance and in five minutes the Box M men, with Larry and his men accompanying them, set out for the ranch house. In front rode the Squire, silent and unsmiling.

It was a grim crew the Squire confronted that night in the Box M office. This sallow, still-faced gambler had looked trouble in the face too often not to be able to estimate his chances but, when he was shoved in a chair, a strong light in his face, and looked over the men before him, he conceded his chance of facing this out was small. Still, he was a fighter, so he sneered.

"Squire, you've got your neck in a noose. You'd better talk."

Dave Martin's voice filled the small room as he intoned the words. He was sitting on the desk directly facing the Squire. Near the door stood Jake Rivers and Larry, the latter tense and watching for the Squire to show signs of weakening. For an hour Dave and Jake had been questioning the gambler who still sat unmoved, now holding a cigarette in his tightly bound hands. Larry had not taken part in this, hoping disconsolately for some way out of the predicament. Now it came to him that he might maneuver the conversation in such a way that Baxter's character would suffer as little as possible.

"Squire," he spoke up, "there's something I haven't told

147

Dave. Do you know how we knew you were raiding tonight?"

The Squire's habitual, expressionless mask changed imperceptibly as he shook his head.

"Crump Mundy tipped us off!"

The gambler's thin, sallow face turned a shade lighter, yet the expression did not change.

"It's a double-cross, Squire. Crump wanted you wiped out.'

The Squire's eyes first betrayed his inner emotion. They smeared over in a dull hatred and seemed to focus on some far point beyond the walls of the room.

"If you talk, we'll see that you get a fair trial. If you don't' — Larry shrugged — "we won't be particular about turnin you over to the boys. Crump says you're back of all this . . . that it's you who's swingin' the sticky loop. We're takin' his word for it . . . unless you've got proof."

"That whippoorwill!" the gambler muttered, his voice low and sharp. "He wanted to cut down on me tonight. To get rid of me! I know too much. All right! I'll talk. The only thing I want is to see him swing before I do! Three years ago Crump started handlin' wet stuff. My back trail would be interestin' to a lot of people north of here, and Crump knew that. So he talked me in on his game. I waited to make my break 'cause cards is my game, and I don't much hanker usin' a vent iron. But Crump paid well, and soon I couldn't afford to leave. Wasn't long before we was runnin' plenty of stuff through the hills over to Pete Rango's place, the other side of Pemmican Buttes. You rannies never will find out how we worked through the hills." He chuckled mirthlessly. "I'm nothin' but an understrapper to that tub o' guts."

"So it's Crump Mundy?" asked Dave. "Baxter'll give a lot to hear that. He's been losin' plenty of. . . ."

The Squire's soft chuckle interrupted him. "Yeah! Baxter's

148

ierds have sprouted wings, too! You *hombres* think Crump's
he big augur? Crump's called the turn, and I reckon I know
vho put him up to it. He's just another understrapper! What
vould you think if I told you. . . ."

Crash!

V

"BEHIND BARS"

The spang of a rifle blended with the sound of the breaking window. Glass splinters clattered to the floor. All except the Squire whirled to face the closed door. Larry's .38 was out as he turned back to flash a glance at the gambler. The Squire's lips were parted, his eyes wide and showing a slow horror. His tied hands raised up to feel his chest then came away bloody and sagged into his lap again as he looked at them. Abruptly his body relaxed, his head dropped forward.

Larry sprang toward the door and tore it open as the muffled beat of hoofs came from out front. He caught a glimpse of a shadow fleeing down the lane of trees that led to the road. Instinctively he knew that the range was too long for his revolver, so he turned back into the room.

They laid the Squire, still breathing, onto the floor.

"Ten seconds more, and we'd have had the answer," mumbled Dave, as he worked over the still figure, tearing the shirt away from the bloody chest.

"We had half the answer," replied Larry, knowing that the shot had given him a feeling of relief. "Crump Mundy."

"He said Crump was understrapper to someone higher up," Dave said and looked at Larry squarely. "Do you know who it is?"

"Give me another day, and I'll tell you," Larry replied, knowing that the time he was playing for would not save him the hurt in the end. "Right now, we'd better look after the Squire. He's our best witness."

Larry stayed with them until they had called in "Doc" Summers, a Box M puncher who once had worked for a vet and who looked the Squire over and ordered him taken into town at once.

"He may live," he said. "Get the spring wagon, Jake, and we'll put him on a mattress. It's goin' to take some careful drivin' to keep us from showin' up in Whitewater with a corpse."

All at once the confining space of the little office seemed to press in on Larry. He walked outside. The chill of the late night air seemed to revive him, to quiet something within him that was strangely disturbing. Here there was nothing for him to do. He was walking off toward the corrals when Dave hailed him.

"We're takin' the Squire into town," Dave told him. "You leavin'?"

Larry nodded.

"We aim to call at the Aces Wild and smoke Crump out. Can I have Quill and Fay? We could stand two fast guns."

Days ago the prospect of seeing Crump Mundy brought to his reckoning would have fired Larry. Now it left him cold, disinterested. Dave, quick to sense that something beyond his understanding was happening, did not urge him to accompany them. Larry told him to take his two men.

After the other had gone back to the house, Larry went to the corral, whistled, and waited until his roan came toward him. He had put up the corral bars and was on the point of mounting when a voice stopped him.

"Larry!"

It was Mona. Facing about at her voice, he saw her coming from the house. The soft light of a waning moon made a playground of shadows on her face and made pale fire where the fine-spun hair framed her head. Her presence filled him with an excitement until he could not trust his voice to answer. In a flash it came to him that she had changed

from the girl he remembered to a woman. She was very
different.

For a lingering moment she too seemed to catch the spell
of this meeting. Then, excitedly, she said, "Larry, I saw him!"

"The Squire?" he asked, fearful that she might have been
sickened by the sight of the wounded gambler.

"No, the man who shot him."

"Did you know him?" Larry blurted out and, on the heels
of his question, he could have bitten his tongue out for
asking it.

"Yes. It . . . it was Sid Baxter."

He hung his head. "I'm sorry about that." Then he looked
at her. "No, I'm not either. Better you know it now than
later."

"You knew about him, didn't you, Larry?" she asked softly.

"Yes."

"And you've kept it from me. Why?"

There was no answer he could make to this — none he
had a right to make — so he remained silent.

Mona said: "I think I know. You thought I loved him and
were afraid of hurting me."

He listened patiently, his face as impassive as he could
make it.

"You shouldn't have done it, Larry." Her voice held something between a reprimand and a caress. "Because I don't
love him. I never did."

He listened blankly, tasting the excitement of those simple
words, and then he reached out and grasped her arms. "Say
that again, Mona," he said huskily.

"I don't love him. I never did."

"Oh, Lord," Larry groaned. "To think I could have stopped
this long ago . . . if I'd only known."

"But why didn't you?"

He could speak now, and he did, simply, bluntly, honestly. Because if you loved him and were happy with him, that's all I wanted."

Mona was silent a long moment, and then she said: "But why did you want my happiness, Larry? Did it mean anything to you?"

"Everything in the world. More than my own," he answered.

"You . . . you . . . how can I say it?" she asked gently. "Do you mean you love me, Larry?"

"Yes."

All at once, she was in his arms, pressed close to him, hugging his body to hers.

"Oh, Larry! What fools we've been. I love you, too. I always have."

He kissed her, but everything in his tired being rose up to deny his right to her until he finished this. He moved her gently away from him. "Not that way, yet. There's still something left to be done."

And then he was gone. As his shadow passed into the misty distance, Mona's eyes glistened with tears of happiness.

The Slash B lay a hundred yards from the bank of the sluggish Rio Falto, deep in a cluster of high cottonwoods. There was a light, Larry saw as he dismounted on the low ridge to the north of the sprawling adobe ranch house. That light would be in the north wing. All the caution, all the stealth he had learned in these two years had been hard bought, but now he forgot them. Sid Baxter was in here, he thought, his rage quiet and consuming. All the guns that Sid Baxter ever owned could not bring him down now.

So he walked down the slope in the open, rubbing an open palm over each gun. Not a sound reached him as he paused beside the outside door of the room where the light was. He reached for the door knob, framing his challenge. The motion was not completed when he heard a sound behind him that made him whirl. As he turned, he bounded sideways and streaked both hands for his guns. A sudden breath-slamming impact, and he knew he had whirled into the man. He twisted his gun, still holstered, and shot, just as a crashing blow flooded his vision with white sheets of light and his knees buckled so that he felt himself falling down, down. . . .

"Let's get him in jail before the boys run into a likely tree," was the next thing he heard over the throbbing drum in his head. He tried to move and couldn't. He opened one eye and, in that brief glimpse, he saw that several strange men were carrying him into a squat, sun-bathed adobe building beyond. Sheriff Parsons was one of them, and he knew the reference to a jail meant that he was in the hands of the lawman. Regardless of the pain, he opened his eyes and struggled with an effort that left him breathless.

"The ranny's showin' life," said a man with a beard. The others grunted, as they carried him through an office into a jail cell.

"It's my duty, Scott, to tell you that anything you say will be used . . . ," intoned Sheriff Parsons, once the ropes were off and he could sit up.

"Where's Baxter?" Larry cut in hollowly.

"Out after the rest of your wild bunch," Parsons told him.

"I want to see you alone, Sheriff."

The remark brought forth a derisive howl of laughter from the four men standing with the sheriff.

"You'll sure enough be alone . . . in here," one jeered. "C'mon. He wants solitude."

"Wait, Parsons!" he called as he saw the lawman turn to leave with the others.

Parsons was frowning as he sauntered back to the cell door. "Talk fast, badman. You gut-shot Jeff Lamb last night at the Slash B, and he was my friend. I'm a busy man. If I don't round up some deputies, you'll be lynched within two hours."

"I was at the Box M last night," Larry told him. "Helped Dave Martin round up some rustlers who were workin' a herd of his east toward the cañons. Dave's likely in town, now. Get him and. . . ."

"Save your wind, youngster!" Parsons sneered.

Larry only then remembered that Dave Martin was one man Parsons hated above all others. It was an old feud, one that had smoldered for years. Once Parsons had been a Box M hand. Dave had fired him for habitual drunkenness. The years had not lessened their dislike for each other nor had they lessened Parsons's liking for liquor. Even now Larry caught the pungent smell of it about the sheriff and knew that there would be no reasoning with the man in his present condition.

"Send for Dave?" Parsons jeered. Then the smile faded and his lower lip protruded in an ugly grimace. "You're seein' nobody. For two years you've been curlin' your tail, swingin' a wide loop that damned near cleaned every ranch in the county. You're poison, and I don't hanker to give none of your friends the chance to get you out of here. I aim to see you brought to trial. After that, I'm goin' to be the one to arrange your necktie-party."

Some inner caution stopped Larry as he was about to tell Parsons what he knew of Baxter. For Baxter had thrown his political influence to help elect Parsons more than tw⸱ years ago, and he recognized that the sheriff would turn ⸱ deaf ear to anything said against his patron.

When the door leading to the office had slammed shu⸱ behind the sheriff's burly figure, Larry knew that he mean⸱ what he said. Tomorrow there would be a trial — unless ⸱ lynching removed the possibility — and there would b⸱ many wanting to rush things through to a quick conclusion⸱ A remembrance of Mona Martin suddenly quieted hi⸱ wrought-up feelings and for delicious seconds he was re-liv⸱ ing his moments with her of the previous night. Few word⸱ had passed between them, yet Larry knew for a certaint⸱ that their lives were pledged to each other. For two year⸱ he had fought, planned, and prayed that he might brin⸱ her happiness. Now it was in his power to give it to her.

Then he abruptly realized that fate was robbing him o⸱ the finest thing that had ever come into his life. There wa⸱ faint hope that anyone or anything could influence Baxte⸱ or Parsons to give him the chance of proving his innocence⸱ Himself guilty of rustling and the murder of Ozzie Weir⸱ Baxter would see to it that all possibility of help reachin⸱ Larry Scott was removed. Parsons, biased by his hatred fo⸱ Dave Martin, would be putty in Baxter's hands. The tria⸱ would prove the outlaw guilty. Larry had seen enough o⸱ Whitewater justice to know that no time would be lost i⸱ taking him to the cottonwood at the cemetery gates. Al⸱ would be gone . . . Dave, Mona, Matt, and those reckless⸱ fearless men who had for two years lived a hunted existenc⸱ with him on the owlhoot.

There came the conviction that all this could not be. Al⸱ at once there returned that reckless, high-born courage tha⸱ had brought him through so many tight places. Twenty-fou⸱ hours to live! Between him and freedom stood the three⸱

oot-thick walls of an adobe jail and the will of two stubborn
nen. Larry's face creased into its old smile as he realized
hat a lot can happen in twenty-four hours.

VI
"DOOMED TO DIE"

The sun-scorched adobes of Whitewater reflected a dazzling glare as Mona rode down the one main street and turned in at Jepson's livery stable. Her horse, Dawn, was almost foundered for he had made the ride of his life in those early morning hours. For a long while after Larry had left, she had leaned against the corral in the dark, numb with happiness. Then, slowly, it had come to her where Larry had gone.

With a strangled cry she ran for the office, where her father was overseeing the handling of the Squire. In a torrent of words she had told him about seeing Sid Baxter, and of what Larry had said. She was sure that Larry was riding for the Slash B to square accounts with Baxter.

Dave Martin knew the truth when he heard it, and he was a man of action. He left Mona standing there, while he called all hands together. In another moment, before Mona could reach the corral, they had thundered out of the yard. She saddled Dawn and followed, only to learn when she got to the Slash B that Baxter had captured Larry and taken him to Whitewater with the Box M men hot on their trail. Sheriff Parsons had been there and gone with Baxter. Ling, the Chinese cook, told her this and assured her the Box M couldn't possibly overtake Larry and his captors.

She followed doggedly. Three hours of hard riding. Now as she turned Dawn over to the stable boy, she knew she and her father had lost. Whitewater in all its history had never seen such activity on a weekday morning. Dust hung like a pall in the still air over the false front stores, churned up by dozens of buckboards, spring wagons, and horses that moved continually up and down its street. She didn't need anyone to tell her that the news of Larry's capture had spread like seeds in the wind.

"Miss Mona!" a voice called, and she turned to see Jake Rivers towering above the crowd on the sidewalk. He pushed toward her and was soon at her side. "You shouldn't be here," he said.

"Jake, where's Dad?"

"He's up at the courthouse trying to see Judge Wallace. I'm just takin' him the news that the judge won't be in town til tomorrow."

"What are we going to do, Jake?" she asked, finding it hard to keep an even voice.

"Come out here," Jake answered mysteriously, leading her out into the street, away from the crowd. "There's too many back there would like to hear what I got to say."

"Can we get him out?" Mona asked and then regretted her question because she already knew the answer.

"No. But we're doin' the best we can. Dave says to lay low until the trial tomorrow. He's sent some of the boys out to bring in Luke McVickers, Rod Halloway, Wes Fenton, and a lot of others who'll help us get Larry a fair trial. Don't you worry, Miss Mona. He'll be all right."

"If Dad brings them, it'll mean guns, Jake."

Jake shook his head dubiously. "We're not breathin' a word about Baxter until the trial. When we do, we'll have guns to back it up."

"Why doesn't Dad go to the sheriff and tell him about Sid?"

"Parsons was out at the Slash B when Larry come bustin' in. He and Baxter is too thick, and you know what he thinks of your dad. He wouldn't listen. Baxter's got his gunnies in town, keepin' an eye on things. They're honin' for gun play

159

and, if Larry was busted out of jail, they'd start somethin
we couldn't finish."

Mona rested a hand on Jake's arm and looked him
squarely in the eyes. "Tell me the truth, Jake. Has Larry a
chance?"

Jake's glance wavered and fell before hers. He muttered
something that Mona did not understand. It was enough.
She turned away and left him, made miserable by her
frustration.

Old Matt Weir had come down from the hills to attend
the trial of his son's killer. He was using this evening as
an occasion on which to drown his sorrows. Just now he
had propped his spare frame against the familiar bar of the
Aces Wild. Crump Mundy was not to be seen, and Matt
vaguely wondered at his absence.

Never had Matt seen so many free drinks. Never had he
been the center of such interest. It was early evening, and
the place was crowded. Ten minutes ago Sid Baxter had
come in to shake his hand and promise him that Larry Scott
would hang for Ozzie's murder no later than the afternoon
of the following day.

"I'll be there to tie the knot, Sid," he had said ominously
"I can build a knot that's slow torture. May Larry Scott's
soul rot in hell!"

That had been his toast, cheered by many in the room
who had drunk it with him. Matt smashed his glass against
the bar and turned to call for another drink, smiling in
wardly at the look on Baxter's face.

A little later he left the place to walk unsteadily along
the crowded street to the hotel, followed by a few of his
more boisterous fellow drinkers. Sober-minded citizens had
gone to bed, so those Matt now met were out for the same

leasures he was finding, and he was greeted everywhere
s something of a hero. They laughed at him and with him,
lad to see that he was enjoying his one, brief moment as
popular idol.

"Turnin' in, Matt?" one of the hangers-on called as he
ntered the hotel.

"Just bookin' a room," Matt answered, thickly. "Be back
n a minute."

The elderly night clerk scowled at Matt as he came up.
Vithout any formality Matt reached over, pulled the regis-
er to him, and scanned the recent entries. He ignored the
till-scowling clerk as he turned from the desk and made
iis way up the stairs. Once the clerk opened his mouth to
ay something to this intruder, but a glance out front
howed him that Matt's friends were waiting, so he wisely
lecided to let events shape themselves.

When Matt reached the upstairs hall, his legs lost their
insteadiness. He walked quickly the length of the hall to
oom 34 and knocked softly upon the panel. The door
ipened, and Mona Martin stood framed in the lamplight
hat flooded out. Matt spoke softly, the door opened wider,
ind he was admitted.

Five minutes later he joined his friends below.

Shortly after midnight Matt looked through slitted eyes
it the men in the smoke-filled saloon. There was not one
iober man among them. At least if there was, Matt had
overlooked something. With a satisfied sigh he turned to
he bartender.

"Ralph, fetch me three quarts of Old Crow. I'm makin' the
ounds."

Ralph tendered three unopened bottles, caught the gold
piece that Matt flipped to him, and stood there to watch
the old prospector weave through the batwing doors. One

of the drunks yelled to Matt, asking where he was going but Matt merely waved an arm carelessly, not looking back

Four doors down was the jail. Matt's steps became more wobbly as he approached it. Out front were three guards lean, flat-hipped, serious-eyed men who scowled until they recognized him then grinned.

"Howdy, old rooster!" greeted Lefty Craig. These were all Slash B men, Matt knew, posted by Parsons and Baxter to guard the jail. Three in front and two out behind. Matt had ascertained that, having walked around the place earlier in the evening.

"Howdy, yourself," Matt answered. "Ain't you boys thirsty?" and he held up a bottle by the neck.

"Naw," answered Lefty, licking his lips.

"Lay aside your cutters, boys." Matt spoke loud enough so that those at the rear could hear. "Ozzie Weir's dad wants to treat you to a drink. Go out back and get the others Lefty."

"Can't do that, old-timer," said Lefty, suddenly serious "Sid would raise hell."

It was then that Matt saw Harmless Ogden. Harmless the frail, stoop-shouldered little man whose guns had snuffed out many lives, was one of the three in front. He had not left his station at the jail door to come and talk to Matt as had Lefty and the other. An uncertainty crept into the back of Matt's liquor-jumbled mind and stayed there like a slow threat.

"Right!" he said, answering Lefty, "it's you boys' duty to guard this place. I'll gun whip your whole outfit if you let that murderin' polecat outta there before his trial."

Matt's threat brought roars of laughter. Even Harmless chuckled. The two guards out back heard and came to stand at one corner, looking on. Matt set two of the bottles on the ground by the wall, opened one, and passed it. When Lefty handed it back to him, it was a third empty.

"Lefty!" one of the guards out back called, "don't we get none of that?"

"Hell, let 'em wait!" growled Matt, tipping the bottle to his lips. It went around again and came back less than half full.

"Damn it, Lefty, send that bottle back here!" came another call. Matt pretended not to hear. He wandered over to Harmless, held out the bottle to the little gunny.

"Drink?"

"Uh-huh."

"Drink to the coals of hell roastin' Larry Scott," insisted Matt. "He beefed my boy."

"Nope." Harmless's voice held finality. "You and the rest have your fun. I'm stickin' here."

Matt gave a careless shrug and walked back to the others. "I reckon Scott can't claw his way around the building to the back."

"Stay here," Lefty ordered the man with him who was following after Matt.

"I want more of that belly-wash," this man answered defiantly. "That's Old Crow, and it ain't often I get a chance at good whiskey. He can't break jail. Let Harmless take care of him."

The two argued until a call came from Matt at the back where they could see him with the bottle tilted up to his lips. A quick glance up the street told Lefty the town was nearly deserted. He tossed the keys to Harmless without a word, nodded toward Matt, and led the way back.

Twenty minutes later the second bottle was nearly gone. Matt heaved himself to his feet from where he had been sitting against the adobe wall of the jail. Lefty, through his

163

stupor, saw the serious look on his face. " 'S matter, Matt?"

Matt pushed his hat back and scratched his head with one long, bony finger. "I want t'see th' pris'ner."

Lefty shook his head solemnly. "Can't do it. No one's t'see th' pris'ner."

Matt passed him the bottle and watched him take a long pull.

"Pris'ner beefed my son. Gotta see 'im."

"Harmless has the keys," volunteered Pete Bassett, the man sitting next to Lefty.

"Don't need keys," answered Matt thickly. "Talk through the window. Here, gi' me a hoist."

"No!" Lefty growled.

"You ornery cow nurse!" Matt bellowed. "I'm Ozzie Weir's old man an' the pris'ner beefed my son. Now, I reckon there ain't no one got a better right to talk to th' pris'ner than me. Gi' me a hoist, or I'll blow th' hell out of th' rest of that likker." Matt drew his .45 and took unsteady aim at the bottle in Lefty's hand.

"Here! Y'old fool! Put up that hog-leg!" Lefty ducked the bottle behind him. "Pete, lift Wild Bill up to thet window, or we'll all be lyin' in our own blood."

Lefty abruptly lost all interest in Matt and focused his attention on the bottle once again. He took a long drink, sighed, and then his head sank onto his chest and his lips parted in a long, slow snore.

Pete made an ineffectual attempt to lift Matt up to the window. It sent them both sprawling. Pete laughed, and Matt cursed, waving his .45. "There ain't no sense in a man lettin' likker get the best of him," he said as he staggered back to Pete again. "Brace yo'self, Pete! You ain't drunk."

"Goddlemighty, what am I then?" Pete moaned, now on all fours under the window.

164

"Let's get this over with and go after s'more rot gut, Pete. Stay set right where you're at! I'm comin'." So saying, Matt steadied himself and climbed onto Pete's back. The .45 Colt was still in his grasp as he reached and pulled himself up to the window.

"Larry!" he whispered, then aloud: "Scott, drag your mangy carcass over here! I got things to say." Inside he saw the vague outline of Larry's head and shoulders.

"Matt!" came Larry's answer.

"Take this!" Matt growled in an undertone. "Look in the empty chamber. Watch out for Harmless Ogden. He wouldn't drink." And before the other could reply, the old prospector had launched into a tirade. "You're the crawlin' sidewinder that got Ozzie. I'm comin' to see your necktie party tomorrow, *zopilote* and, after you've quit kickin', I'm hopin' they fill your carcass with hot lead an' sink your head down in the ground. You ain't . . . ," his words abruptly cut off as Pete flattened. The two of them piled up against the wall, Pete laughing quietly. After they had picked themselves up, Matt said, "Let's go up the street for 'nother snort."

They tried to rouse Lefty and the other two, but three quarts of Old Crow had done their duty. So Matt and Pete staggered their uncertain way up the street, this time to the far end. Matt, as he walked away, cast one glance to where Harmless was sitting on the steps of the jail office. He shook his head sorrowfully.

When they were standing at the bar, he sighed: "Now I c'n get sozzled."

VII
"JAIL BREAK"

Watch out for Harmless Ogden! Those five words hammere‹
at Larry's brain as Matt and Pete went around the corne‹
of the building and out of his sight. Their voices faded int‹
the still air, and the quiet held. Idly he fondled the Col‹
Matt had thrust at him through the bars, thinking o‹
Harmless. He could remember the lazy drawl, the gray eyes
the boyish face of the Slash B gunnie, and knew him to b‹
the deadliest killer of all that wild crew Baxter had gathere‹
around him.

Strangely enough, he found no trace of fear when h‹
thought of meeting Harmless. He groped for an idea tha‹
would show him a way of escape. Several came, but h‹
discarded each one, knowing the man who was against him

Watch out for Harmless Ogden, Matt had said. *H‹
wouldn't drink.*

Now the words were full of meaning. Harmless would b‹
clear headed, alert, and naturally suspicious of anythin‹
his prisoner might do or say. He could not be taken in b‹
an ordinary ruse. Abruptly Larry recalled Matt's referenc‹
to the empty chamber in the Colt and decided there migh‹
be something there to help him. He spun the cylinder
pushed the ejector, and forced out through the loading gat‹
a tightly rolled slip of paper. It was pitch dark in the cell
but his eyes, accustomed to it, made out the writing:

> Larry:
> If Im luckey ther wont be anybody garding the jail
> when Im gone. Walk right out. Mona has steaked a

horse out in the arroyo behind the cort house. Head for the hills. Squire is going to live. Hes in bed at Doc Roberts house. The boys will get Baxter. The Squire has agreed to tell Parsons all he noes. Gud luck.

Larry crumpled the note, his mind racing over the impli-cations of Matt's message. If Baxter discovered that the Squire still lived, he would make another attempt at killing him. Parsons might even help him to hunt down the Squire. It was certain that he wouldn't take the Squire's story against the word of Baxter.

No, there were two things Larry could do. He could break jail and hightail it, letting Baxter get the Squire out of the way and remain the big augur of this country. It would mean that Larry Scott was on the owlhoot forever. Or he could break jail, get the Squire and Parsons together, and make the sheriff believe the story. It was his only chance for freedom and happiness — with Mona.

He stepped over to the window and could see the three sleeping gunnies below. They were out of the way. Out in front would be that gun-slick, sober killer, Harmless Ogden. Between them was the office. Every moment he lingered, he knew Harmless would be getting more suspicious about the silence of the other guards.

He stepped to the cell door and brought the Colt up, held its blunt snout within two inches of the lock. The bellowing roar of the shot seemed to rend the walls apart. He fired once more, pointblank, then sent his weight crashing against the bars. The door gave way, and he half way fell through it as it swung open. He caught himself and leaped for the office door, tearing it open, sidestepping. The deaf-ening thunder of a gun blast greeted him, seemed to throw him back as he felt the air rush of a bullet fan his cheek.

He stepped swiftly out. Harmless fired again, and Larry caught the slug in his left upper arm. His own .45 bucked in his hand, waist high, at the purple flame lance that came from Harmless's gun. Two, three times he squeezed the trigger then threw the empty gun at the place where Harmless should be. With a bound he was in the office and away from the door.

It was then he heard the thick, pulpy cough and knew his bullets had found their target. He stood unmoving for many seconds. Abruptly a piece of furniture scraped crashed hollowly to the floor and there followed a thud that could have been nothing but a man's body falling. He waited seconds more. He yanked his own guns from the hook on the wall and left.

At the rear of the jail yard he struck an alley and ran down it toward the edge of town, hesitated, then went on to the next alley. He cut into the street, yet stopped as he came to the front of a house. There he crouched and waited wondering if he had come too late.

He did not have long to wait. From inside the sound of someone moving about served to quiet his fears. Suddenly the door swung open, flooded a brief rectangle of light into the night, and closed behind the figure of a man. It was Sheriff Parsons who stood there, looking up the street swinging about his burly waist a belt, weighted down by two holstered, ivory-handled Colts.

Parsons took two quick steps toward the street before he felt the gun jab into his back. He froze in his tracks speechless, while swift hands flipped his guns from their holsters.

"Quiet, Parsons! Put your hands down and step lively. We're callin' on Doc Roberts."

Parsons moved, turned up the street, and they walked

arther toward the edge of town.

"You'll hang for this, Scott!" the sheriff said huskily when
.e had picked up the courage to speak.

"The second time you've mentioned that. Save your wind!"

Behind them from the jail came the excited sound of
oices. Once Larry told Parsons to hurry as he heard the
ound of horses moving up the street. But the riders went
he other way, and then they were turning in at the doctor's
.ouse. A voice from out of the shadows of the porch stopped
hem.

"That's far enough. What'll you have?"

"Let us in, Quill," answered Larry, knowing the voice. The
.ther didn't answer, but Larry caught the quick surprised
ntake of breath. Before they entered, Larry said to Quill,
I want to know where Baxter is. When you find out, come
.ack and let me know."

Dave Martin was inside with the doctor. His face was lined
.nd drawn, but as soon as he saw Larry a smile erased the
.ook.

"Matt told me you'd be here," he said, causing Larry to
vonder how Matt had been able to guess what his actions
vould be.

Dave's glance took in Larry's bloody sleeve, and he came
.ver to look at the wounded arm.

"Never mind that, Dave. Take us in to the Squire."

The sheriff had not moved since he entered the room. Now,
.t Larry's words, he fidgeted nervously, sensing in them
.omething ominous. Dave indicated a door at the rear, and
.arry motioned the sheriff toward it. In a plainly furnished
·oom they found the Squire. He smiled wanly as he saw
vho it was that came in. His face was pale, and Larry had
.n indefinable regret at what he knew the little gambler
vould be facing once he was well enough to leave his bed.

"Can you talk, Squire?" he asked.

The Squire nodded.

"Then tell Parsons who it was killed Ozzie Weir."

The Squire gave Parsons a long look then said simply "Baxter!"

The words struck Parsons like a whiplash. He gulped and swallowed thickly.

"You knew it, didn't you?" Larry asked, suddenly convinced that more than surprise showed in the sheriff's face.

"Me?" Parsons queried, hoarsely. "If I'd have known. . . ."

"Cut it!" snapped Larry. "Go ahead, Squire. Tell Parsons why Ozzie was beefed."

"He knows," the Squire told them. "Ozzie had Baxter's hide-out spotted . . . knew where he was runnin' the herds he lifted. Baxter's the one, lawman. Stretch his neck and this county's beef will stay in home pasture."

The sheriff mumbled an oath, trying to pick up his courage. "Scott, if I'd known. . . ."

"What would you have done?" Dave cut in, his level gaze fixed on the blubbering lawman.

"He'd been arrested long ago," said Parsons with a show of bravado.

"We're askin' you to do that now!" Dave intoned the words.

Parsons started to speak, then his jaw clamped shut as some inner emotion guided him. His bearing of confidence gave way and before those who watched him he seemed to shrink into himself.

"Baxter's in town," Dave put in, and the words put a trace of fear in Parsons's eyes.

"I can't go after him tonight," the sheriff said lamely groping for a way out. "Every ranny he's hired is in town tonight."

"They're mostly drunk," said Larry. "No trouble there."

170

"There's Harmless Ogden. . . ."

"Dead!"

The one word went unquestioned, yet every man in the room connected it with the dull roar of gunshots they had heard minutes ago. Parsons thought for long moments, until the quiet of the room oppressed them all with a sense of indefinable embarrassment.

"You're yellow, Parsons!"

It was the Squire who spoke quietly, accusingly. Parsons whirled on the gambler, glad of someone on whom to vent his wrath.

"Yellow! By all that's holy, you low-lived. . . ."

"Parsons!" Larry's single word stopped the sheriff like a blow in his face. "I'm goin' after Baxter."

Parsons was not the only one who stared at Larry. Dave, too, looked at him as though he had not heard right.

"You can't, Larry! You'll be one against twenty."

Quill entered the room at that moment, walked over to Larry, and spoke in an undertone. Larry nodded, looked once more toward Parsons, and said: "I'm leavin', Parsons. Don't interfere!"

He was out of the room before Dave, helpless in the face of this recklessness, could utter a word to stop him. Hardly had the door closed behind Larry when Dave reached for his Colt, raised it from the holster, and leveled it at Parsons.

"You and me are goin' to stop this killin'," he said.

VIII
"GUNMAN'S LAST DRAW"

"Crump Mundy's ridin' point for the border," Quill told Larry as the two walked toward the lights that winked up the street. It was an hour before dawn, yet the town was alive with people who would not seek their beds again this night.

"Anyone tailin' him?" asked Larry, only half way interested.

"He cut out alone . . . on a high lonesome."

Larry accepted the news, not caring. Crump's luck would give out on him one day, and death would take him, probably at the hands of one of his victims. Below the border they knew his breed.

For the first time Larry noticed his arm. It was when the blood had run down and onto his hand that he realized he must be losing a lot of it. He stopped, asked Quill to tie up the arm above the wound. Then they went on again, neither of them speaking. The arm was starting to throb.

A little further on Quill said, "I sent Fay to round up the Box M crew."

"I can do this alone, Quill."

"Huh-uh! You're crowdin' your luck too much."

He did not answer, admitting to himself that it mattered little how many guns faced him or were in back of him in this encounter. He would meet Baxter and that was all he wanted. For a moment a thought of Mona crowded in on him, and there was a pang of regret at what he was going into, a regret intense and painful.

"Better take to the walk," Quill's voice interrupted his

houghts. They were nearing the jail. Larry nodded, for on
he walk they would have only one flank exposed. "Baxter
ent most of his gunnies out scrubbin' the brush for you."

The news should have been reassuring, but again Larry
lid not care. The edge was wearing off the nervous excitement he had felt for the last hour, and he knew he was
ired, weary to exhaustion. He cursed softly, trying to
ummon that quick energy he knew he should feel at this
moment, but it would not come.

Along the street they passed groups of men who were
liscussing the jail break, others who voiced their wonder
it Parsons's disappearance. So intent were they in hearing
and telling of the events of the night in the murky darkness
hat Larry and Quill passed by unnoticed.

As they came abreast the Aces Wild, Larry thumbed loose
he butts of the two .38s and made for the doors. He edged
hrough, and Quill came directly behind. The quiet in the
oom warned him something unusual was taking place. His
eyes shuttled quickly over the crowd until they found
Baxter. The Slash B owner was standing at the bar, one
arm extended, and with that arm was clutching Matt Weir
by the shoulder. As Larry looked, Baxter shook the old
prospector easily, as though it were no effort. It was plain
o see that Matt was not pretending this time. He was dead
drunk. Baxter's voice broke through the silence.

"Here's the man who helped Scott escape!" He slapped
Matt alongside the face so hard that all could hear the click
of Matt's teeth. "You're a pack of sneakin' coyotes if you let
his man live 'til sunup."

Baxter looked up then, his dark face twisted and ugly,
and by chance his glance rested directly on Larry. His
expression broke, changed, and he pushed those on either
side of him away. Matt, free now from Baxter's grasp,

reeled and pitched to the floor.

Baxter's next action was instinctive. He shot a quick glance around the room to see how many of his men were there. The glance reassured him, for he took two steps forward, planted his feet apart, and sighed aloud: "Scott!"

Others looked now, and there were those who knew Larry and told the others. Then all of them, seeing what was coming, backed out of line of the expected bullets.

"Fill your hand, Baxter!" Larry said quietly, and something within him hardened his nerve until he gloried in this moment.

"You looked for it, Scott. You'll get it! Save the county the expense of a trial." Baxter's words cut through the hush of the room.

Larry waited, knowing the futility of words, sensing that the other's talk signified an uncertainty. There was nothing, no warning whatever, that gave away Baxter's sudden move! All Larry knew was that his start for his own draw was a split-second behind Baxter's. Yet his confidence was supreme, his movement one lightning-smooth flow of muscle. His down-hanging hand flicked upwards, and no man there would see the smooth play of motion that flashed the .38 hip high, crashing out! Baxter lurched from the impact of the bullet even before his own Colt cut loose, yet it was not enough to spoil completely his aim. A blow smacked Larry's thigh, high up, throwing him backwards. He steadied himself, firing again, and saw the blood gushing from the hole in Baxter's throat. The man was falling, but the five slugs that tore into him kept him erect — until the hammer click told Larry his gun was empty. Baxter sank to his knees, tottered there an instant, then sprawled full length in his own blood.

"Hold it!"

174

It was Quill who shouted, catching a Slash B man in the act of drawing. He covered the man with his Colt. Steps sounded on the board walk outside, and Larry shifted sideways, bringing the door within his vision. His other .38 was in his hand as Dave Martin burst through the doors, six-gun in hand. Parsons followed after him, stopped dead in his tracks, and stared, bewildered.

It was then that the familiar faces of several Box M hands detached themselves from the group and stepped forward. Eight men with leveled, menacing guns stood lined up alongside Dave Martin when the room began to spin before Larry's eyes. He blinked wearily, tried to hold objects in focus, and then blackness settled down.

It was as though he had waked from a deep, restful sleep. Above him the *vigas* of the room slanted away to a white-washed adobe wall. There was no pain — nothing but a sense of peace. Then, slowly, his mind was crowded with the blast of guns and the smell of powder smoke. He tried to move, but the effort was too great, so he lay there slowly letting the torment subside.

He felt a touch on his arm. He turned his head and saw Mona. She had been sitting there, watching him. The perfect oval of her face was outlined against a window where geraniums grew. The blue of her eyes was deep and spar-kling like the color of the sky above mountains at dusk. He drank in the vision of her loveliness, and then she bent toward him. Her kiss told him what he had to live for.

In 1940 Dodd, Mead & Company co-sponsored a competition with Street & Smith's *Western Story* for a first Western novel. The winning novel would be awarded a prize of $2,000. It would be serialized in *Western Story* and published in book form by Dodd, Mead. Although Jon Glidden's first stories were published in 1936 and numbered over sixty in all by the middle of 1940, he had yet to write a story longer than 40,000 words. Jon set to work with his customary industry on a novel he titled THE CRIMSON HONDO. It combined, as would many of his subsequent novels, a mystery within a Western setting. Jon's submission was awarded the prize. Its title was changed to "The Crimson Horseshoe" when it ran serially in seven installments in *Western Story* (11/16/40 - 12/28/40). Dodd, Mead published the book version under the same title in 1941. "Lost Homestead" was written shortly after this first novel was completed. It was submitted to Jon's agent on September 9, 1940 and was purchased by *Western Story* for $270 on December 1, 1940 even as his first novel was being showcased in that magazine's pages. It was published in the issue dated April 5, 1941. Henceforth, the name Peter Dawson, either as the author of four more novels serialized in installments or of stories of varying lengths, became a staple in *Western Story*. "Lost Homestead" was later selected for reprinting in Street & Smith's *Western Story Annual* for 1943.

LOST HOMESTEAD

I

"GUN-BLOCKADED WATER"

Late afternoon of that still, hot day saw dust hanging lazily at almost the exact center of Los Alamos Basin. Down out of the north, from a jagged line of peaks, wound a stream's silvery ribbon. It was marked by a broad green line of trees and lush grass. Half way across the basin, having followed its eastern edge along a maze of drab, torn badlands, the stream swung west past the town of Tres Piedras. Beyond, it bisected the grassy lowlands for close to twenty-five miles. A low notch in the heights to the west marked the place where it left the basin and coursed downward to the desert's lazy floor.

The tail-like streamer following the dust cloud deep in the basin pointed east, in the general direction of a trail that would eventually have a man back across Navajo country and into upper New Mexico. For many days now the center of that dust haze had crawled west along the trail, almost from its beginning at Santa Fé. Ten miles a day, occasionally twelve, at rare intervals fifteen, the progress of the four-hundred longhorns whose hoofs churned up that visible sign had been a relentless, onward surging. This afternoon the herd had slowed for the first time in over sixty days. The reason: its goal lay in sight.

Red Knight, owner of the herd, was riding drag, a bandanna tied half way up on his lean face against the dust when Clem Reynolds, his aging *segundo,* appeared through the haze to call sharply above the thirsty bawling of the cattle: "Fence ahead, Red! Only way to the river is down a damned lane! Do I go 'round it?"

Red cuffed back his Stetson to send a sifting line of dust down off the hat's back brim onto his wide shoulders. He scrubbed his forehead with his hand, and his gray eyes narrowed in speculation as he listened to the bawling of the herd. His answer was: "Go down it, Clem!"

That reply only hastened a happening that, either way would have been inevitable. Red's two wing riders pressed in on the flanks and presently, after a perceptible slowing the thirsty animals were hemmed in on either side by the stout lines of a four-wire fence. Red held his roan back until the dust had settled somewhat then put him on at a walk between fields of new corn, ankle-high wheat, and bright green patches of chili. A low 'dobe appeared out of the dust an overalled figure standing in its shaded yard, leaning on a hoe. Red lifted a hand in greeting, got no answer, and rode on, puzzled by the show of unfriendliness that had met his first wordless interchange with a man of this country.

But he had little time to dwell on this puzzle, for the next moment he heard shouting ahead and the drag slowed, the longhorns impatiently milling and bawling. Then Clem Reynolds appeared once more out of the dust fog, quirting his brown gelding, bellowing at a steer that blocked his path. His pony rammed the steer's flank and came on shying from flying hoofs. Clem, face flushed angrily, pulled rein.

"We're stopped!" he said in a grating voice. "Right at the river! Bunch of jaspers loaded down with artillery! They say we can't go on!"

A rock-hard gravity took Red Knight's ordinarily good-humored face. He eyed his foreman as though wanting to make sure no joke lay behind his words. Then: "Let's go have a look." He started ahead, retracing Clem's route along the crowded fence to the left. A swing rider appeared out of the og close at hand, and Red called: "Get back and hold 'em, Ed. Send Tex up front!"

The roan, wise to his business, nicely avoided the arcing horns and the angered rushes of the saltier bulls going along the crowded lane. The smell of water was strong in the air, and the herd, thirst crazy, pressed vainly against the leaders. Red finally rode clear of that dusty welter of packed animals to find two of his men, Jim Rhodes and Frank Phelan, holding the lead steers at the mouth of the lane that emptied down onto the sands along the river bank. Gathered below, along the rush of the clear-water stream, were twelve riders headed by a massively built man mounted on a black stallion. This individual sat with a Winchester sloped across the horn of his saddle. There were more rifles behind him. Not a man of the dozen lacked a high holster. A few wore two.

"Keep 'em there!" Red called to Phelan and put the roan down toward the men who blocked the way.

He was keenly aware of his empty thigh. This morning, on breaking camp, he had ordered all guns checked in with the cook who had driven his chuck wagon on ahead and now had obviously also been stopped at the river. Red's motive in taking the guns from his men had been distinctly honorable. It didn't seem friendly to come riding into strange country wearing weapons.

He stopped ten feet above the man on the black. "What's the trouble?" he inquired mildly.

"You don't go across," was the prompt answer. The speaker appeared to be close to Red's age, crowding thirty. He was handsome in a blunt way, his square, good-featured face darkly bronzed. Tall, he lacked an inch or two of Red's height, which was six two. But he was heavier and, in contrast to Red's dusty outfit of worn boots and faded denims, his whipcords, fancy-stitched boots, and blue-and white checked shirt were glaringly immaculate. One thing completed the contrast. His hair was black, Red's a bright sorrel.

"How come?" was Red's steady query.

The man lifted massive shoulders in a shrug. "We say so."

"You're sheriff?"

The man laughed, shook his head. "Just plain Duke Clanton."

There was a touch of arrogance to Clanton's looks that galled Red. But he didn't give any outward sign of that as he drawled: "These critters haven't tasted water for three days, Clanton. That's about as far as they can go without it."

"Tough," Clanton said with mock-sorrowful expression. He let it go at that.

There was something here Red couldn't understand. He tried to find his answers by saying: "I'm Knight, from Texas. I was in last fall filin' on graze across there." He lifted a hand to indicate the low westward hills. "Had a man on it all winter, workin' on a tank and stringin' wire. Now I'm bringin' in stuff to. . . ."

"You ain't," drawled Clanton. "And Spence left here in March."

At Red's elbow Clem Reynolds asked sharply: "Why would Ned do that?" Clem counted Spence, the man Red had left on the homestead, his best friend.

"Climate wasn't right for his health," was Clanton's answer.

"Let's get this straight." Red held down his anger. "I'm on my way across the river. I'll water and keep straight on, if that's what's worryin' you."

"Was I worryin'?" came Clanton's smooth drawl. "We say

ou don't cross the river. You don't even water here."

It was bluntly put, a challenge Red had no way of answering. Once again he was aware of his empty thigh. He was
also aware of the bawling, crowding herd behind, of his tired
crew.

"You can't deny a man water," was the only reply he could
think to give Clanton. "These critters can't go back. They
wouldn't live to do it! What law . . . ?"

Again that coarse laugh of Clanton's rang out. "What
about the law? We make our own! Brother, you got a few
things to learn! First off, we don't want cattle north of the
river. Stay over here with the nesters, if you want, but don't
set foot across there." He jerked his head toward the narrow
stream's opposite shore.

"We can settle that later," Red said. "Right now you can
let me through to water. I'll keep my stuff on this side."

"Damned right you will! All the way. We shoot the first
critter that dips snout in this creek!" Clanton's rifle nosed
up.

But for the thing that happened then, Red Knight might
have led his crew to a disastrous end. A steer broke through
the two point riders and charged toward the stream. Lazily
almost, Clanton lifted the Winchester to his shoulder, following the animal's loping charge. The steer waded into the
stream, and his head dropped to drink. Clanton's rifle spoke
sharply. The steer stiffened, lunged a step, and fell over on
his side, his blood darkly clouding the clear water. Clanton's
bullet had smashed his heart.

Then, as Red's boots were swinging out to gouge the roan
into a charge at Clanton, a voice called from behind: "Hold
it! Knight, come across here!"

Turning, Red caught the nod of a man in bib overalls
leaning on the corner post of the nearest fence. The man

added: "Don't commit suicide!"

Red gave Clanton a long level glance which also showed him several drawn six-guns in the rank of men behind. He lifted reins and brought the roan wheeling around to the fence.

"My handle's Jennifer," the man in overalls announced. "Toad Jennifer. I own this farm." With a gesture he included what lay behind the fence he leaned on. He looked up squint-eyed at Red. "Better go easy with Clanton. He's boss on the Circle D."

Red remembered having heard of the outfit. "Tom Dennis's?"

Jennifer nodded. "Was Tom's. But the old man died this last fall, leavin' his daughter owner. Clanton rods for her. Sheepman!" His last word was added scornfully.

"Sheep?" Red's glance went to Clanton again. "I thought Dennis was a big name in cattle."

"It was. But Clanton talked the girl into stockin' the layout with woollies. Ain't you winded the stink yet?"

Red heard someone approaching and turned to see Clanton coming up on them. Clanton eyed Jennifer sourly. "Don't get any ideas, Toad," he drawled. Then, to Red: "And don't pay him to let you water stuff inside his line. That won't work either."

Jennifer flared: "I guess I got a right to. . . ."

"To do exactly as we say." Clanton slapped the oiled stock of the rifle. "Knight, turn around and go back! We don't want any more ten-cow outfits in this country!"

Clem Reynolds rode up, saying: "Red, we can't hold them much longer!" He looked at Clanton, his old face apoplectic. "Shuck them guns and step down, and I'll beat your liver white, mister!"

"Easy, Clem!" Red said quickly. "Better start pushin' 'em

ack." He saw that his old foreman was on the verge of causing serious trouble. Clem glared a last time at Clanton then rode back to the head of the lane to give orders to the crew.

"That's showin' sense," Clanton observed suavely.

"I'll repeat that invitation," Red drawled, openly running his hand along his weaponless thigh.

"Another time." Clanton rode back to join his men.

"Callin' that gent a skunk is abusin' the name of a noble animal!" Jennifer muttered. "Well, I tried. Was only goin' to charge you a nickel a head to let you water inside my fence."

"Thanks," was all Red could think of to say. He was about to join Clem and the others when a thought made him say: "We'll be camped out on the flats tonight, Jennifer. I'd appreciate knowin' more about this. The food ain't so fancy, but I'd like to buy you your supper."

"I'll be there," was Jennifer's answer.

II

"ADVICE FROM A BASIN MAN"

The lights of Tres Piedras pinpointed the night off to the
northwest, seeming feebly to mirror the star-sprinkled and
vast reach of cobalt sky that was crystal clear except for a
long belt of thin clouds in the west. The chuck wagon was
a faint grayish blob below the redly glowing fire. The night's
stillness was ridden with the plaintive bawling of the thirsty
herd. Red, a generous supper under his belt, listened to the
off-key chant of a night rider and wondered if those clouds
off there meant that it sometimes rained in this dry country.
He glanced at Clem then at Toad Jennifer.

"So we really are licked," he mused. "I thought I'd find a
way around it."

Jennifer shook his near-bald head. The three of them had
had the fire to themselves these last twenty minutes. The
others had either gone back to riding circle around the herd
or to their blankets for all were worn out by the trying
three-hour battle of pushing the stubborn longhorns back
up the narrow lane and out across the flats to this spot
three miles from the creek.

"There ain't any way around it," declared Jennifer. "This
Clanton has guns to back him. He's got all them outfits
north of the creek to raisin' sheep. They're makin' money
and they'll fight."

"But this Dennis girl," Red insisted. "Her old man was half
longhorn, if what you say is true. Where's her pride?"

"Burned out, same as old Tom's was. He took a lickin' two
years runnin' on a bad drought. It whittled down the outfit
some. He left the girl with a loan at the bank and half his

186

ange burned out. It must've been easy for Clanton to swing her over. Add to that his courtin' her and her likin' same and you have your answers. There ain't an oversupply of men hereabouts that could fill Duke Clanton's boots."

"Where's your law?" Clem asked, his voice sounding tired and dried up.

Jennifer chuckled softly. "Where it's been for the past ten years. Tom Dennis put Harvey Jenkins in office, and Clanton's bunch will keep him there. Anything the Circle D does is right by Harv. Same as it was before Dennis cashed in. Someone swung a powerful big sticky loop in here last year. Seemed partial to Circle D stuff. When Dennis blamed us small outfits, Jenkins backed him. That's another thing."

"What is?" Red asked when the basin man hesitated.

"This rustlin'. Dennis's guess was way wide of the mark. I know my neighbors. They're honest. They didn't have to steal to make a livin'. All the same, we got blamed. It's just one more reason why Gail Dennis let Clanton sell her on sheep. Now she thinks she's gettin' even. They've made the creek a boundary. No cattle north of it. Rammin' it down our throats, so to speak."

The silence ran out, broken only occasionally now by the bawling of a thirsty, wakeful animal. Red's tanned face was a mask of gravity as he stared into the coals of the fire. Finally he drawled: "And I'm stuck with four hundred critters that'll be four hundred carcasses unless they get water within the next two days, three at the outside. Well, I won't sit here and take it!"

"I've been thinkin'," Jennifer said. "There ain't but two parties in the valley that could help you any. One's Doc Masker, owner of the saloon in town. He might buy up your critters and take a chance on turnin' some money resellin' em. He'll drive a hard bargain."

"Who's the other?" Red queried.

"Gail Dennis."

Red sat straighter. He laughed, a laugh that sent Toad Jennifer's eyes down to the gun at his hip. Toad had noticed that the whole crew now wore guns and was privately thankful they hadn't when meeting Clanton's bunch, which outnumbered them.

"That's a hot one!" drawled Red.

Jennifer cocked his head speculatively. "She might buy. I can't get it out of my craw that she don't know how you was treated today. She ain't hardhearted enough to deny a man water for his animals when they're near dead from thirst. It's an idea, Knight. You might try and see her."

"How would I go about it?"

"See Doc Masker first. Then go to the girl. Get 'em to biddin' against each other."

"But whichever way it goes, I lose."

Jennifer nodded reluctantly. "Seems like you do."

Red came erect, thumbing alight a match and holding it to a newly rolled cigarette. "Clem," he drawled, "we're takin' a slight *pasear* around."

"Where to?"

"Down to the river."

Jennifer shook his head. "Not a chance. Clanton's men are ridin' the creek. Poke your head in there and you'll run into the same trouble you did this afternoon. Only more of it."

"That's what I'm after tonight. Trouble!"

"Suit yourself." Jennifer shrugged. Then he looked up at Red. "How come you ain't inquired after Spence?" he asked.

"Too many other things to think about," Red admitted guiltily. Strangely enough, he'd almost forgotten Spence, the man he'd left on the homestead last fall. "What do you know about him?"

"Only that the last time he was seen was in town, at Doc Tasker's place. Duke Clanton and four or five of his men cleaned him down to his boots and underwear in a stud game. Next mornin' he'd disappeared. The day after his bighead was found down on the desert, draggin' the hull under his belly. That was three months ago. No one ever found him."

"Dead?" Clem asked in a hollow voice.

Again Jennifer shrugged. This time he added no word to that gesture.

Clem stood up, looking at Red. "What're we waitin' on?" he said acidly. "I got to do somethin' to keep from goin' loco!"

As they walked out of the dim circle of firelight, Jennifer called after them: "Mind if I wait here till you get back? I'd sort of like to know how you come out."

"Help yourself to blankets," Red said, waving in the general direction of the chuck wagon. Then, as they went to the rope corral and got their ponies, he forgot about Jennifer, too preoccupied with his other troubles to give the man another thought.

III
"THE WOMAN IN THE HOTEL"

The town of Tres Piedras, so named for the three rocky buttes that rose half a mile to the south of the creek behind it, seemed only half alive as Red and Clem rode its street at nine-thirty.

"Some dump! Walks rolled up already," Clem observed sourly, as they came between the rows of false fronted stores. He nodded ahead. "Would that be Masker's joint?"

"Looks like it." Red swung across, and they put their ponies in at the saloon's tie-rail. A barely discernible painted sign on the face of the broad wooden walk awning read **Rosebud Bar** and below it **R. J. Masker, Prop.**

"Funny," Clem observed, as they ducked under the tie-rail and crossed the walk, "but I hadn't expected ever to hit a town as dry as this and want a drink less."

Red made no reply but shouldered in through the batwing doors, his eyes squinted against the rude glare of overhead lamps that cut the thin smoke fog of a barn-like room. The Rosebud was unpretentious, even for so small a town as Tres Piedras. Wider than it was deep, the bar and a doorway occupied the back wall. To the right were faro and blackjack layouts, to the left two poker tables. Half a dozen men were at the bar, four more seated around one poker layout. Red's glance went to the latter and remained there.

Duke Clanton was one of the four, sitting with his back to the saloon's side wall. As the doors swung shut behind Clem, Clanton's glance lifted and met Red's, and a slow smile broke across his wide face. Seeing that smile, the others turned and also looked toward the doors.

Sudden decision started Red across there. Under his breath, he warned: "Stay set, Clem!" He stopped close to he nearest chair at the table, looking at Clanton and drawling: "This is luck!" He was at ease, feeling better than he had any time during the last six hours. Here was his chance to even the score with Clanton. Clem had his back covered, and a cool nervelessness was settling through him. No one at the table made a reply, yet wariness touched the eyes of all four.

"Go for your iron, Clanton!" Red said abruptly, deciding not to waste more words.

Clanton's left hand folded his cards and then lay on the table. "No dice," he said. "I ain't lookin' for trouble, Knight."

"I am! All you've got!"

"Don't let him ride you, boys!" Clanton said none too steadily.

Here, sitting calmly before Red, refusing to fight, was the man who was costing him his future in this country. He heard Clem drawl behind him: "Keep your hands in sight, apron!" and was aware of the barkeep raising his hands.

Then, still sure of himself, Red hooked a boot over the rung of the nearest Clanton man's tilted chair and pulled. The chair skidded from under its occupant, and the man went down heavily. Yet, instead of taking offense, he scrambled to his feet.

"You can't make me mad, brother!" he said quickly.

Once again Red thrust sharply with his boot, this time against the table edge. The table caught Duke Clanton in the stomach and tilted sideways away from him, spilling chips, money, and cards onto the floor with a rattling thud that made the planking tremble.

Still Duke Clanton made no move. His smile returned, and he drawled: "We could talk this over, Knight!"

Just then a voice that Red recognized as his foreman's gave a painful grunt. Then Clem was swearing saltily and another voice was saying: "Lift 'em, stranger!"

Red didn't turn until the wary tightness of Clanton's smile relaxed, and the Circle D man said blandly: "You've got a gun lined at your spine, Knight!"

Facing about, Red was brought face to face with a man standing close behind him. In one hand the man held a gun lined at him. In the other hung Clem's horn-handled .45. Clem, off to one side now, was pale and holding his right wrist. It was obvious to Red that his foreman had been surprised by the entrance of Clanton's man through the doors behind him.

A chair scraped. Red faced Clanton again. The Circle D foreman pushed the overturned table aside and came in close to Red. "I ought to fix you for a set of store teeth, Knight," he drawled. "Instead, I'm makin' you a proposition."

Red stood there silently, trying to judge where he could hit Clanton to make the most of the one blow he felt was all he'd be able to throw before getting a bullet in the back.

"You'll like it, too," Clanton said. "I want to buy your herd. Or rather Miss Dennis does."

Red shook his head. "No deal."

Clanton's bushy black brows raised slightly in surprise. "Thinkin' of Doc Masker?" he queried. "Because if you are, you're fresh out of luck. Doc's away. He'll be gone a week."

"It's still no deal."

"Isn't Gail Dennis's money as good as Masker's? I can offer you spot cash within an hour. Within ten minutes, if you'll wait while I go across to the hotel and see if she's available."

"What the devil, boss?" said one of the trio, a dark-faced half-breed who'd been at the table with Clanton. "She's. . . ."

192

"Shut up, Pete!" Clanton snapped in the first show of utright anger Red had seen him display. "Want to see her, Knight?" he queried pressingly.

Reason was beginning to dissipate Red's anger. Clanton vas offering him the only way out of this predicament. It alled him to give in to the man, but after a moment he odded his answer.

"I'll be right back," Clanton said and stepped around Red nd across through the doors which swung shut sharply behind him.

Red looked back at Clem and, ignoring the others, said: How about that drink, partner?"

They stepped unchallenged across to the bar. As the barkeep set the bottle before them, he said in a hoarse vhisper: "Stranger, you better make tracks while you got he chance!" He nodded toward the alley door nearby.

Red smiled wryly, poured their drinks, and emptied his lass at a gulp. Ordinarily he felt no need for whiskey. But he warmth of the liquor seemed to steady his nerves and, Clem's glass also empty, he poured another. He knew that Duke Clanton had level-headedly put aside a personal rudge for some obscure reason. His long acquaintance with rouble and the ways of men in trouble told him that omething unexpected was going to happen, something so mportant that it made Clanton willing to ignore an insult.

He was draining the last drop of that second drink when Clanton reappeared at the doors. The Circle D foreman said briefly: "She'll see you. Across the street."

"Come along, Clem," Red said and went out the doors.

Following Clanton across the street, Red was aware that Clanton's men were coming along behind him. Clanton made no pretense at friendliness but walked up the broad teps of the hotel verandah and into the lobby. He nodded to a door in the right corner of the lobby, saying briefly "She's in there. Go ahead."

The room Red entered was small, furnished with cheap deal chairs and tables, a writing room. A woman sat behind one of the tables near a window, and Red's first glimpse of her made him halt in surprise a moment before he came on into the room.

He had expected something different, a woman with more looks, refinement. This woman had a coarse appearance, her face, rouged and powdered, might once have been pretty but now showed age.

"Miss Dennis," Clanton said, "this is Knight."

The woman nodded. "Sit down," she invited.

Red took a chair, annoyed at the familiarity of the smile that accompanied her words. Clanton came over, carrying another chair, calling back to the door: "It's all right, boys. We don't need company." He gave Clem, who stood leaning against the wall alongside Red, a scowl and sat down. "Better let him have it straight out, Gail," he said.

The woman nodded. "That's the way I do business. Take it or leave it!"

Her manner irritated Red. His opinion of the late Tom Dennis suffered some revision. His opinion of Toad Jennifer changed somewhat, too, for the homesteader had spoken respectfully of Gail Dennis.

"Take what?" he inquired.

"Her offer." Clanton gave the woman a look. "Tell him."

"Twenty-five hundred," she said flatly. "And that's every damn' cent you'll get!"

Profanity from the mouth of a woman was something Red had rarely heard outside the walls of a saloon. But he overlooked it as his mind took in the shock of her words. Twenty-five hundred dollars for his herd!

"That's barely six dollars a head," he drawled. "These critters of mine are fat, even if they are thirsty. No old cowbaits, either, most of 'em three-year-olds! They'd bring thirty dollars on the open market."

"This isn't the open market," Clanton reminded him.

In the following silence a fly buzzed at the hot chimney of the lamp and fell wing-burned to the table top. Street-ward sounded the clop-clop-clop of a fast-walking horse. Clem shifted his position, his shirt sleeve rubbing audibly against the wallpaper. Red looked up at him.

"Take that or nothin'!" Clanton put in.

"What'll you do with the herd?" Red asked the woman.

She shrugged, and her look was undecided. Her hand went up to smooth down a lock of her lusterless mouse-colored hair.

Clanton put in quickly: "Get it on its feet and drive south to Tucson. Make money."

"While I take my lickin'."

Clanton nodded. Red looked at Clem. A barely perceptible lift of the shoulders told him that Clem was as much at a loss as he was himself.

Abruptly, Red said: "You spoke of payin' cash."

Clanton gave the woman a meaningful glance. She reached down under the table, and her hand came up and tossed a tight roll of paper money across the ink-spattered table. "Count it!"

"And give us a bill of sale," Clanton drawled.

Red counted the bills. Twenty-five hundred dollars. He lunched sideward toward Duke Clanton as he pushed the roll deeply into a pocket of his Levi's.

Suddenly, his shoulder close to Clanton's, he threw his body to the side and up in a swift lunge. His shoulder caught Clanton on the jaw, throwing him off balance as he tried

195

to dodge. Then Red was on his feet.

Braced that way, he put all the drive of his tall fram
behind the swing of his right fist. The woman screamed
Clanton's hand dipped toward his thigh. His big fist wa
closing on gun butt as Red's knuckles slammed his jaw. Th
blow lifted Clanton's heavy frame half up out of the chair
His body went loose, his eyes rolled to the whites, and h
sagged down and sprawled at full length on the floor. Befor
he had straightened out, Red had stooped to snatch hi
heavy .45 from holster.

Red pivoted toward the door in time to catch a Clanton
man coming through it. The woman, on her feet and cring
ing back to the wall, screamed again as the .45 in Red'
hand exploded. The man in the doorway choked out
startled groan, and his right arm hung limply. He lunge
back out of the door, colliding with a second man as Re
sent another bullet after him.

"The window, Clem!" Red said. Picking up the chair he'
been sitting on, he hurled it through the lower sash of th
nearby window.

Clem climbed through the jagged opening. Red followe
feet first, pausing astride the sill to shoot again into th
lobby. Then he jumped, his legs took up the drive of hi
six-foot fall, and the two of them ran down the passagewa
between the hotel and the adjoining building. Coming ont
the street two buildings below and across from the saloon
they chose a pair of horses at the nearest tie-rail an
pounded out of town before the first shouts announcin
their flight echoed along the street.

A mile from town Clem drew close to Red's pony to say
"Did you bust his neck?"

Red grinned broadly at his foreman. "He'll live." Then h
asked, shouting above the pound of their ponies' hoofs: "Di

ennifer say what color Gail Dennis's hair was?"

Clem looked puzzled. "No. Why?"

"Want to make me a bet?"

"Depends."

"That the woman back there was not Gail Dennis!"

"I'll be hornswoggled!" was all Clem Reynolds could think o answer.

Twenty minutes later, when they had wakened Toad ennifer out of a sound sleep at the cow camp, Red was sking: "What does Gail Dennis look like, Toad? What olor's her hair?"

Toad frowned, muttering under his breath at the rough andling the last few seconds had given him. "Who in arnation cares? It's light, corn-colored."

"And this woman could have been mated to a mouse." Red aughed long and loud.

"What woman? What's so funny?" demanded Jennifer.

"Tell you later. Right now we've got to move."

"Where to?" Jennifer was reaching for his hat.

"Anywhere but here. We're movin' the herd. On west. I've ot an idea."

"It'd better be good!" drawled Clem, leaving to rout the our sleeping members of the crew from their blankets.

Red was looking toward the west where what looked like high bank of hills now blotted out the stars. Those dark asses, backing the hills that edged the desert, hadn't been here an hour ago. They were clouds. Red Knight was ambling on them.

IV
"RED'S GAMBLE"

"Clem, get the herd movin'," Red told his old foreman a
soon as the crew was gathered at the now nearly dead fire
"Push west, fast as you can. Nels," he spoke to the cook, "hitcl
your team. I'm going with you. Tex, your job's the horses
Every man take a rifle. If you're stopped. . . ." He hesitate
a moment then added: "But you won't be. It'll take 'em ;
while to find the camp. By then we'll be gone."

"What's all this addin' up to?" Clem asked.

"Water," was Red's cryptic answer. "When you get out ;
ways turn those two horses loose. The ones we came ou
on."

"How about me?" Jennifer asked. "Ain't you got anothe
job?"

Red's glance went to the basin man gratefully. "I want t
move the herd five miles, better seven," he explained. "I
there a wash off there you're sure will run water if it rains?

"Why sure, Red," Jennifer said, "they all run . . . if it rains
But it ain't goin' to. Those clouds don't mean a thing."

"Maybe not. But you ride the chuck wagon with Nels an
me. And if your back's strong enough to heave some dirt
you can help us throw an earth dam across a wash an
catch the run, if there's rain."

"You're doin' this for nothin', Red," was Clem's gloom;
reminder. "You sold those critters."

"Clanton can't produce a bill of sale," Red said.

"But there's still the sheriff," Jennifer reminded him.

"And there's Gail Dennis," was Red's reply.

"What about her?" This from Clem.

"I don't know yet. But I do know I won't let these critters ry up and blow away. Get goin'! If the law stops us, we've ried anyway."

The next hour seemed interminable to Red Knight. Sitting he jolting, swaying seat of the chuck wagon between Nels ansen and Toad Jennifer, he studied the dark cloud bank o the west until his eyes ached. He vainly tried to catch he taint of rain riding the cool night air, but only the tang f dust and the smell of horses and harness leather blended ith its freshness.

"It never rains this late in the spring," Jennifer said once. "But it's going to tonight."

After that they sat in silence, the cook following Jennifer's rief instructions. The miles fell behind. They climbed to nore broken country where the hills were bare and treeless nder the starlight.

Finally Jennifer said, "This ought to do," as they brought he dark gash of a deep wash in sight. "This thing'll run vater if she rains a drop south of the creek."

Red swung around from a wheel hub as the team came o a stand. "Drag out the shovels, Nels," he ordered. "Then ake a horse and go find Tex and have him bring his bunch cross here." The cook would have little difficulty in finding he wrangler, for they had come directly west since leaving he camp ground.

Work was the only thing that seemed to ease Red's mind, nd work he did, bending over a shovel at the bottom of the igh-banked wash. He channeled out a shallow trough cross the bed of the arroyo, marking the line of a dam to e thrown up. Jennifer also began to work. For an hour and . half they shoveled in silence. Red paused only twice and oth times climbed the far bank to stand on the wash's rim nd peer upward at the sky. The last time he saw the clouds

199

advancing darkly, their upper reaches almost directly over head.

"Want to lay money on it, Jennifer?" he called. But the only reply that came to him was a solid grunt as the basin man strained against the weight of his shovel.

Shortly after that Nels Hansen slid down the bank and spelled Jennifer. In ten more minutes Tex Olds was there with another shovel from the chuck wagon. No one spoke.

They heard the herd moving up out of the east a long time later. By then the bank of dirt and gravel running across the wash had risen knee high. And only then did Reed surrender his shovel.

"Keep at it!" he called, climbing the east bank.

Weariness was cutting him bone deep. His shirt clung to his back wetly, and his curly red hair was sweat plastered as he took off his Stetson to blot his forehead. In the saddle of Tex's pony, swinging out from the chuck wagon in the direction of the sound made by the herd, he felt a splashing drop of rain strike his left hand. He reined in quickly. A fitful gust of wind whipped another drop in at his face, then another struck his right shoulder with a weighty drive.

All the weariness went out of him as he touched Tex's gray with a light spur. He felt like shouting, singing, riding fast to feel the whip of the now strengthening breeze cut his face, but he took his time, his thankfulness a sobering thing. Then, gradually, his elation was wiped away by the knowledge that he'd gained only a temporary victory. The pressing bulge of the money roll in his right pants pocket was a grim reminder of things to come.

When he had found the herd and his old foreman, Clem said: "You must've brought along one of them crystal balls to gaze into, fella. What do we do?" They both wore ponchos now against the gusty flurries of rain.

Red took him on ahead, pointing out the wash at a place where it widened and the bank sloped less steeply. "Hold 'em here till it runs, Clem, then let 'em work down. Not too far or they'll tramp down the dam. Send a man to help us throw up more dirt when you've got 'em settled."

The rain was coming in fitful, wind-driven squalls when Red got back to the chuck wagon. He slid down the bank to take Jennifer's shovel and worked with a new strength, ignoring a broken blister on his hand. Frank Phelan appeared to announce that the herd was being held in the wash. Frank got to work with a shovel, and from then on the earthwork dam grew fast.

Red was thankful that lightning and thunder didn't come as the storm hit. A driving, straight-down rain settled in at last. He stood up, leaned on his shovel, and called: "That's all! Now all we have to do is wait."

He looked with satisfaction at the four-foot slanting wall of earth that crossed the wash. There was no trickle of water yet, for the hungry soil in the uplands was soaking in the rain as fast as it fell. But soon now there would come a trickle then a rush of water. If the herd was placed right, if the dam held half an hour, better forty minutes, the animals would be watered and safe on the unstaked graze of this open country.

As they wearily climbed the bank of the wash, they saw a glow shining through the gray curtain of the rain. Coming up on it, Red saw that the cook had built a cedar fire under the wagon. A piece of sheet iron wired below the wooden bed protected the dry planking.

"Got a head on his shoulders, that grub slinger," Jennifer commented admiringly as they lined up to take steaming hot tin cups of coffee.

The wash began running after the rain had stopped, as

the first hint of the false dawn was graying the far horizon
They were all there to see the herd moved slowly down. U
the wash sounded a low roar. Then, around a bend above
came a foot-high and foaming wall of water rushing slowl
down, filling the wash from bank to bank.

"Hold 'em," Red called and spurred his pony down the fou
hundred yards to the dam. There he worked feverishly witl
a shovel for five minutes, gouging a notch into the dam
Minutes later, when the foaming, debris-strewn wate
dropped slowly into sight, his effort was rewarded. Th
water hit the dam, filled in behind it quickly and woul
have overflowed and washed it away but for the notch tha
let the overflow escape. Even with the notch, a pool som
sixty feet broad was gradually filling in behind.

Clem and his men let the herd drift down to the pool. Soo
they stood heads down to the muddy water. Presently, Re
saw the flow slackening and used his shovel again and fille
in the notch. The water rose slowly and in another hour
when the sun's disk edged over the eastern flats, the poo
was full to within a foot of the top of the dam.

Jennifer, who had stood on the bank above, called sud
denly: "Trouble comin', Red!" There was an edge to his voic
that made Red climb quickly up the bank to stand besid
him.

Jennifer pointed valleyward. Red saw a knot of rider
topping a rise three miles away in the direction of the town

"Clanton and the sheriff, I reckon," Jennifer commented

"You'd better hit for home and stay clear of this, Jennifer,
Red said hurriedly. "Thanks for all you've done. I'll dro
around the first chance I get."

Then he was off at a run for the chuck wagon where
black gelding was tied. "Clem, get up here!" he calle
sharply. He was swinging into the saddle when Clem rod

202

p over the bank. Red pointed at the oncoming horsemen. Better tell the boys not to get proddy," he said. "If Clanton wants the herd, let him have it. If he's got a warrant for me, tell him anything you want. Tell him I've started south or Tucson. Remember, we don't know a thing about those two jugheads someone stole in town last night."

"Where you goin' if it ain't to Tucson?"

"Across to pay a call on Gail Dennis."

Clem whistled. "Askin' for trouble, ain't you?"

"Clanton's crew will be with him. That means I shouldn't have any trouble getting in to see her."

"When you see her, then what?"

"I don't know." Red turned the black away toward the nearest rise that would conceal him from the advancing posse. Then he paused to add: "Better get yourself some extra tobacco, Clem. You're liable to run short in jail."

"Hey," Clem called as he went away. "You can't let 'em lock me up!" But as Red skirted the rise and rode out of sight, a wide smile broke the severe planes of the old man's mustached face. "Like Hades he don't know what he's doin'!" He turned to the cook. "Nels, you got any extra makin's?"

V

"QUICK SALE"

Red crossed the river west of Tres Piedras, close in to the low hills that edged the desert. Once beyond the stream the look of the country changed indefinably, although it had the same rolling, grassy, tree-dotted outline as that to the south. All at once Red realized what it was that was different. Bunches of sheep grazed in the distance. The white cones of herders' tents showed here and there. Occasionally Red glimpsed a herder and his dog. It was strange not to see cattle grazing a vast, rich stretch of country like this. Something seemed to be lacking, and an impotent anger gradually took Red. Cattle-bred, he couldn't admire a man — or a woman! — who would sell out a range like this to sheep.

With two things to judge by, her foreman and her business, Red could feel little respect for Gail Dennis. The fact that she had let Clanton talk her into forsaking cattle for sheep convinced him that the girl must be weak willed at best. He was convinced, too, that this errand would be a fruitless one. He tried to think why he had left the chuck wagon, left Clem to the mercy of the posse, and couldn't He had acted on impulse alone, curious about the girl.

It didn't dawn on him that there was little point in seeing Tom Dennis's daughter, until he had already asked a herder the way to the Circle D. Then, because he would have had to ride ten miles back to the chuck wagon but only three more to the ranch, he went on.

Circle D's headquarters bore the unmistakable signs of good living as Red first looked down on it from half a mile' istance. The house was built of rock, slate-roofed, shaped like a crude U. A quadrangle line of cottonwoods bordered grassy yard. Outbuildings lay at a generous distance elow the house which crested a long slope.

Red came in along a lane between whitewashed pasture ences. A big buckskin stallion was the lone occupant of a mall meadow on his right. Across the land, two fine mares nd their foals raised their heads to watch him pass. Once gain he had a moment of strange anger. Fine horses and heep didn't seem to go together.

Closer in, the layout had a deserted look. Red came in arily. Not until he'd left the head of the lane and was assing the biggest of the corrals did he see anyone. The nan was evidently the cook, for he came out of a small 'dobe ut and emptied a bucket into a shallow ditch nearby. He aused a moment to look at Red then disappeared through he door. Red's appearance seemed to have caused no more han casual interest.

Climbing the slope from the outbuildings to the house, ed rode a graveled path to the tie-rail outside a picket ence that enclosed a patio. He sat the saddle stiffly a noment, wondering if he was being observed. Then he wung aground and went through the gate and up to the road, white painted door that was shaded by a wide ortal.

His knock went unanswered a long moment. Then the oor swung open on a broadly smiling Chinese who tilted is head graciously and waited for Red to speak.

"Miss Dennis in?" Red asked.

"I see. You come in?"

"I'll wait here."

The door swung shut. Red sauntered over and leaned against a roof post. He built a smoke, feeling the tautness

of nerve strain ease out of him. It was pleasant here, cool
the fragrance of flowers filling the air. He revised hi
opinion of Gail Dennis somewhat. Every sheepman he ha
known had lived in near squalor, close to his pens, his outfi
pervaded by the stench all cattlemen recognized as part o
the business. The contrast between what he now found an
what he'd expected brought a slow smile to Red's bronze
face.

The door opened abruptly again and the girl who appeare
in it caught a trace of that smile. Later, Red was to b
thankful for that good beginning, for Gail Dennis in turn
smiled and her "Good morning," was as pleasant as thoug
she were speaking to an old acquaintance.

His " 'Mornin', ma'am," was a trifle slow in coming. Thi
girl had a freshness and a look of vivaciousness so foreig
to his expectation that he stood a moment in awe of her.

Tall, her figure willowy and with a trace of boyish angu
larity, Gail Dennis's laughing blue eyes seemed to mock a
his former certainties of her. She wore a light blue percal
dress, tight waisted, sprigged with a yellow daisy pattern
And her hair was a golden blond, not corn-colored. It wa
brushed back in a sweeping pompadour gathered in a kno
at the nape of her slender neck.

Red's first impression was of a beautiful face. Then h
decided that there was more character than beauty in it
The girl's generous mouth lacked the shallow rosebu
quality of surface prettiness, and the sun had tanned he
skin a deeper olive than he knew was considered fashion
able.

As he hesitated, a slight flush rose into her face. "Yo
wanted to see me?" Her voice had a lilting musical qualit
that made him eager to hear it again.

"I was told you were the person to see about a certai

matter. Fact is, I'm new here and not acquainted with the rules. It's about. . . ."

"You must be Knight, the man who took out the homestead north of here," she said, as he stumbled for an explanation.

Red nodded, puzzled by her continued cordiality.

She went on: "Duke . . . Mister Clanton, my foreman . . . mentioned you."

"He did?" Red's puzzlement was mounting. "Tell you anything in particular?"

"Only that he'd persuaded you not to bring your herd across the river. I suppose that's why you're here, to discuss the sale."

Sheer astonishment held Red speechless a longer moment than was necessary. There was something he wanted to know, and his next question sought that answer: "What if I've decided not to sell?"

The girl's head tilted gravely as she met his glance. "In that case there's nothing I can do about it. But we'd hoped to keep the river a boundary between the sheep and the cattle. Mister Clanton says they don't mix."

Red stifled his amusement. Clanton obviously omitted details in telling Gail Dennis of their meeting. "So they say," he drawled. "I've been wonderin', ma'am, just why you gave up your father's business."

Her laugh rippled pleasantly. "Wasn't his a rather old-fashioned theory? There's more money in sheep. Dad tried for years to lift his debts by raising cattle. I'm giving sheep a trial."

Red digested her explanation in the sudden knowledge that Clanton was playing a game of his own. He felt the urge to mention exactly what had happened but ruled that out for a selfish reason. Clanton had evidently been ordered to make the attempt to buy up Red's herd rather than let

207

the newcomer take up his homestead. Red intended now to find out what kind of a deal Clanton had been ordered to make.

"I might sell," he said slowly, "but I have a crew to take care of and. . . ."

"I'll be fair with you," the girl put in quickly. "What's your price?"

"Twenty a head. Let's see," — Red made a mental calculation — "that comes to an even eight thousand. You'll be able to sell for thirty a head this fall, providin' you graze 'em right."

Gail Dennis smiled, and a small sigh escaped her. "I was afraid you'd ask more." Abruptly she held out her hand. "It's a bargain, then! Eight thousand. Would you rather see Mister Clanton again or will my check do?"

Red swallowed with difficulty and met the firm clasp of her hand. He got out: "Your check's good, ma'am. If you've got pen and ink, I'll write out a bill of sale."

At that moment she looked beyond him, out the lane and the trail that led southward toward Tres Piedras. "Here comes Duke now," she announced.

Red turned, saw a line of riders in the distance. He did some quick thinking that made him say: "Might be a good joke on Clanton to have everything signed, sealed, and delivered before he gets here. I'll leave without him seein' me, and you can have it as sort of a surprise."

The girl frowned. Red added quickly: "You might as well know the truth, ma'am. Clanton's offer last night was lower than yours by a good bit."

He had guessed shrewdly. This time the color that mounted to the girl's face was brought on by anger. A bright emotion Red couldn't fathom was mirrored in her eyes.

"Sometimes I don't quite know Duke," she murmured then

ave Red a look of guilt, as though she'd spoken out of turn. "You can't blame him for tryin', can you?" he said. "Nor ne for turnin' down his offer. Shall we sign the papers now?" Ie didn't want Clanton to interrupt the completion of this ransaction.

The girl turned and went in the door. She was gone less han a minute, returning with a pen and ink, a box of letter paper, and a checkbook. They sat down at a table alongside broad window. Red wrote out his bill of sale, she a check or eight thousand dollars on the Tres Piedras Bank.

Folding the check, Red thought of something else. "There's story goin' the rounds that you're on the outs with your eighbors across the river," he said. "It isn't any of my usiness, but I wondered why."

"When Dad was alive, he had enemies," the girl told him villingly enough. "He claimed that the ranchers across here stole cattle from him. But that's all over now. Duke as persuaded the ones who hated Dad to bury the hatchet."

With this added proof that Duke Clanton was nicely oncealing his dealings with the small ranchers from the irl, Red said good bye, went out to the tie-rail, and untied he black. Swinging out from the picket fence, he called: I'm headin' out the back way so Clanton won't see me."

Gail Dennis laughed and waved to him.

VI
"CLANTON BACK TRACKS"

An hour and a half later Red was riding the main street in Tres Piedras. He turned into the walk awning that fronted the bank. Crossing the walk, he saw a man wearing a pearl-gray Stetson, whose dark face was vaguely familiar straighten from his slouch against an awning post and turn to hurry away down the walk. Sure that he had been recognized, Red went in the bank and presented Gail Dennis's check to the cashier. The man examined the check with a frown, said, "Excuse me a moment," and walked over to go in a door with a frosted glass panel lettered PRESIDENT.

He reappeared in a few moments with a banded sheaf of paper money. "I didn't have this much on hand," he explained. He counted out eight thousand dollars and pushed the bills through his wicket.

Red said, "Thanks," and went to the entrance. He glanced down along the walk. Far down he sighted the man with the light Stetson who had reacted so strangely to his appearance. Accompanying this individual was another from whose shirt front metal glinted brightly in the sun light.

"Better make tracks, fella!" Red mused aloud but thought of something else. He stepped past his gelding into the street and continued obliquely on across to the hotel. Short of the steps he turned aside to the passageway he and Clen had used in escaping last night.

As he'd expected, the broken window was unrepaired. He looked through it into the empty room. Voices came from the lobby beyond the door. The chair he had thrown through

210

he window last night leaned brokenly against the near all. The table was pushed out from the wall. Near its outside edge stood a wastebasket Clanton had somehow missed overturning in his fall.

Red took from his pocket the rolled bills Clanton's woman friend had given him last night. He tossed the money in through the window. It struck the edge of the wastebasket, hung there a moment, and fell down out of sight inside.

Recrossing the street, he was lifting a boot to stirrup a quarter minute later when a gruff voice from behind on the walk called: "You, Knight!"

Red turned. The man who had spotted him less than five minutes ago stood closest, his dark half-breed's face set in sneer. Beyond him was a spare old man, grizzled, hawkish of face and with pale-blue eyes now stony of look but giving hint of shiftiness. This one wore a sheriff's silver star.

As Red turned, the lawman stepped slowly forward. "I'll handle this!" he said flatly to his companion. Then: "Goin' someplace, Knight?"

"I thought I was," Red drawled.

"You are. Only it ain't where you think. You're under arrest."

"What for?"

"Robbery, horse stealin', attempted murder!" The sheriff's gun rocked suddenly up at Red. "Get his hogleg, Pete!"

The half-breed eased around Red and took his gun. Then he planted his hand in the middle of Red's back and roughly pushed him toward the walk.

Red caught himself, stiffened, and was wheeling on the man when the sheriff said sharply: "Hold it! No rough stuff, amigo! There's Duke down at the office. Come along, Knight."

Red gave the half-breed a brief, unreadable look before he

stepped onto the walk. The sheriff seemed momentarily puzzled over his docile acceptance of his arrest and growled a warning as they started on, side by side: "We're goin' to make this stick, Knight."

Red shrugged, more interested in Pete who flanked him on the other side, walking even with him. The half-breed swaggered, his manner arrogant after his rough handling of the prisoner. Their passage along the walk occasioned some interest. Passing the saddle shop, they had to walk close together to edge through a group that eyed them curiously. Red suddenly slowed his stride. Then, too quickly for Pete to anticipate it, he thrust his leg out and tripped the man with a hard blow at his swinging knee.

Pete stumbled and fell. Red's hand flashed down and recovered his gun thrust through the half-breed's belt. He swung on the sheriff to catch him flat-footed, his hand barely raising toward his now-holstered gun.

Red dropped his own .45 into leather and drawled, "You two go on ahead!" as Pete, his face black with anger, picked himself up off the planking.

For a brief moment, all three stood without moving. "Want to make a try for it?" Red invited.

All the lawman said was: "Don't be so doggone proddy, Pete!" And to Red: "You comin' or ain't you?"

"Think I will," Red said. "But after you."

Laughs came from the group nearby as Sheriff Harvey Jenkins turned and, with the Clanton man, preceded his prisoner. In them Red had his first hint of the lawman' unpopularity. It brought him a little relief to think that thus the odds against his getting out of this spot were lessened.

Before the sheriff's office, a plain board shack built onto the near end of a substantial stone jail, Red saw Duke

Clanton's sleek black stallion standing hip shot at the hitch rail. He smiled faintly as Jenkins opened the screen door and called: "No sidesteppin', gents!" His warning made the half-breed, following Jenkins in through the door, wince visibly.

Duke Clanton's big frame was slouched in a swivel chair behind the small room's rolltop desk.

"Where the devil you been, Harv?" he said querulously. Then, seeing Red coming through the door, he stiffened.

Without preliminary Red said: "Tell him why I'm not under arrest, Clanton!"

Duke Clanton's broad face took on an angry color as his eyes fastened on Red's holstered gun. He gave the lawman, then Pete, a questioning look.

"Had some trouble with him," Jenkins muttered.

Clanton's manner abruptly changed. He smiled openly. "Now don't get us wrong, Knight," he began suavely.

"He's trumped up some charges against me." Red nodded to the sheriff, having noticed the swollen lump on Clanton's jaw where his fist had connected last night. "Supposin' you explain 'em."

"You'll admit we could make those charges stick," Clanton said.

"How? When did I steal a horse? And what's this about robbery?"

"You headed out last night with twenty-five hundred bucks of my . . . of that lady's money," Clanton corrected himself quickly. "You swiped a couple of jugheads to make your getaway. You. . . ."

"Didn't you find the money?" Red asked blandly. "I tossed it into the wastebasket. Or maybe you weren't seein' much right then." The taunting remark brought instant anger to the Circle D man's face. "As for the two horses, you didn't find 'em at our camp this mornin', did you?"

"Then how the devil did you get out of town?" Jenkins flared.

"We could've walked. You can't prove we didn't. We weren't in possession of those horses this morning."

"Turned 'em loose, that's what you did!" the sheriff grumbled.

"Pete, go look for that money in the wastebasket in the hotel writin' room," Clanton said tersely. "If it's there, I want it all. Understand?"

Red leaned against the wall by the door as the half-breed went out. "Now how about this attempted murder?" he said.

Jenkins started to say something when Clanton waved him to silence. "Skip it, Harv! We're too late. He's seen Gail Dennis." There was a hint of grudging admiration in the glance he fixed on Red. "Well, what happens now, Knight? You leavin'?"

"I may, or I may hang around. I'd sort of like to know what happened to Spence."

He was watching Clanton closely as he mentioned the man he'd left on the homestead last fall. He could not be sure of Clanton's reaction, except that one moment the man's glance was open and unguarded and the next inscrutable with wariness.

"Spence?" Clanton's expression went pious. "Tough luck about him. He was a good man."

"You said yesterday the climate didn't agree with him."

Clanton shrugged. "I was talkin' through my hat. Don't know what happened to him."

"You can forget I mentioned it. Only I won't." Red eased out from the wall as the door opened and Pete reentered the room.

The half-breed handed Clanton the roll of bills. Clanton

214

ounted it and thrust it in his pocket. "Withdraw the charges, Harv," he told the sheriff. "It was a misunder-standin' all around." He gave Red a shrewd look. "You played it smooth, Knight. How much did you tell her?"

"Enough." The eagerness Red detected in Clanton's casu-lly put question convinced him that Gail Dennis had given her foreman some uneasy moments out at the Circle D.

Clanton shrugged. "Let that old duffer out of there, Harv," he said.

Puzzled, Red watched the sheriff reach for a bunch of keys and unlock the padlock on the solid steel-paneled jail door. The lawman opened the door and disappeared into the half-lit interior of the jail. In there unoiled hinges squeaked, and the sheriff's voice sounded in some unintelligible re-mark.

Then Clem Reynolds's querulous tones shuttled out to Red: "Maybe I've been in a worse jail, but I'll be hanged if I know where!" He came out the door, blinking against the stronger light. Then he saw Red, and his old seamed face took on a broad grin. "You didn't forget me after all?" When he spotted Clanton, the smile vanished. "How come you're shinin' up to this polecat?" he asked Red.

"We've been talkin' over a few things. Among them, Ned Spence."

"What about Ned?" Clem barked.

"Clanton can't seem to make up his mind."

The old lawman wheeled on Clanton so abruptly that the Circle D ramrod edged back toward the wall. "Your bunch was the last to see Spence alive," he drawled tonelessly. "What happened to him?"

"I wouldn't know," Clanton's face even bore a trace of regret, "except that we saw him ride away that night."

"The devil you don't!" Clem scoffed.

"Easy, Clem," Red cut in. "We'll find out sooner or later. He nodded to the sheriff. "Give him his gun."

At a nod from Clanton, Jenkins reached to a shelf over his desk to take down and hand across Clem's full-looped shell belt and holstered gun.

"Let's be goin'," Red said.

The ramrod took his time cinching the gun about his flat waist, all the while eyeing Clanton darkly. Before he followed Red out the door, he drawled: "Somethin' tells me I'm one day havin' to even things with you for Ned, Clanton. When that day comes, you'd better have your joints oiled for some sudden shootin'!"

VII
"THE SKY'S THE LIMIT"

Outside, on the walk, Clem asked Red: "Get anything out of Clanton?"

"Not much. What happened this mornin'?"

"Clanton took the herd. The boys were headed for Jennifer's the last I saw of 'em."

They walked on, Red acquainting his foreman with developments since their parting at dawn. When he mentioned Gail Dennis's buying the herd, and the price she'd paid for it, Clem gave an astonished whistle. "Not bad!" he conceded, then went on to post Red on what had happened with the arrival of the posse. "Clanton was cocked for trouble, ravin' mad when he found you'd hightailed! Madder when he saw our critters had had water. Threatened us with everything from a bull whip to hangin'. But I took it and let 'em put the handcuffs on me and told 'em to take the herd. That got Clanton's goat. They brought me in and locked me up. Wouldn't even buy me any breakfast. I'd give a month's pay for a big steak right now!"

"Let's get one," Red suggested, and they turned toward a restaurant.

Finished with a good meal, Red asked: "What happened to the horses we left here last night?"

"Feed barn. I'll take 'em out to Toad's directly."

Red reached into his pocket and brought out his money. He thumbed four hundred dollars from the roll of bills and gave it to Clem. "Here's enough to last you and the others until tonight," he said. "I'll be back by dark."

"Where you goin'?"

"To the homestead. Maybe I can run on to somethin' that'll tell us what happened to Ned."

Clem looked at the bills, a slow smile breaking across hi face. "We're liable to give this town's tail a mighty goo(twist with this much to go on."

"Twist it all you want," Red grinned. "You're due a goo bust."

They parted at the entrance to the Rosebud, Clem saying "I'm goin' to have one before I go out after the boys."

"Only one, though," Red warned him good naturedly, a he left.

He was to remember his remark later. He would hav(found it even more significant had he noticed the man wh(stood nearby along the walk and witnessed the exchang(of money and overheard what he said. That individua hurried down to the jail where he spent some moments i earnest conversation with Duke Clanton. Presently he wa back again, shouldering his way into the Rosebud.

Clem found Toad Jennifer bellied up to the saloon's bar Relief was plain in the basin man's glance when he saw th other.

"Am I seein' right?" he demanded. "It ain't you, packin' a iron, free as the breeze! What happened?"

Clem ordered whiskey. Over three drinks he posted Jen nifer on what had happened since early morning.

"Reckon we ought to go out and collect your side-kicks t start the celebratin'?" Jennifer said finally.

Clem never answered that question. For at that momen a lanky, range-outfitted 'puncher sauntered up to the ba and called loudly for whiskey, adding just as loudly: ". . . t get the stink of sheep out of my craw! Who's the two-legge(polecat that sold out this country? My last trip it was ru by white men!"

"Which sentiments are mine exactly!" drawled Clem, pushing away from the counter and thrusting out a gnarled hand. "Shake, partner! We're drinkin' for the same reason."

The stranger shook. Presently, after the proper introductions and much talk, the stranger, whose name was Reese, said: "How about me buyin' this round?"

He bought. Clem bought, then it was Toad's turn. Two more congenial souls joined the trio, both agreeing readily to the now belligerent belittling of the business engaged in by all outfits north of the creek. After Clem's sixth drink, when talk got around to the merits of stud as against draw poker, Reese's suggestion that they settle the argument by a friendly small-stakes game met with complete agreement.

The barkeep accordingly lit the lamp over the nearest table, broke out a new deck of cards and a rack of not-so-clean chips, and all five men took chairs. The game started at a two-bit limit. Clem won. The limit was raised to a dollar. Then, finally, as Toad began to win his share, and Clem's luck was holding, Reese plunked a fat wad of bills on the felt and drawled: "The devil with this penny-ante stuff! Any reason why the sky ain't the limit?"

Clem smacked his roll down alongside his hefty stacks of chips. "No reason at all!"

So the limit was forgotten. Also forgotten was Clem's luck. It didn't desert him swiftly; but as the afternoon dragged on his chip stacks dwindled. To counterbalance this, Toad Jennifer's luck started running high along about dark. Once he leaned over and whispered to Clem: "Don't let this bother you. I'll make it good if you'll stick and help me make a cleanin'!"

So Clem's conscience, badly troubled, eased somewhat. He told himself that he'd get the rest of his pay from Red and easily pay the crew. Besides, he'd owned two dozen head of

219

the herd Red had sold this morning.

They sent a swamper out for sandwiches at supper time ordered another quart, and kept the game going. At nine Toad Jennifer was amazed to find that he'd won slightly more than two thousand dollars. At that point Reese and the other pair tossed in their cards, and Reese expressed the sentiments of all three when he said: "Fun's fun, gents but it's got to stop sometime, and mine stops before I have to throw in my boots to cover a bet. That agreeable with you, Jennifer?"

"Sure is." Toad let out a long, relieved sigh.

Reese rose and stretched and yawned, noting the empty table in front of Clem. "About busted you, didn't it, old timer?"

"Just about." Clem was cashing in thirty-four dollars in chips, all that remained of his four hundred. He said ruefully: "Let's be travelin', Toad."

They all had a last drink and left. Clem parted company with Toad, whose horse was at the livery corral. They agreed to meet on the way out of town. Down the street Clem was about to climb into the saddle when Reese came along and called: "How about a night cap, partner? Got a bottle in m' room 'cross at the hotel."

"Uhn-huh!" Clem shook his head. "Got to be gettin' out to meet Toad."

"Wha's matter?" Reese's tongue was thick after his day long bout with the bottle. "Ain' my liquor good 'nuff?"

"Sure. But. . . ."

"No buts 'bout it!" Reese threw an arm about Clem' shoulders. "Drown our sorrows, that's what we will! We're sure a couple pikers to let that dang sheepman clean u out."

"Toad ain't a sheepman!" Clem protested.

220

On their way across to the hotel, he carefully explained just who Jennifer was. Presently, with a couple more drinks, he forgot all about meeting Toad. He was in the hotel forty minutes. Those forty minutes were all that were necessary to decide a certain something the Clanton man wanted to make sure of. Toad Jennifer started home alone.

VIII
"SHOTS IN THE NIGHT"

Fourteen miles across the valley was the shack Ned Spence had lived in the past winter. Going through it for some hint as to Spence's disappearance and then calling on the nearest neighbor, a sheepman, took Red until dark. He couldn't turn down the sheepman's invitation to stay for supper, and it was eight before he started back to town, expecting to find Clem and the crew well on the way to a memorial celebration after sixty days on the drive.

But the more he thought about it, the less he wanted to join in the fun tonight. He was dog-tired. He was uncertain of the future, and he wanted to be alone to think things out. Should he break his unworded bargain with Gail Dennis and buy another bunch of cattle and stock the homestead? Or should he forget it entirely, homestead in another part of the country, and take his crew with him. After all, he'd promised them jobs.

He chose to wrestle with his knotty problem rather than join the crew in town, swung off the town trail, and headed for the river, intending to find where Jennifer lived and spend the night there. In the bright starlight he studied the dark horizon and tried to strike the creek at the point the herd had yesterday, at Jennifer's fence. He rode slowly, enjoying the night's peaceful stillness and the crisp, bracing air. In the next hour the only foreign sound to break the stillness was what seemed like a faint, far off shot. He forgot it a moment after he heard it.

Red felt a small regret over the decision he finally reached — to leave the basin. The past years of footloose wandering made him yearn to settle down somewhere, that had been his reason for coming here. In only two days he'd grown to like the country. Yet, common sense told him that this pleasant hill-bordered valley wasn't to become his home. Sooner or later he'd have another run-in with Duke Clanton. Sooner or later he'd follow the impulse to see more of Gail Dennis, to get to know her.

This girl had attracted him strangely. There weren't many like her, he reflected, then bitterly remembered Jennifer's statement that Gail Dennis and Duke Clanton would one day be married. It galled him to realize that Clanton was deceiving the girl. Yet it wasn't his place to inform her of her foreman's deceit. That would be someone else's task. She probably wouldn't know the real Clanton until it was too late and then would begin years of bitter disillusionment for her.

Well, he'd had his share of trouble here and enough luck to counterbalance it. He'd met a girl he liked uncommonly well. He'd forget her. He'd made some money. If he didn't waste time, he could put a second herd on another range before the end of summer.

He rode his roan across the creek toward a high sandy spur he thought close to the place where the herd had tried to cross yesterday. Once on the other side, though, the look of the night-shadowed land was unfamiliar. There was no lane where the lane should have been. Irritated, Red rode south, knowing he'd come to the road running toward town. At the road he made his guess on which way Jennifer's place lay and turned east, riding leisurely, glad that this star-studded, bracing night was one that would cleanse a man's thinking.

All at once Red heard a sound close ahead, one he couldn't identify. He was riding the line of a fence and decided it might be the gentle swing of a loose wire against a post. But suddenly an elongated shadow showed on the trail ahead. Instantly he recognized it as the outstretched figure of a man.

He vaulted from the saddle, dropping the roan's reins. As he was kneeling alongside the man, the sound came again. It was the racking, indrawing of breath into choked lungs. Turning the man over, Red looked down into the face of Toad Jennifer. Blood made a glistening line at one corner of the basin man's mouth. Toad's eyes were closed. In this new position, his breathing came easier. Tearing open his shirt, Red saw the small dark blotch of a wound high on the left side of his chest.

"All right, Toad?" he asked when Jennifer's eyes opened briefly. His answer was a vacant stare. Jennifer was still unconscious.

Tying his bandanna over the wound, Red was thinking of getting Jennifer quickly into town when the muted hoof thud of a trotting pony shuttled down along the trail. He stiffened, came erect, and drew his gun. His glance went quickly to a stunted piñon that grew close to the trail. Quickly he led the roan behind the tree. There he stood wariness high in him, for he knew now that someone had tried to murder Toad Jennifer tonight.

The sound of the oncoming pony strengthened quickly. Then came something else, a high thin voice crooning the strains of "Red River Valley." Red knew that voice. It was Clem Reynolds's! Instantly he was reassured and stepped out from the concealment of the tree.

Clem was drunk, not roaring drunk but pleasingly so. He was within ten feet of Red before he saw him and even then found nothing strange in a lone dismounted rider blocking the trail, for he called heartily: "Evenin' stranger. Got a drink handy?"

"It's me, Clem. Better get down and help."

Somewhat sobered by the flat tones of Red's voice, Clem obeyed quickly. "Who's that with you?" he asked as he came up.

"Toad."

Clem chuckled. "Passed out, eh?"

"No. He's been shot."

"Shot!" Clem was really sober now. He stared down helplessly at Jennifer, trying to explain: "Him and me met up with some regular gents and had the best game. . . ."

"Tell me about it later," Red cut in, trying to keep down his anger. He knew that somehow Clem had failed to keep his promise of the morning. "The thing now is to get Toad to a doctor. He's hurt bad. Here, give me a hand."

As gently as they could, they lifted Jennifer's loose bulk so that he straddled the roan's withers. Red, in the saddle behind him, held him erect.

"You go on ahead and be sure there's a doctor ready," he ordered Clem. "I'll stop at the first house and get a rig to carry him in. Hurry!"

Clem went up into the saddle and was wheeling the pony around when Red felt a light blow strike his left cheek. An instant later the sharp *crack!* of a rifle cut across the stillness, and he knew that the blow on his face had been the air impact of a passing bullet. Instinctively, he put spurs to the roan, calling: "Ride, Clem!"

The roan's lunge carried him on past the other man. Suddenly, creekward, sounded the explosions of two more guns. Red swung away from them, hearing the pound of Clem's pony behind. With the roan at a run it was hard steadying Jennifer's loose bulk. He covered a hundred yards before more shots sounded, this time the lower-toned blasting of a .45 fired four more times. And now he couldn't any longer hear Clem's horse. He looked back over his shoulder to see Clem's dim shape streaking along the line of the trail from which he had been angling. Far behind Clem the red stab of powder flame cut the night's blackness, and Red made out vague hurrying shapes back there. Clem, realizing the predicament of Red's roan caught carrying a double load, had evidently decided to decoy the killers away. He would make out all right. He'd had a good start on his pursuers.

Red swung even more sharply away from the trail, riding the abrupt-sloping bottom of a deep gully for a good half mile. He had circled, starting back this way, intending to take Jennifer to his farm. Then suddenly he reasoned that whoever had tried to kill the basin man would doubtless be watching the layout. That thought brought him up out of the gully to strike a straight line to the river. Crossing it twenty minutes ago he'd seen a light a mile or so away on the north side. He should be nearly on a line with that place now. It was important to get help for Jennifer.

He thought once that Jennifer's spare frame straightened under his hold. That was shortly after the roan crossed the stream and headed out across the flats beyond, going toward the light, now in sight. But when he spoke to Jennifer there was no answer, and the man's weight was as limp as it had been before.

The light shone from a shack, a sheepman's. Below the shack was a roofless barn, a corral, pens, and a windmill whose spidery bulk towered blackly against the heavens. Red drew his Colt and held it in his rein hand as he walked the roan in across the barn lot. Then a dog barked savagely and dashed out of the nearest pen, snarling at the roan's heels.

The roan shied and narrowly missed unseating him. Red was swinging his gun around to shoot so as to frighten off the dog when a voice called sharply from the direction of the windmill: "Down, Mike!" Immediately the dog quieted and slunk away in the darkness. "Lift 'em, stranger!" came the voice again, its note ominous.

Red tossed his gun to the ground but didn't lift his hands, since he had to hold Jennifer erect. "Can't," he drawled. "He'd fall off if I did."

"Who you got there?" came the voice again, and now Red could see the speaker standing a few feet from the windmill's nearest leg.

"Toad Jennifer."

The man breathed an oath of surprise. "Toad! What's wrong with him? What was all that shootin' across the creek?" He advanced toward Red slowly.

"It was meant for us. I got away with Toad. He's shot."

"The devil he is! Why didn't you say so? Here, let me lift him down!"

The man rocked his rifle down from the crook of his arm, laid it on the ground, and reached up to catch Jennifer's weight as Red let him go. Red came aground. The man called sharply, "Jim, open up!" The shack door opened on a boy's slender figure, a feeble wash of lamplight coming out across the littered yard.

The man looked at Red and gave a visible start. "You're Knight, ain't you?" he queried.

Red nodded and said: "Let's get Toad in a bed."

The shack was a single room, poorly furnished, lacking any feminine touch. Double bunks ranged one wall, a stove and packing-box cupboards the one opposite. There were a table, two chairs and a crude plain chest. Nothing else.

"Get a fire goin', Jim," the man said, as he and Red laid

Jennifer on the lower bunk. He pulled Jennifer's shirt aside
saw the bullet hole, and looked questioningly at Red. Re
told him briefly what had happened.

"I'm Sewell. This is my kid, Jim." The sheepman nodde
to the gangling youth laying a fire in the stove. The hint o
a smile broke the gravity of his long face. "Maybe you'v
heard of me?"

Red shook his head.

"Toad and me is friends, even if I do live the wrong sid
of the line," Sewell explained. "I was at Masker's place las
night when you called Clanton's bluff. Your talk sure di
me good. That highbinder needed takin' down!"

"Hadn't one of us better get to town for the doctor?" Re
put in impatiently.

Sewell looked down at Jennifer. He shook his head. "N
can do. The sawbones left for the Wells today to help
woman with a baby. Won't be back till toward mornin'."

"But we can't let Jennifer die!" Red flared. "He's bad hurt
There must be someone else."

Sewell's look was thoughtful. He turned to his son. "Jim
get a bridle on Bessie! You're goin' for help."

"Where?" the boy asked, already on the way to the door.

"Tell you later," Sewell said. As the door swung shut o
the youngster, he turned to Red again. "You wouldn't lik
what I'm doin', so I'll keep it to myself. Now what abou
that scrap across the river?"

Red told him of his sale of the herd, of leaving Clem i
town this morning. Sewell interrupted at that point to say
"I can tell you part of what happened. Three of Clanton'
men were in a poker game with your side-kick and Jennife
at supper time tonight. Toad's luck was goin' strong. You
man's was not."

In a few more moments, as Red finished, Sewell said

You'll want to go back, won't you, and see what happened to Reynolds? Go ahead. The boy'll bring help, and I'll look after Toad." When Red hesitated, he added: "Don't think I'd give Toad away. I hate Duke Clanton's guts as much as I like the girl he works for."

In these few words Sewell did much to ease Red's worry over leaving Jennifer in unfriendly hands. Sewell was to be trusted. He had also hinted that Clanton was responsible for the ambush across the river.

Red went out into the yard, found his .45, and mounted the roan again. Leaving, he saw the boy lead a hackamored mare up to the shack and stand talking to his father. Before the darkness hid them, the boy had climbed onto the mare and was headed out in the direction opposite the one Red was taking, riding fast.

Back across the river, Red was undecided what to do. Finally he turned upstream again, this time following the creek bank, determined to find Jennifer's layout and see if his men were still there. He came to Jennifer's lane, followed the fence in, and found a gate. Beyond it, a faintly marked trail led in through a dense cottonwood grove then climbed steeply to a knoll on which stood a pole cabin, barn, and corrals. The gray outline of his chuck wagon showing in the deeper shadow of the barn convinced him that this was Jennifer's place. There was no light in the cabin. Red approached warily, keeping to the cover of the small trees.

He was within fifty yards of the cabin when a gruff voice, off to his left, said mildly: "That you, Red?"

"Nels?" Red answered, recognizing the cook's voice. He reined the roan off there and saw the cook's heavy shape come out of a nearby tree's dense shadow. "How come you're roamin' around out here?"

"Trouble, boss," Nels told him. "Bad trouble! A while ago

we heard shootin' off toward town. We'd been in Toad' kitchen, tryin' to work up some fever over a stud game waitin' for Toad to come home. That shootin' sounde(suspicious, so the boys went out to saddle up and go se(what the ruckus was about. They was all crowded in th(corral when half a dozen jaspers rode out of the trees an(threw down on 'em. Caught 'em cold! I was still in th(kitchen and managed to duck out the front door and ge(away."

"What happened to the others?"

"Gone!" was the cook's ominous answer. "They lined 'en up and headed out the road. I heard one jasper say they'(have a hard time findin' enough cots in the jail to g(around."

IX

"LYNCH FEVER"

Red's astonishment prevented his immediately taking in the full significance of Hansen's words. "Jail!" he echoed.

"That's what he said. It don't make sense, unless they're tryin' to even it up with all of us for the rumpus you and Clem raised in town last night."

Red's thinking was coming a little clearer now. "That isn't it," he said and sat considering a long moment, having to make a choice between two decisions. He wasn't quite sure any more that Toad Jennifer was in safe hands and was already blaming himself for having left the basin man. Then there was the crew. And Clem! He didn't know what luck Clem had had in getting away. Nor what Clanton hoped to accomplish by having the crew jailed. He wanted to get to town and find some answer to this mysterious and unexpected development.

He had a thought that made him ask: "Has anyone had a good look at you, Nels? Any of Clanton's bunch, I mean? You weren't there yesterday when they stopped the herd. How about this mornin'?"

Nels frowned thoughtfully. "I was at the wagon the whole time," he answered. "They wasn't close enough to see me."

"And they didn't get a look at you tonight?"

The cook shook his head.

"Then get a hull on a horse and head for town. Go straight on in and see if you can pick up anything on Clem or the rest. They'll. . . ."

"Clem?" Nels cut in. "What about him? Ain't he in jail?"

"No. Tell you about it later. Right now I need information.

231

You're the only one who can get it. I'm meeting Jennifer across the river in a few minutes." To save time Red was going to wait and tell Nels about Jennifer and Clem later. He glanced up at the wheeling stars. "It's close to eleven now. At midnight I'll be waiting for you half a mile this side of town near that old barn with the caved-in roof. You can't miss it."

"There's an awful lot here I don't understand, Boss!" Nels protested. "Why . . . ?"

"Later, Nels!" Red interrupted. "We've got a whale of a lot of work to do. See you in an hour." He reined the roan around and went back down toward the river through the trees.

A quarter hour later he was riding in on Sewell's place. The dog again barked savagely but seemed to remember the roan and, after a few last half-hearted yips, stopped worrying the animal. The shack door opened as Red dismounted close to the small, roofed stoop. Sewell stood in the doorway, and beyond him his son crossed the room carrying a steaming basin of water.

"How is he?" Red's query was urgent.

"Doin' all right." The sheepman stepped aside to let him enter.

The light of the unshaded lamp, sitting on the table alongside the bunk where Jennifer lay, blinded Red for a moment. Then, as his eyes became accustomed to the glare, he made out a figure kneeling by the bunk beyond the table.

At the instant he knew who it was. Gail Dennis turned and looked at him. The lamplight edged her head with spun gold. Her prettiness was breath-taking; color heightened the olive hue of her cheeks. In spite of her clothes, a pair of waist overalls and a dark red cotton shirt open at the hroat, and her wind-blown hair, she was still utterly eminine.

"He's going to be all right," she said softly, and her smile was a reminder of this morning's meeting.

Red knew now why Sewell hadn't warned him of whom he was to find. It was natural that the sheepman would believe his antagonism toward Circle D's foreman would carry over o its owner. As evidence of this, Sewell said questioningly: "You ain't sore, Knight?"

Red shook his head in a brief negative. He crossed the 'oom to stand at the head of the bunk, looking down at Jennifer. Toad now lay propped up on folded blankets and a pillow. Gone from his face was the deathly pallor of an hour ago. His breathing was even.

"He's asleep," Gail Dennis said in a hushed voice. She nodded to a bottle of whiskey on the table. "He took a good drink of that. It'll keep him quiet, stop the chance of a hemorrhage. If he rests, he has a good chance." She gave Red a look of near pleading. "Sewell's told me some things I didn't know. About Duke. I . . . I didn't realize what kind of a man he was. He did this to Jennifer, didn't he?"

Red was uncertain, half embarrassed. "Let's wait until we find out," was all he could think to say.

"You don't have to try to cover up for Duke!" Gail told him. "I can see things now I couldn't before. Perhaps you were kind not to tell me. Is there anything I can do to help?"

"Not a thing except to look after Toad. We're pullin' out as soon as we can," Red lied. "I reckon when we leave, things will go back to normal."

The girl's glance clung to him, seeming to see beneath his mask of indifference. "I want you to know I'm sorry . . . very sorry for the way this has turned out," she said finally. "You should be taking up your homestead. I shouldn't be running sheep." She shrugged restlessly. "You have my promise tha[t] things will be different from now on. I'm having it out wit[h] Duke."

"Better go easy with him. You wouldn't want trouble."

Gail's smile was enigmatic, somehow lacking in amuse[-]ment. "I still have a few friends I can call on," she said.

Red held out his hand. "I'll be leavin'."

The pressure of her fingers tried to make up for the thing[s] she was leaving unsaid. She breathed, "Good bye," and the[n] he left her.

Sewell followed him out into the yard. "I couldn't hel[p] tellin' her, Knight. Someone maybe ought to take a heft[y] kick at the seat of my pants, but I'm glad I did it."

"That doesn't matter now. What does matter is that sh[e] has some friends to count on."

"Don't think she ain't! Maybe we're makin money at thi[s] stinkin' business but, for me, I'll take cattle and starve if [I] have to. There's a few besides me thinkin' the same way[.] We all knew old Tom Dennis, and we'll stick by his girl."

"Well, here's wishin' you luck."

Red went astride the roan and out into the night. Onc[e] again weariness settled upon him, but it was a differen[t] feeling now. His wind was played out, and a heavy depres[-]sion was settling on him. He had said farewell to the on[e] girl who, in contrast to all others he had known, ha[d] prompted in him a feeling deeper than reverence. He wa[s] riding out of her life because he saw no possible way of thei[r] ever becoming more to each other than they were now, mer[e] casual acquaintances. Perhaps she hated him for havin[g] exposed the man of her choice. It had seemed inevitabl[e] since their meeting that this should happen, inevitabl[e] because all Red's hopes in coming to this country had bee[n] blasted in the space of two days.

He forcibly put her from his mind, looking ahead to his meeting with Nels Hansen. His lean face sobered to a stern, rock-like gravity as he grimly faced the solution to tonight's dilemma. There would be more trouble. He was almost glad to be riding into it.

"They've got the whole dang bunch locked up!" were Hansen's first words after meeting Red. "You didn't tell me they let Clem go this mornin'. He got tangled up with three Clanton men in a no-limit game at the saloon an' they took him to the cleaner's while Toad was the heavy winner. Now they're sayin' that Clem shot Toad for his winnin's. Claim they found Toad's money in Clem's pocket after they'd shot Clem's horse out from under him in that fight down the road tonight. They're makin' lynch talk, and they've got a reward out for you! You're supposed to have got away with Toad's carcass." Hansen paused, out of breath, having put together more words in one piece than Red had ever thought possible for the ordinarily untalkative man.

"What about the crew?" Red asked. "Why are they holdin' them?"

"Rustlin'!" Nels said harshly. "They tried to run off the herd tonight, accordin' to the story. And I dang well know they weren't within ten miles of where Clanton was holdin' those critters!"

"It's beginnin' to make sense now," Red breathed.

"What is?" Nels demanded testily. "Clanton's taken over the saloon, set up a second bar. Does that make sense? Drinks are sellin' at half price, for nothin' to them that can't buy! The town's wild! If they don't bend a good cottonwood limb with Clem at the end of a rope before mornin', I'm a coal-black Swede!"

"We'd better get in and see what we can do." Red's tall

body was erect in the saddle as he stared off toward the winking lights of the town.

"What good'll it do us? We're two against half a thousand! And that bunch of drunks ain't foolin'!"

Red shrugged. "We'll see. How about the jail?"

"Guarded front and back. What really happened to Toad?"

Nels had almost forgotten the basin man.

Red told him, then: "We'll work down along the alley across the street from the jail."

It wasn't difficult to reach the dark alley. The few men they met had indulged too heavily of Clanton's free liquor and were probably on the way home to sleep it off, for they paid no attention to Red and Nels. But at the head of a narrow passageway between two stores, as Red looked out onto the street, he saw that Clanton's whiskey was having a different effect on nine-tenths of the town, most of whose citizens seemed to have forgotten their beds for the duration of the night.

Two crowds were massed along the street's broad length. One was centered in front of the Rosebud. The other, the biggest, completely filled the street in front of the jail. This last was the most noisome and ominous looking. The wall and the hitch rail in front of the sheriff's office were clear, being paced by two deputies armed with sawed-off shot guns. They ignored the taunting jeers and mocking laughter of the onlookers. But it didn't take much imagination for Red to see that the mob, restless and still undecided, would in the end take the chance on rushing the jail to lay hands on a man they considered a murderer, Clem Reynolds. And unless Red's hunch was wrong, the deputies would offer little resistance.

He and Nels stood for minutes in the shadowed entryway to the passage, watching the traffic that moved along under he walk awnings. Red was trying to think of a way to get Clem and the others out of the jail. He recognized the sobering fact that nothing less than dynamite would clear he street or sway the crowd from its grim purpose.

Nels finally broke the silence, voicing Red's worry. "We in't got a Chinaman's chance, Boss! I once heard of a ashier firin' a house at the edge of a town to draw away a nob makin' a run on his bank. But even that wouldn't work ere. These jaspers got their hearts in their work. And don't igure to stick your neck out by walkin' across there with a un. You wouldn't live to pull a trigger twice!"

"Not a chance," Red agreed, and in that moment hope nearly left him.

Clanton's reason for this iron-bound frame-up was obcure. But Red had no doubts that this was Clanton's doing. 'he fact remained that the Circle D foreman had laid the roundwork for a revenge that was out of all proportion to Red's having come off best in the sale of the herd. Clanton evidently took Red's small success as a personal affront. Ie'd framed Clem with murder and come close to taking Jennifer's life. He had saddled Red's crew with a charge of ustling that would be almost impossible to prove false. Lastly, he had put out a reward on Red to make sure that he couldn't help his men.

There weren't any loopholes for Red to work through. He vas outlawed. Clem would probably die at the end of a rope, even though Jennifer lived to tell his story, for the truth vould come too late. Red considered for a moment the possibility of forcibly taking several townsmen out to see Jennifer on the possibility that the wounded man might ave regained consciousness. But there was no assurance hat Jennifer could talk, that he wasn't dead by now. And even if Jennifer could speak, Red couldn't be sure of getting back to town to rescue Clem before the hangman got him

Sheer desperation turned his mind to another possibility "Nels," he said gravely, "we've got only one chance. Here i is." And he stepped back into the passageway and spoke t his crewman earnestly for long moments.

When he had put his last question, Nels's answer cam on the heels of a long-drawn gusty sigh. "I reckon it's bette than standin' here watchin' it happen. Sure I'll help. Bu we may be too late."

His words added to Red's urgency as they rode out th alley to the west limits of town. Red pushed the roan har along the trail, irritated at having to hold the animal in s that Nels, on a slower horse, could keep abreast. Th three-mile ride that brought them within sight of a redl glowing light in the distance seemed to take an eternity But at last they were close enough to make out that ligh as a big camp fire, the dark sprawling shadow of bunche cattle beyond it telling Red he had guessed correctly on thi being Clanton's cow camp.

"Remember, we ride straight in." He added a last warnin word to Nels. They were close enough now to see a man' shape momentarily outlined against the big blaze. Th man's walk was uncertain, and Red thought he saw a bottl in his hand. He drew his Colt and held it in his free hand cushioned in his lap behind the generous swell of his saddle Nels, seeing his move, did likewise. They were within hundred yards of the fire, Red going on with the roan at trot. Here, close at hand, was his one chance of saving hi men, the one wild gamble left him.

Thinking that, he rode boldly in. He and Nels were we within the range of the fire's broad circle of light before the were hailed by one of the three men lying or sitting o blankets close to the blaze. The man who gruffly called t hem merely rolled over onto his elbow and looked in their direction, his shout more a greeting than a challenge. His oice was thickened by whiskey, his words hardly intelligible. Red answered that hail with "Who's got a drink?" and kept oming on.

He had now spotted the fourth man, the one he'd seen ross before the blaze a moment ago. This one was now pproaching the fire from the far side with an armload of lead cedar.

"Tarnation, it ain't . . . ," began one man as he recognized Red.

His hand stabbed toward the gun at his thigh a full second oo late. For Red cocked his weapon up from his lap, lrawling: "No . . . it ain't!" His .45 arced around then in ime to catch the man on the other side of the fire as he lropped his armload of wood to draw.

Nels, alongside Red, said flatly: "Go ahead! Make a try for t!" His hard-set face and the .45 in his hand were compelling enough to make the trio on the blankets lift their hands.

Red swung to the ground and sauntered over there to elieve the three of their weapons. One wore a pair of .38s, naking the count of surrendered pistols four. Two rifles lay against a saddle nearby. Red took them. Then he went around the far side of the fire and took from the fourth Clanton man a pair of silver-mounted .44s.

"Where'd you pick these up . . . at a circus?" Red drawled s he thrust the weapons with the others through his belt. A growl of impotent rage was his only answer. Red motioned is prisoner across with the others. "Hunt up some rope," e told Nels.

The cook, gone a brief moment beyond the wide circle of he blaze's light, reappeared with three coiled riatas.

"There's a buckboard off there," he told Red. "We could

239

tie 'em to the wheels."

Less than five minutes later the four Clanton men, gagged
with their own bandannas, sat each at the foot of a wheel
arms extended and roped to spokes, legs tightly wound with
many turnings of the manila.

Red gave them a last inspecting glance, told them: "Some
one'll be out in the mornin' to cut you loose." Nodding to
Nels, they both hurried back to their horses. There, Red
handed Nels the half-dozen six-guns and the rifles.

There was no need for them to speak as they set about
their work. They rode out to the margin of the herd and
circled it to the point farthest from the fire. Outflanking
the last bald-faced steer, Red cautioned Nels only once
saying: "Not too fast!" Then both of them shouted, spurring
their mounts at the nearest sleeping animals.

Wakefulness ran through the herd. Downed animal
lunged to their feet; those standing shied away from the
pair of riders and drifted off into the night. A lead bull shook
his shaggy long-horned head and plodded straight for the
lights of Tres Piedras. The animals nearest him followed in
a long thick line. Soon the others, urged from behind, got into
motion. Within five minutes the whole herd was on the move

"Easy!" Red cautioned once as Nels's horse swung sud
denly aside to cut back a steer that broke from line. "Le
the salty ones go. We don't need 'em."

"What happens when we get close in, Red? How're we goin
to put 'em where we want 'em?"

"Fences," Red answered. "It was fences that helped Clan
ton make his play yesterday, and they'll help us make our
tonight. All that land this side of town is under wire."

"Ought to be a cinch." Nels's momentary skepticism wa
forgotten.

"If we work it right," was Red's reservation.

X

"CATTLE DRIVE DOWN MAIN STREET"

Duke Clanton had just finished a long talk with Tres
Piedras' mayor, Tom Higgins. Several minutes ago he'd
taken the mayor, full of dubious misgivings, into Doc
Masker's office. Over a drink and much persuasion, he'd
convinced Higgins that the course the mob was taking
tonight was the right one. This stranger, Clem Reynolds,
had killed one of the basin's most upstanding citizens.
Furthermore, Knight's crew had had the gall to try and
steal the herd Knight had this morning sold to Gail Dennis.
It was obvious that the normal workings of the law weren't
fast enough to take care of a situation like this.

"To blazes with the courts!" Clanton had finally worked
up the boldness to say. "In the old days they didn't wait on
the courts to condemn a killer, did they, Tom? We ain't
waitin' tonight!"

Higgins was convinced in the end. So convinced that just
now he stood on a chair under the big chandelier at the
center of the Rosebud's main room, addressing the crowd.
He was a trifle drunk, but his words came loud and clear.
Instead of constraining the mob, his speech was to do more
than any one thing so far to spur it on. He was privately a
little concerned over having sent a man out to the Circle D
an hour ago to inform Gail Dennis of the treachery of her
foreman, for Clanton's maneuvers now seemed honest and
above board. Higgins was trying to make up for his lack of
faith in Clanton who last year had helped vote him into
office.

As his stentorian voice rolled on, holding the attention of

the crowd, a brief inscrutable smile played across Duke Clanton's face. He saw Pete Hernandez on the edge of the crowd and sauntered over behind the half-breed, touched him lightly on the shoulder, and just as casually sauntered back to his place at the office door again. Presently Pete was standing beside him.

"Go tell Jenkins to get ready." Clanton's voice was barely audible over the bellow of the mayor's. "It's comin' any minute now. Tell him he's to throw up his hands and give in. We don't want no one hurt."

Pete's head tilted down in a brief affirmative. He left Clanton's side, working his way inconspicuously toward the swing doors up front. Out on the walk he unobtrusively pushed his way through the crowd listening to the mayor's harangue. When he was in the clear, his stride lengthened and he started for the jail.

He had taken only a dozen steps when he saw a rider break through the outskirts of the crowd in front of the jail and come streaking down the street, recklessly threatening to overrun anyone who got in his way. Pete recognized the rider as a Clanton man and hailed him.

"Find the boss quick!" the rider said breathlessly, as he drew his nervous pony to a stand beside the half-breed. "Hell's busted loose! It's the herd!"

"Forget the herd," Pete drawled. "We got somethin' else to think. . . ."

"Forget 'em! When they're headed down the street? There!" He raised a hand and pointed. Pete, looking toward the jail, saw the crowd beginning to break into a wild flight. Beyond, in a dark oncoming mass topped by rocking, glistening horns, the street was jammed, walk to walk, with cattle whose lumbering gait seemed like the onrush of a tremendous slow flood along a dry riverbed.

Pete turned and ran. Behind him shouts and curses and cries of terror struck over the undertone of low-thundering hoofs. Far down the street, beyond the mass of cattle, a six-gun exploded. The lead steers broke into clumsy lope. Pete tried to claw his way into the crowd in front of the Rosebud, but others were doing the same thing.

Red Knight had a moment ago lifted his Colt and fired it over his head in a blasting crescendo of sound that struck terror through the herd lined down the street. Luck had been with him and Nels. The fenced pastures out beyond the street's far limit had formed a perfect aisle down which to drive the four hundred animals. Now, in full light along the main street, the herd was like a ramrod thrust down the choked barrel of a muddied shotgun. Up ahead the two separate crowds were fast melting off the street. Saddle horses and teams, terrified, lunged and broke out from the tie-rails, threatening to run down pedestrians.

The crowd caught first, in front of the jail, was in the greatest danger. For along those two rows of facing buildings nearest them there were no passageways and few inset doors offering shelter. Tres Piedras' citizens, ranchers and sheepmen alike, turned and ran for their lives. Through the dust Red made out Nels Hansen's blocky shape. He reined over there, close to his cook, and shouted: "Make it fast, Nels!"

Nels needed no urging. As Red reloaded his Colt, the cook was already spurring his horse in through the animals of the drag, pushing on up deeply into the main body of the herd. He was risking being thrown and trampled, but he rode solidly, the bullets in his gun belt and his buckles glistening dully in the reflected light of a store window he passed, a rifle cradled across the swell of his saddle. He struck out viciously with rein ends to prod animals out of

243

his way and shot once or twice when some unruly stee
jammed his horse against another.

All at once, Red looked up the street to see it clear ahea
of the leaders of the herd. Miraculously, the crowd in fron
of the Rosebud had melted in through the doors. The alle
out behind the saloon must be jammed. The jail crowd ha
somehow managed to find cover, too. There wasn't a man
in sight ahead of the long line of the charging cattle, now
loping in terror-stricken flight down the long straight aisl
between the buildings.

Red saw Nels, up ahead, charge in before the front doo
to the sheriff's office. An instant later the cook was out o
the saddle, kicking in the flimsy screen door, his horse lef
to his own devices. Seeing the cook safe, Red sighed in kee
relief. As the first muted blast of gunfire sounded from
inside the jail, he set about accomplishing his own job. Nel
would have Clem and crew out of their lock-blown cells i
another thirty seconds. It was Red's turn to push up int
the herd, past the scattered animals of the drag. No prod
ding was needed now to keep the steers on the run. The
had stampeded and would run until in the clear beyond th
far limits of the town.

He used his gun twice, reloading each time. The roan
worked tirelessly, nimbly, as a good cutting horse will whe
in danger of being pushed off his feet. Once he would hav
gone down but for Red's lifting his head so that he coul
find his footing again. Red shot and killed the steer blockin
the way, and the roan jumped the falling carcass and wa
clear of the death-slashing hoofs the next instant.

Slowly, the roan crowded his way towards the street'
south walk. Under firm rein, he lunged up onto the wall
and in under the awning. Ahead and opposite a stee
crashed into an awning post, broke it, and a thirty-foo

244

tretch of awning sagged down and was splintered to kin-
lling as the herd hit it. Red, riding the other walk, felt the
lackles rise along his back at the thought that he might be
aught under a similar obstruction.

The saloon windows lit the backs of the animals twenty
ards ahead. The roan had nearly stopped. Cattle jammed
he walk where the wall of the building beyond the Rosebud
utted out to make an impassable pocket. Red lifted his Colt,
aimed at the up-curving horn of a steer caught in the pocket,
and squeezed the trigger. The steer's head tossed violently.
Then with a bellow of pain and rage, the animal charged
out from the wall. The ones packed behind charged also.
The jam melted away, and Red rode in toward the light of
he Rosebud's doors. Thirty feet short of them he stood in
he stirrups and reached above to catch a hold on an awning
oist. The roan went on, pushed from behind by the relent-
ess surge of the herd. Red swung up until he lay flat across
he joist, his body in the shallow opening made by that joist
and the smaller up-slanting roof support that gave the
awning its slope. He wormed his way across and on to the
next and lay there so that one joist supported this thighs,
he other his chest. There, gun in hand, looking down and
n through the small rectangle over the saloon's swing doors,
le waited while the frenzied cattle lunged past below him.

He could see a narrow wedge of the Rosebud's room packed
vith men's bodies clear to the doors. Below him the last
animals moved past and up ahead. The thunderous volley
of their hoofs striking the thick walk planks gradually faded
as the street and walks cleared of animals. Red tensed,
vatching the saloon doors.

From up-street came the sound of voices, the slam of a
screen door. Red leaned down and looked back and out to
see a group of shadows moving across from the jail toward

him along the hoof-churned dust. Except for the slurrin
sound of boots, an ominous silence seemed to follow in th
wake of the herd's receding tumult. Those men would b
his crew: Nels, Clem, Ed, Tex, Frank and Jim. Countin
himself, they were seven against whatever guns the Rose
bud would shortly disgorge.

Lying there across the awning joists, Red thought bac
over his plan. He had risked much in this attempt at freein
his crew from jail. Now he was risking even more i
stepping into a shoot-out with Clanton and his men. Hi
hunch had been that the men responsible for tonight's mo
violence would be the first to set foot on the street agai
after the herd's passage. He was gambling on that hunc
and on the presence of his own men on the street as
surprise.

Still he was confronted with the responsibility for the live
of his men. Here he was, leading them into danger whe
he, and they, could have ridden straight out of the countr
and had satisfaction in looking back on having got the bes
of Clanton. But in this moment Red knew that neither h
nor his men would turn tail to run from what they no
faced. Clanton had thrown down the gauntlet of a challenge
Not one of his men would have wanted to let pass thi
chance.

"Spread out!"

That hushed word, drifting across the street's gatherin
silence, was uttered by Clem Reynolds. Red heard it, an
the touch of sheer confidence in it did more to wipe out hi
doubts than anything. Hardly had that group of shadow
fanned out to cover a fifty foot wedge of the street's widtl
before another voice, this one from the saloon, spoke ou
sharply:

"Ben, Sid, Pete! All of you! Get up here!"

It was Clanton who gave that curt order. Looking down over the doors, Red saw men shifting aside, others taking their places. As he had foreseen, Clanton was accepting the responsibility of making the first appearance on the street.

Someone said: "Duke, there was shots across at the jail."

"I know," Clanton snapped. "It's Knight tryin' to break his bunch out. Pete!"

He was having trouble marshaling his men, but the big man threw the doors wide in a solid thrust. Before the doors had swung shut again, he was through them, a six-gun in each hand, stepping warily aside and out of the lamp glow that flushed across the walk and into the street.

It must have taken Clanton a few seconds to see into the darkness, for in the following brief interval no word was spoken. Then suddenly his voice grated out: "Who's that? Sing out or we shoot!"

He was standing less than ten feet from the spot below which Red lay. Red sensed immediately that his men were in plain sight and in danger of being cut down, so he drawled flatly: "Up here, Clanton!" It would give his men the time they needed to meet this threat.

On the heels of his words a man on the opposite side of the doors fired suddenly. Two shots of his .45 had blasted the stillness when a gun from the street answered. Its lone reply brought the Clanton man pitching outward and sprawling in a broken fall to the walk. Clanton, who had a moment ago looked upward, wheeled quickly away and out of line. His gun lifted. It's lancing flame licked upward in the direction of Red's voice.

Red had had his Colt lined down on Clanton, the hammer thumbed back, trigger finger tightening. But all at once, even with the odds against him, shooting Clanton cold-bloodedly seemed like murder. He had an advantage up

247

here, having chosen it to get clear of the herd more than for the reason of surprising the Circle D crew. As he was thinking this, Clanton put the line of a joist between himsel and Red's gun, and Red had lost his edge.

Once again Clanton's gun exploded aimed upward, his bullet flickering a splinter from the roof that gouged Red's forehead. Red was suddenly impatient at being robbed of a target as other guns cut loose. He reached out, lifted his legs off the joist, and swung down. Letting go his hold, he hit the walk in a crouch. Clanton, seeing his shape suddenly appear out of the shadows, whirled and threw three thought-quick shots at him. The first bullet took Red in the left shoulder. It spun him halfway around, put his side to Clanton's gun. The next tore the left sleeve of his shirt. The third went wide of its mark for, as Red's body turned, his gun arced down at Clanton. His gun beat Clanton's last shot. He saw the big man's stooped body straighten rigidly as his gun fired. A man behind Clanton went down, stopping a slug from the street. Another behind him staggered drunkenly to the side to grasp the support of an awning post. Yet another ran in through the doors, two more down the walk. Red thought he heard the pound of hoofs down the street blended with the guns. The acrid stench of powder smoke was strong in the air as his men blasted home their small advantage of surprise.

Clanton's stiffening was brief. The next moment he was again crouching, right arm limp at his side, left hand blurring up. Red thumbed the hammer of his weapon again It exploded in unison with Clanton's. Red went down to his knees under the numbing wrench of a blow at his right thigh. Clanton, as though caught in the stomach by the hoof of a kicking bronc, bent double and fell face downward on the walk.

Some mighty inexhaustible force seemed to possess the Circle D man. He straightened his bent body, lifted head and gun arm, and laid his sights on Red again. Red slumped sideward, and Clanton's bullet stirred a breath past his head. He fired then, taking time to look across his sights. Before his gun had bucked up out of line, he saw the hole that dead-centered Clanton's forehead and brought the big man's frame flat to the planking in sure death.

It was over then, over but for the snap shots from the street that lent speed to the heels of the last three Clanton men left standing. As the boot pound of their hurried flight faded into the after-echo of the guns, two things happened almost simultaneously.

Harvey Jenkins, the sheriff, called loudly from behind the saloon doors: "Duke, are you there?" As he spoke two riders appeared out of the obscurity on the far side of the street. The leader of this pair, small of body, reined in suddenly as Clem's voice called: "Lift your hands, you two! Who are you?"

"Gail Dennis. Is Red Knight with you?"

Red felt weakness go through him as the girl spoke. His shoulder stabbed with pain as he pushed himself up on an elbow, trying to stand. His bad leg buckled under him, and he fell again, trying to call out to her.

Weariness and loss of blood dulled his mind as he lay back on the walk. He was vaguely aware of the crowd spilling from the saloon and gathering about him. Dimly, too, his eyes made out Gail Dennis's face, looking down into his. That was the last he remembered as he struggled to try and find the strength to speak to her.

The room was airy, light, and it hurt Red's eyes to open them. For long minutes he stared upward at the whitewashed ceiling. Then, curious, he turned his head and looked toward the wall with the window in it. The wall was clean and light, too. Near the window was a small steel table covered with a white cloth. Bottles and an enameled basin sat on it.

"Hospital!" he breathed. The feebleness of his voice made him smile.

"Yes, Red," came a voice that made him turn quickly. It was Gail.

She was wearing the dress she'd worn that first day at the ranch, the blue one. Her hair was done the same way, too, only more loosely now than then. And, looking into her face, he was instantly worried at the tiredness he saw there.

"You've been very sick, Red," she said. "Try not to talk."

"Then you'd better," he said, and she smiled.

"Don't worry. Clem and the others are all right. Jim Rhodes came out of it with a broken arm. It's mending nicely. You see," she added, "you've been here three days now."

"How about Toad?"

"The doctor doesn't know why, but Toad's going to live. Gravity touched her glance. "Toad remembers. Duke Clanton shot him then left him lying in the road, while he waited for Clem. And something else about Duke. Pete Hernández, one of his men, talked before he died that night. Duke had hired him to steal cattle from Dad two years ago. It was Pete who hunted down Ned Spence and turned his horse loose on the desert. At the end, Pete said something about Duke's wanting to marry me and afterward take over the whole basin." She tried to smile again, but the expression was lost against the soberness in her eyes.

He lay looking up at her, not wanting anything to change. For the moment there was nothing more he desired. Gail

250

was looking down at him with a tenderness that could mean only one thing. He loved this girl, and she might one day love him.

There was something more she had to say. "I . . . I've had your men take the herd across the river and put it on my graze." She hesitated, as though making up her mind to something. "I don't know how you'll take this, Red, but I've offered them jobs until you're on your feet again. I want to offer you one, too."

Red did his best to nod. He wanted to say something but was afraid to.

Gail's glance didn't meet his now. Then she was saying: "I need a foreman and a crew that knows cattle. All Dad's men quit when I brought in the sheep. Now I want to go back to cattle. Could you stay on and . . . and would you help me get started again, started the right way?"

Then she was looking at him, a pleading in her eyes. Red lifted his hand and held it out to her. Sudden thankfulness brought her smile back again. Her hand met his.

"We'll get along, Red!" she murmured.

Peter Dawson is the *nom de plume* used by Jonathan Hurff Glidden. He was born in Kewanee, Illinois, and graduated from the University of Illinois with a degree in English literature. In his career as a Western writer, he published sixteen Western novels and over 120 Western novelettes and short stories for the magazine market. From the beginning, he was a dedicated craftsman who revised and polished his fiction until it shone as a fine gem. His Peter Dawson novels are noted for their adept plotting, interesting and well developed characters, their authentically researched historical backgrounds, and his stylistic flair. His first novel, *The Crimson Horseshoe,* won the Dodd, Mead Prize as the best Western of the year 1941 and ran serially in Street & Smith's *Western Story* prior to book publication. During the Second World War, Glidden served with the U.S. Strategic and Tactical Air Force in the United Kingdom. Later in 1950 he served for a time as Assistant to Chief of Station in Germany. After the war, his novels were frequently serialized in *The Saturday Evening Post.* Peter Dawson titles such as *High Country, Gunsmoke Graze,* and *Royal Gorge* are generally conceded to be among his masterpieces although he was an extremely consistent writer and virtually all his fiction has retained its classic stature among readers of all generations. One of Jon Glidden's finest techniques was his ability after the fashion of Dickens and Tolstoy to tell his stories via a series of dramatic vignettes which focus on a wide assortment of different characters, all tending to develop their own lives, situations, and predicaments, while at the same time propelling the general plot of the story toward a suspenseful conclusion. *Dark Riders of Doom* (1996), *Rattlesnake Mesa* (1997), and *Ghost Brand of the Wishbones* (1998) are his most recent titles.